DEADLY SIGN

The thrashing was loud, and it came from the river. They ran in the direction of the sound and found the deer in its death throes, at the river's edge. Drouillard slit the soft throat for the final kill. "I do not do with the gun what I can do quietly with the knife." His dark eyes glared under drawn brows at some saplings farther upstream that parted where an animal trail cut into the embankment. He motioned Collins to follow as he went to investigate.

It started to rain, first a soft misting, then a heavier pelting that washed the sweat away. Collins took off his shirt and hat to let the welcome water slosh over his healing back. Drouillard approached the base of the trail silently as a cat stalking his next meal. He stooped down suddenly, ran his fingers in the wet soil, and brought them up to his nose. "Blood. And by the smell of it, human, not animal. . . ."

River Walk

Rita Cleary

LEISURE BOOKS NEW YORK CITY

A LEISURE BOOK®

September 2001

Published by

Dorchester Publishing Co., Inc.
276 Fifth Avenue
New York, NY 10001

Published by special arrangement with Golden West Literary Agency.

ISBN 0-8439-4922-8

Visit us on the web at www.dorchesterpub.com.

ACKNOWLEDGMENTS

My appreciation to The Lewis and Clark Trail Heritage Foundation; its members and friends, who always knew the answer or knew where to find it; to The North Dakota Lewis & Clark Bicentennial Foundation; and to the Missouri Historical Society. Thanks to Captains Meriwether Lewis and William Clark; Sergeants Charles Floyd, Patrick Gass, and John Ordway; Private Joseph Whitehouse; and all the others whose exploits, journals, books, articles, and letters demonstrate the breadth and width of our great land.

Introduction

Sergeant Patrick Gass in his journal entry of April 5, 1805 wrote:

> . . . [W]e ought to be prepared now, when we are
> about to renew our voyage, to give some account of
> the fair sex of the Missouri; and entertain them with
> narratives of feats of love as well as of arms. Though
> we could furnish a sufficient number of entertaining
> stories and pleasant anecdotes, we do not think it
> prudent to swell our Journal with them; as our views
> arc directed to more useful information.

In RIVER WALK, I have gone beyond "useful information," and tried to restore what could have been the "enter-
taining stories," the unscientific but human elements which
ignite the incredible journey's progress.

In 1805, emotion was a private affair. Meriwether Lewis,
William Clark, Charles Floyd, John Ordway, Joseph
Whitehouse, and Patrick Gass all wrote journals of the Lewis
and Clark Expedition. They restricted their accounts to dry
fact. Their story is fascinating. But the story did not end
there. They barely skimmed the fears, loves, joys, bonds of
friendship, antagonisms, and personal struggles for fulfill-
ment that these brave men must have experienced. Many are
lost to history. Conjecture and hearsay surround others.

In RIVER WALK, I have attempted to recreate these men

as the brave individuals they were. I have tried to rekindle what could have been—what one young member of the expedition might have felt in his heart—how he might have reacted. John Collins was eager and feisty, strong and healthy. He could shoot straight, run fast, drink with the best of them. He could not write his name. What rushes of adrenaline and hormones, what courage and youthful enthusiasm impelled this man to disobey, to rebel, to befriend, to deny, to fight, to love, and ultimately to conform?

If he were alive today, I would think of him and his peers as a combination of irresponsible fraternity brother, resourceful Marine, and tough gang member. The age is right, and so is the attitude. Collins and all these men worked hard and played hard. They chased girls, drank themselves stupid, gambled, played pranks, sang, danced, and devoured an incredible amount of red meat. They suffered, and I'm sure sometimes they fought. But they were a very effective unit, led by the sure and able Captains Meriwether Lewis and William Clark.

Rita Cleary
Oyster Bay, New York

Chapter One

The river was wide. The water gushed and eddied. John Collins held Bourgeron by the hair of his head. Collins was a strong man, and his iron grip pulled the black hair back from the Frenchman's bony temples. He jerked Bourgeron once, high enough to let his lungs suck air, plunged the face back into the muddy stream, and growled: "You Frenchmen squawk like geese . . . all flap and no bite!" Then he grinned like a clown.

His friend, Georges Drouillard, held the wagers. The dark, lanky frontiersman draped himself over the long barrel of Collins's gun, a .45 caliber, Kentucky flintlock rifle. He cradled his own rifle under his free arm. "Johnny, *mon ami,* you have won. But watch your back! If you let him drown, they'll kill you!" Collins let go. He had bet good money on himself. He knew he'd whip the wiry little Frenchman. He knew he'd win.

Jacques Bourgeron surged up, fists flailing. He coughed, sputtered mud and weed, and swore. "*Crapaud! Bâtard!* You violate my sister! You insult the name of Bourgeron!" The crowd on the riverbank booed and threw insults thick as black flies back at Collins. Bourgeron's blows fell short. He was a short man, French and Indian, feisty as a cat, slippery as an eel. The lanky Collins held him easily at arm's length, but the scrappy Frenchman scrambled out from under.

Drouillard frowned, and the crowd cheered. They had bet heavily, and they loved a fight, especially a duel over a woman. It swelled their Gallic sense of chivalry and the combative pride of their Indian heritage. John Collins stepped back a moment and bowed. Bourgeron erupted from the earth and landed a hard right on Collins's clean jaw. Staggering but not falling, Collins grabbed the black mat of hair once more and shoved the Frenchman backwards into the water. "Who are you, her jailer? Let her dance with the man she chooses!" He was screaming.

Drouillard stepped forward and called: "Johnny, leave him be. He cannot hear you with his head underwater! They know you are the victor, and they must forfeit their wagers!" Drouillard's mellow voice filtered through the shouts like a cool breeze in the hot summer air.

Bourgeron surfaced breathless and subdued, with the lingering grimace of hatred in his black eyes. "She is promised to Calderon, not you, *diable!* I forbid her to marry English!"

Collins clamped his mouth shut, biting his lip. The taste of blood angered him. He splashed cold water on his face and bellowed back: "Not English! Irish! My ancestors fought with Celts against Saxons, and I left your sacred sister purer than the lilies on your blessed altars! I have three sisters and a mother I love and respect! It was one of your own soiled your linen! You want to clear your name, talk to Villon! Now give me my money." He held out his hand. Drouillard handed him his winnings. Collins shoved the winnings under his shirt.

At that, Bourgeron struck out again. Collins landed a giant punch to the side of the head, and Bourgeron fell unconscious into the water. He didn't get up. Collins picked him up by the collar, dragged him to shore, and dumped him in a soggy lump in the soft mud of the riverbank. He addressed the circle of onlookers: "He accuses innocent people and treats his sister like a mule in harness."

The crowd did not sympathize. Hard, Gallic eyes glared from the limp form of their countryman back to Collins. A voice screeched: "A mule in harness is stubborn and slow and needs the whip!"

Drouillard shouted back: "A mule in harness is a beast of burden. A sister is kin and has an immortal soul! Your priest should teach you that!"

Drouillard moved up, handed Collins his rifle, and steered him up the embankment, away from the crowd. "Enough! Leave the mad dogs snarling before they catch me by the tail and hamstring me, too."

"You're their countryman. They have no argument with you."

"They thought you were *Colin*. They pronounce it the same as your Collins in their tongue. The *Colins* are a large family with many cousins on the river. They look at you, and they know you are not *Colin*. They don't want their money going to an English, and they suspect me for handing it to you, even though it was a fair fight and they lost. Many owe their livelihood to the power of Spain and know I am engaged by Captain Lewis, the enemy of Spain. To them, all Americans are infidels, heretics, instruments of Satan who murder and plunder, the same ones they quartered and burned in the Inquisition. They hate Captain Lewis! They have never heard of Mister Jefferson! They think I have betrayed the name of Drouillard. They do not love me."

Collins had just arrived on the Mississippi from Maryland and one month's duty at Fort Massac. He did not understand the unraveling of politics and family ties that enmeshed his friend and that impelled these impulsive inhabitants of Louisiana. This was not Maryland or Virginia. Drouillard worked for Meriwether Lewis, who came from a respected family in Virginia. Lewises were neighbors of President Jefferson, and Meriwether Lewis had been Tom Jefferson's secretary. Collins had heard the name Lewis uttered with quiet respect even in the drinking halls at Fort Massac and on the way here at Kaskaskia and Cahokia. He had never met the man. He was on his way to meet him now, with the Frenchman, Georges Drouillard.

Meriwether Lewis was enlisting young men for a grand exploration into the unknown reaches of Louisiana, across territory claimed by Spain and Britain. He hoped to find the Northwest Passage. It was a dangerous undertaking. Others had tried, like the Spanish Company of Discoverers and Explorers of the Missouri, and had failed miserably. Clamorgan, the Creole, and Spanish Governor Carondelet in New Orleans, and Lieutenant Governor Don Carlos Delassus in St. Louis would lose their lands and power, if the Americans gained sovereignty. To Collins's untutored mind, the entrenched rulers of Louisiana were like the English overlords who had driven his family from Ireland. They represented tyranny and oppression.

Drouillard had signed on with Lewis in Kentucky and had recruited Collins. The younger man was impetuous and untutored, but he was unattached, physically strong, eager to smell the salt wind that blows off the western ocean from the farthest corners of the world. He was a dead shot and brave to the point of rashness. In fact, the smell of danger excited him.

Collins took off his hat, shook the weed and water from his hair, and wrung out the hat like a soggy sponge. Tall and straight as the mast of a square-rigged ship, with shoulders broad as yard-arms, and long, supple arms and legs, he moved with the graceful stride of a Thoroughbred and the agility of a lynx. He had soft, penetrating blue eyes, and blond, curly hair that he wore long, like a badge of honor. His square jaw and straight nose added to the symmetry of his features, and yellow hair fell like silk over his ears. He was roughly handsome and generally exuberant. Ladies loved him, an attribute that caused him difficulty with jilted lovers and overly protective brothers.

Bourgeron was sitting up now, blinking dumbly. Collins looked back down the embankment and shouted testily: "Tell 'im he should wish his sister happiness, *bonheur* like you say . . . love and life! Marry Calderon and she'll dress in black before she's twenty and end her life barren as a empty keg!"

Drouillard herded him ahead like an unschooled colt. "Quiet, Johnny Collins! Don't provoke them or they'll come after you!" Drouillard was older, wiser, tamer with a Gallic sense of expediency. "Calderon is rich. Her father has died. Bourgeron is her eldest brother, *tête de famille* we call him, a man of import in the village. She is headstrong and beautiful, and he does not understand the poundings of her heart, but his word is law."

"His word is unjust."

Drouillard shrugged. "Not to them! They are creatures of law, used to living with authority. They have a governor who dictates. They had a king who ruled. Now there is an emperor who commands them like God. Louise is a vixen and needs direction. Bourgeron only exercises his right as eldest, and, when you shout at him, you degrade him, make him less a man. He will want to fight you again to preserve his dignity."

Collins still seethed. "Is he more a man for forcing his sister to marry a grandfather?"

The Frenchman narrowed his black eyes. "She is his sister. She must do as he says."

"And if he is wrong?"

The older man turned callused palms upward and raised his bushy brows. "Bourgeron is considering her welfare for many years to come. The marriage is a pretext. She will marry Calderon, and he will die within the year. She will inherit the land he has from the King of Spain, which extends to the far

13

horizon, and she will be free to marry whomever she chooses. You can marry her yourself."

"Me?" John Collins blinked and coughed. "I'm too young!"

Drouillard was serious. "You look like English, and you do not love her. But for her, love or no love, marriage is not so bad a compromise . . . a *mariage de convenance* we call it. Marriage to an older man is a small sacrifice for a larger benefit. She will endure, and he will not. Only a little while and the suitors will flock to her door like crows to the cornfields, because she will be not only beautiful, but also rich." Georges Drouillard did not smile. He grimaced casually at his young friend. "*Mon ami,* Johnny, we must spirit you away from the wrath of the brother and the song of the siren sister! Get your horse. He is too fine an animal to let stand in the mud. Move quickly before Bourgeron finds his knife. He is a demon with the knife!" He shoved the young man toward a sheltering grove of trees. "Have you thought what you will do with your winnings? Have you thought of what you will say to Louise? Bourgeron will tell her that you won and that now you are rich and will ask for her hand to protect her innocence and save her from Calderon." Drouillard chuckled under his breath.

Collins stopped short, squared his shoulders, and arched his neck. It was a posture of resistance. "I'm not getting married!" He had only just met Louise at a village ball. He couldn't speak French, and she was the only person at the ball who spoke English. Women and their imaginings and the machinations of these strange folk who inhabited the Mississippi settlements were an enigma to him, as great an unknown as the tortuous rapids of the northern rivers. He could no more read the workings of their hearts than the crude maps of the western territories. In fact, he could not read at all. Nor could he understand the torrents of patois French that issued from their gushing lips.

He liked Louise. She was pert and round with a bright, inviting smile. She had seemed pleased that he had asked her to dance. He had treated her with polite agreeableness, and they had talked in English. She had not mentioned Calderon or introduced him. This Bourgeron, the brother, could have prevented the whole misunderstanding. But marriage! Not here, not now! Not to that little temptress! Never!

He and Drouillard looked back again from the top of the embankment where the horse was tied. He grabbed the shank that tethered the horse, frowned once at the menacing cluster of rivermen below, and stalked off into the sheltering woodland after Drouillard.

Drouillard set a grueling pace, then came to a halt after a few miles, out of sight and sound of the crowd. "Bourgeron will not forget. He will seek *la vengeance!*" His black eyes darted from side to side, alert to every shadow. "They will pump the water from Bourgeron's lungs, and he will come after you. Do you remember the bearded, old man who sat in the armchair at the ball?"

John Collins shook his head.

"Calderon. He did not dance. He is too crippled. . . . What did you think, that he was her father or grandfather, Johnny Collins, that you could cross-tie him and let him stand like your stupid beast? He was the *fiancé*." Drouillard's words sniped like musket shots.

John Collins defended himself. "I didn't think. I didn't see. There was no reason."

Drouillard snorted derisively. His voice sliced, like a sharp blade. "There is good reason to think, Johnny, all day and every minute of the poundings of your heart and the future your emotions will create for you! In the wilderness, you must always think. Thinking will show you where to lay your traps and the direction from where the predators come . . . . You might have asked if she was spoken for. Calderon was not amused, and they will blame only you . . . the foreigner . . . the American or Englishman, or whatever you are."

"Irish! Friend to Catholic France! No friend to England!"

"No matter. Her brother will have to revenge the insult because old Calderon is a friend of the governor and is too old to defend himself." Drouillard shook his head wearily and walked steadily up the path, herding Collins and the horse ahead of him with a switch. He was still grumbling when he added: "But you did not kill him, so they will not kill you." He stopped and swallowed a long stream from a wineskin slung over his shoulder and pursed his lips. "The wine is turning. Drink now, before it sours." He held it out for Collins. "And guard your beast lest Indians steal him in the night."

John Collins squirted a stream of red liquid into his mouth and grinned stupidly back. He never refused a drink, but the wine puckered his lips like rotten fruit.

Drouillard took another drink and spat it out. "You must learn to distinguish the good wine from the bad, the virgin from the whore! You have created an *affaire de sang,* a red blot on Bourgeron's name, redder and more bitter than this vinegar we drink! The French and Spanish are jealous of their women, jealous of the lands we take from them, jealous of their power over the inhabitants of the river. They are greedy lords of Louisiana. They will not let us go easily to join Captain Lewis. They will not let Captain Lewis proceed easily on his journey." Drouillard's lips contorted sideways in the matting of his beard. A quiet gurgle rose from the cavern of his chest. He burped. "You see their deviltry in the delays and losses. They refuse permissions and passports. They short-weigh and pilfer the stores." He stared ominously at Collins through dark slits of eyes, but his final words were reassuring. "You were poor, my Johnny. You had only your rifle and powder horn and horse and the skins on your back. No traps, no swift canoe, but you have won your bets. Louise Bourgeron will only marry for a considerable payment and with the approval of her brother. Lose your winnings and marriage with her is not acceptable."

Collins protested loudly. "I keep what I win!"

"Keep it and this will not be the end of it. They will revile you because you are friend to me, and I am the hired man, the *engagé,* of Captain Meriwether Lewis."

Collins didn't answer. He had come west to escape the clutches of too many sisters and adoring women. But he had also come west to seek his fortune, not to throw it away. He threw back his head and emptied the wineskin and spat.

Georges Drouillard mumbled on: "You guzzle sour wine and your brain clouds and your eyes dim, Johnny Collins. If you come with me, I can give you back your future. But if you work for Captain Lewis, you must control your tongue and the cravings of your lust, and you must think clearly and obey. You will be a soldier under his command on an important mission." He smacked his lips and shot a sidelong glance at the young man. Drouillard sensed the futility of his counsel and ended the harangue. "You have tasted the wine and it has addled your thinking, but do not lay excuses for your foolishness on me."

John Collins did not answer. He hadn't listened. He grit his teeth, shouldered his pack, and handed the empty skin back to Drouillard. Thoughts floated in his brain like flotsam on the surface of the water. They collided with powerful emotions, swirling and eddying and tumbling against each other.

The two men walked up the path through a thick wood

that bordered the flood plain, then turned inland. Hills rose, layer upon layer of huge sentinel elms and stately oaks. The slant rays of the autumn sun filtered weakly through the tall trunks and merged gradually with the forest undergrowth, until Collins doubted if Drouillard knew where he was going. They reached a clearing where the older man had a wagon stashed, and they stopped to drink and rest. Collins led the horse to water and submerged his own head in the pool to wash off the sweat. He took off his shirt and rinsed it clean. Tiny goose-bumps speckled the white skin of his back. He ran damp fingers through his hair and tied it with a twine behind his ears. When he pulled the shirt back over his head, the wet buckskin clung like netting to the furrows of his back. It was clammy and cold. His muscles rippled, and his teeth chattered uncontrollably.

Drouillard sat cross-legged on the ground and watched. "My horse has cracked his hoof. I gave him to a farmer to mend."

The implication was obvious. Collins offered without resentment. "My horse will drive. He can pull your wagon."

Drouillard nodded. "I am in your debt. . . . The sticks are dry. I will build a fire."

The horse's head jerked up suddenly, ears pricked. A suggestion of vibration in the earth underfoot and a shadow of movement along the trunks of the trees signaled that they were not alone. Another horse neighed from the dark shadows of the trees. Drouillard's eyes flicked a warning as he reached for his rifle. The animal was scraggly brown, a dark silhouette against the background of leafless branches. Its hoofs were unshod and its step soft on the cushion of wet, fallen leaves. Like the horse, the outline of rider blurred against the gray-brown of the late autumn woods, until they both emerged into bright shafts of oblique, evening light.

"Louise!" John Collins's jaw dropped.

Louise Bourgeron rode bareback, astride a fat, pregnant mare. Her skirts and layers of petticoat bulged from beneath her thighs, and her bare calves and feet dangled alluringly on either side of the horse. She wore a man's blue coat two sizes too big that opened loosely at the neck revealing a white swath of cleavage. A fringed shawl held the coat closed and defined a trim waistline. A knitted cap cocked jauntily over a profusion of curls, the red color of the fox. Her bare toes wiggled temptingly. The curl of her lip and the curve of her bust made John Collins swallow hard. The tip of her tongue protruded from between even white teeth. She was smiling.

Drouillard ran forward to seize her horse's bridle shouting: "Brazen girl, daughter of Eve, what are you doing here?"

Louise slapped his hand with the end of her rein, and kicked the horse forward with a shrill laugh. "You're not my keeper, Georges Drouillard, and I'm not a queen bee you can confine to her chamber to produce eggs. I can read and write in French and English and ride a horse and shoot a musket every bit as well as you." Her husky voice raked the air. "I came to see Johnny Collins, not you."

"If your papa were alive, he'd pen you like a sow in season!"

"My brother tried that! Jacques only wanted to hunt and ride and throw a knife. He burned my books and sold my writing desk because he was too lazy to chop wood." She lifted her chin and turned full lustrous eyes on John Collins. "You've treated me more kindly than I have been treated since my father died, *Monsieur* Collins. I came to thank you." She dismounted, walked up to John Collins, put one hand on each of his shoulders, pulled herself up, and kissed him full on the mouth.

19

Georges Drouillard's frog eyes bulged. John Collins staggered numbly and licked the sweet moisture from his lips. A drop of blood oozed over his tongue where his tooth stabbed involuntarily, but he was grinning stupidly from ear to ear. He was about to kiss her back when she pursed her lips and drew away. She appraised the full length of him: his wet hair, his clothing, a tear in his sleeve where the threads unraveled, his swelling lower lip where her brother's fist had struck and her kiss had pressed.

She touched a finger to his lips, withdrew it, and licked off the blood. "You've been fighting, John Collins, but it has not soured the taste of you."

Drouillard jumped between them. "You show intellect, Louise, but you have the morals of a mongrel bitch. You disgrace the holy values your father taught you. Confess and Father Poirot will assign you penance."

Louise Bourgeron burst out laughing. "Father Poirot sits like a hen in his confessional box. He does not comprehend the beatings of my heart. It takes more than sitting to produce eggs."

Drouillard's jaw dropped. "You speak blasphemy, girl!"

Louise Bourgeron hunched her shoulders and tossed her pretty head. "Father Poirot is a celibate priest. He lives on his knees like a monk or galley slave. Blasphemy is a sin against God, not against a fat, ignorant priest."

Drouillard raised his hand as if to hit her, but John Collins caught his arm. "No, Georges! Not a woman! My fight is with her brother, not you, not her."

Drouillard pulled back his arm in disgust. "You don't know the brother and his friends, Johnny Collins! I told you! They don't love me. To them, I'm a traitor because I am American and work for Americans." He turned back to the woman, shouting in French and waving his fists in the air.

Hands on hips, Louise tossed her head back and returned his rantings word for word.

John Collins stood dumbfounded, trying to catch some glint of meaning, a gesture there, an inflection here. He thought back to his childhood and the eligible maidens of Frederick, Maryland who spent their days with bake pans and milk pails. Skill with the spindle and needle was what they needed to attract a man. Louise Bourgeron was a different breed of woman, excitable, alluring, with an exotic mixture of barbaric Gaul and war-like Indian. Like most of the inhabitants of Louisiana, notorious for quick tempers and impulsive wills, she was more free with her favors, more shameless in her desires. Or was it that she lived on the edge of an untamed land, in the company of rowdy men, on the brink of what he knew as the civilized world, that made her more willful and appealing?

Collins had noted the difference in the habits of men, too, as he had floated down the Ohio from Pittsburgh to New Madrid. The farther west he'd come, the more set apart the towns, the more resourceful, independent, and willful the people. Here on the west bank of the Mississippi, at St. Louis, in the sparsely populated territory now owned by Spain but made up of French-Indian half-breeds, the population assumed the wild spirit of the land around it.

The spirit was contagious. Collins felt it in himself. He was young; he was healthy; he no longer owed allegiance to family or church. Every muscle and bone felt the surge of unchecked power. Drouillard be damned if he didn't approve! If Louise Bourgeron had said—*Come to my bed.*—at that moment, with scowling Georges Drouillard as witness, John Collins would have picked her up and carted her off. But he could distinguish only thin meaning from the angry words that flew like darts between the Frenchman and the girl.

Devoir and *honneur* spiced Drouillard's accusations. Louise countered with *amour,* and the one word Collins did understand, *liberté.* His blood boiled; beads of sweat spread over his brow. The sexual surge of a young man's lust, the propulsion of curiosity and daring, inflamed him. It drove him to desire forbidden ecstasies at once exciting and compelling.

Suddenly, the shouting stopped. Louise Bourgeron cocked her head and locked flirtatious eyes on him. "You know what he is saying, *Monsieur* Collins? He is reminding me that I am a woman . . . of the inferior sex . . . that I am meant to serve and obey my masculine lord, that only marriage will give me the freedom I seek! He condemns me to marry Calderon! I say that marriage to a toothless gelding like Calderon is worse than an iron collar, the kind they weld around the necks of rebellious slaves." She opened her mouth and the pink of her tongue appeared between even white teeth. "You are handsome, *Monsieur* Collins. Your father fought a war for independence and won. We women are not so lucky. We must marry to be free like you. Slavery first, then doubtful freedom." She placed her hands on her hips and threw back her head defiantly. "When I marry, I will gnash my teeth when my brother snaps his fingers." She laughed at that. "If not you, then I will couple with the old one." Her voice softened with disappointment not remorse. "Calderon will be no husband at all, and after Calderon, I will choose the man I desire. I am young. A year, two years. Drouillard says it will take only one turn of seasons. But Drouillard is older, and his years seem shorter." She wrinkled her nose to show her disgust. "After Calderon, I may choose you, my handsome *Monsieur* Collins . . . if you do not die first." These last words slipped sweetly but coolly off her tongue as her face widened into an enveloping brilliance.

John Collins's head swam. He swayed on his feet and swallowed hard, afraid that even the slightest movement would overcome him and he would fall upon her, carry her off to a wooded bower, and ravish her passionately. Saliva, like the vinegar-wine, burned the length of his gullet.

She was still teasing lightly. "I go now. If my *frère* Jacques catches me, he will beat me. But I'm not afraid that you will tell, Georges Drouillard, nor you, my handsome *Monsieur* Collins." She gathered her skirts and pulled herself back into the saddle.

"Louise, wait!" Collins seized the rein. Too much was left unspoken, but he drew back under the harsh scrutiny of Drouillard.

Drouillard stood with brows locked together over his bulbous nose, staring at them both like a wrathful god. "Let her go, Johnny! She is sweet to taste but bitter to swallow, the serpent with the apple who will expel you from paradise. You have made one enemy because of this woman. Bourgeron believes you have despoiled his sister. Do not make it the truth."

Louise turned on Drouillard. "You are a disagreeable beast, Georges Drouillard. You excrete bile like snake venom." She lashed the horse with the end of the rein and trotted off into the woods.

John Collins followed her with his eyes. Siren, temptress, instrument of the devil—Drouillard was right. He could feel the inexorable enticement of a sorceress. Drouillard grimaced irritably and scrounged another wineskin from his pack. "Drink, *mon ami!* It stills the drumming of the heart. You are well rid of her. Bring the horse."

Collins raised the wineskin to dry lips and squeezed. Cold water ran over his tongue. The sun shone down through the bare branches of the elms and warmed his back. Its taste was sweet and sharp. It puckered his lips and chilled his insides. His stomach heaved, and he choked.

Drouillard nodded. "Cough it up! Spit out the witchery of the woman, *mon ami,* and count yourself fortunate. She has loved and betrayed many before you." Drouillard crossed himself. "There is another wine we make from apples, stronger than your corn liquor, powerful enough to drown the temptations of Louise Bourgeron."

"No more!" Collins's stomach was already churning as he weaved up the trail after Drouillard.

Chapter Two

Don Carlos Dehault Delassus, Spanish Lieutenant Governor of Upper Louisiana, banged his silver-tipped cane on the hard tile floor. He was a lordly man, tall and thin with cold blue eyes, coal black hair, and a long slide of concave nose that sniffed disdainfully down at lesser mortals. His beard was groomed to a fine point. He wore a black waistcoat, a frock coat of dark navy blue, black polished boots, and dark gray britches that emphasized the ascetic thinness of his frame. A silver-link chain with the medallion of his rank hung around his neck, and several large gold rings set with a family seal, adorned his fingers. His thin lips seemed frozen in a haughty frown. It pulled at the edges of his eyes so that, at the sides of his face, the skin seemed to fold in pleats, like a worn drapery.

When the rapping of his cane failed to attract attention, he rose from his chair, limped impatiently across the room to the door, and shouted: "Pedro!" He turned back to his massive desk in front of a blazing hearth fire, sank down, and arranged the surface with the same precision with which he administered the Louisiana Territory. His enamel inkwell and tray, with the matching blotting pad behind them, he pushed to his right. His ledgers, his missal, and a silver decanter of Spanish port with matching goblets, he squared carefully to the left, leaving the center expanse bare.

A manservant appeared.

"A quill, Pedro, and paper if you please?"

Pedro bowed meekly and retreated, then returned and

placed the requested paper and quill in the center of the desk. "*Señor* Clamorgan to see you, Your Excellency." He waited for an answer.

A ray of brilliant summer sun illuminated the polished desktop as Delassus flipped up the tails of his coat, seated himself regally, smoothed out his paper, and dipped his quill in ink. **Sir,** he began. He struck it out, threw the balled paper into the fire, and rewrote:

> **Your Excellency,**
>
> **Copy of the formalities transferring Louisiana to the Emperor Napoléon and thence to the United States were received yesterday. I have laid them aside and denied Captain Meriwether Lewis and his party passports, so that, should they venture into Mexican territory, appropriate measures, arrest, and seizure, will be implemented summarily. But I regret to inform you that my orders from Paris, orders which the French Consul at New Orleans has transmitted, do contradict your instructions. I cannot prevent this Territory's public transfer to the seventeen United States. I can only delay it. Derailing the transfer would obviate the wishes of our esteemed Emperor, Napoléon. Nor can I prevent the departure of Mr. Lewis and his cadre of adventurers. However, I urge vehemently that an armed battalion leave Santa Fé immediately with the express mission to intercept the Lewis party and restore this Territory to her proper overseers. The battalion should extend Mexican territory to its maximum limit, east to the Mississippi, west to the Pacific, and north to the British dominions. It should contain and compress any possible expan-**

sion of the seventeen American states beyond the Mississippi River. For the present, the battalion should co-operate with the British North West Company's and Hudson Bay's efforts to extend trade south from Canada.

Suffice to say that the American Expedition is largely ignorant of the hazards of exploration. Their maps are inferior; their equipment unsuitable. The men are undisciplined, and their leaders unversed in the art of placating natives. The whole effort will melt like snow in spring at the first sign of armed opposition or natural disaster. But the surge of American immigration is another matter. We must with all due haste populate the Territories of Illinois and Louisiana with citizens of our own choosing.

I assure you that I will do all in my power to forestall the American invasion and to insure the failure of Messers Lewis and Clark. I trust you will match my every effort in diligence and dispatch.

I remain your most humble and obedient servant

He stopped and reread the whole before signing it with a flourish, folding and sealing it with wax, addressing and handing it to Pedro. "Take it immediately to Captain Guiterrez. My seal will gain you entry. Tell him to choose a fast horse and deliver it personally into the hands of Governor Carondelet." Pedro bowed meekly and padded from the room.

The room was cold. Delassus poured himself a glass of port and pulled his chair closer to the fire. One hand gripped the cane; the other massaged a knee, then reached for a goblet of the wine. He sipped but did not swallow, allowing the cloying liquid to dilute the bitterness on his tongue. Events had not devolved according to his wishes or the wishes of his superiors in Cuba. He cursed the Emperor Napoléon's greed which he blamed for Louisiana's sale. Now he considered how best to retrieve the lost territory for Spain and conserve the considerable wealth he had accumulated personally in his position as Territorial Lieutenant Governor. He downed more wine, then dashed what remained into the fire. The drops of liquid fizzled and swiftly evaporated in a puff of smoke. Delassus willed the Americans to disappear as swiftly.

He smiled at the thought of their demise. It was a thin, scheming curve of lip. How to engineer a disappearance in the wilderness of the entire American Expedition? It had happened before to the Sieur de La Salle and Don Silvestre Velez de Escalante. It would happen again even without his intervention. He set about plotting the fate of Captains Meriwether Lewis and William Clark, like manipulating pawns in a game of chess.

A slave entered, clicked his heels, and announced: "*Señor* Clamorgan, Your Excellency, he has been waiting."

"Usher him in." Don Carlos positioned himself behind the desk. When Clamorgan entered, he rose languidly and held out his hand. "Clamorgan, I did not know you were waiting! We have much to discuss."

Clamorgan, a short, dark Creole of West Indian Island extraction, bowed. He was not alone. "I have taken the liberty, Carlos, of bringing another with me who may be of immeasurable help to us. Your Excellency Don Carlos Dehault Delassus, may I present my countryman, *Señor* Jacques Bourgeron."

Delassus was French like Bourgeron, but an aristocratic refugee of the French Terror. Even in exile, he did not consort with peasants. His blood was blue and his skin milk white. He flicked a nod to Bourgeron and spoke to

Clamorgan. "Not many reach Saint Louis from the Indies. Be seated, my friend." The single chair was for Clamorgan. There was none for Bourgeron.

Bourgeron pushed rudely forward. "I come from New Orleans, Your Excellency, and I am of fine French stock." Bourgeron's implication was obvious. He meant that his breeding was whiter than Clamorgan's, that he deserved greater recognition. Don Carlos turned his head slowly to stare haughtily at the pompous Frenchman. Clamorgan ignored the insult and took his seat.

"Some port to fortify the blood, gentlemen?" Delassus poured with flourish into three gleaming silver goblets. Bourgeron reached immediately to seize his, while Clamorgan was sitting back and beginning to speak. "Jacques has good reason to detest the United States' expedition, Carlos. One of their party has debauched his sister."

Don Carlos focused on Jacques Bourgeron with renewed interest. "Perhaps, *Señor* Bourgeron should explain the difficulty himself."

"With pleasure, Your Excellency." Bourgeron paused, straightened, then sputtered his words in short, staccato spits. "My sister is very beautiful. Our father is dead. I am her guardian, head of our household. She met a man, Your Excellency, a member of this Lewis and Clark company. They are an unruly bunch, infidels, thieves and pirates, with no respect for decency or the law of Almighty God! The man's name was Collins." He pronounced it coal-an. "I had to fight him to free my sister from the blot of disgrace and restore respect for her virtue." He puffed out his chest with assumed importance and continued: "I married her off immediately according to the rite of Holy Mother Church, to a man of prestige among you, a man of your acquaintance. He is *Señor* Jaime María Gustavo Calderon de Ruiz." The abundant syllables rolled out with the precise beat of a drum.

Don Carlos cast a sidelong glance at Clamorgan and leaned forward toward Bourgeron with concern. "So now you are Calderon's brother-in-law? And when he dies and she is widowed, she will inherit his property, and it will be you, head of the family, who will administer Calderon's lands and wealth. Congratulations, *Señor* Bourgeron! You have used your sister admirably." He chuckled lightly, fingered his quill, and turned to the Creole. "Have you apprised him of our purpose, Clamorgan?"

"He knows I've recruited men to shadow the American expedition and prey upon it wherever possible. I told him we will pay."

Impressed with his importance, Bourgeron interrupted once again. "It is not the money, Your Excellency. For me and for my sister, it is *la vengeance.*"

Don Carlos was smiling sardonically now. His voice oozed officious courtesy. "You have high ideals, *Señor* Bourgeron, and great concern for your sister and for Calderon who will not live to enjoy your revenge.

"He will see the justice, Your Excellency, and glory in the honor from his place in heaven."

"For justice and honor, *Señor* Bourgeron, I pay well." He thought—*As old Calderon will also pay.*—and continued: "Spain is a generous mother. Emperor Napoléon is a munificent conqueror." Charles Dehault Delassus de Luzière was the son of a French noble family who had fled for their lives during the French Revolution and settled in the Catholic Spanish colonies. He was a royalist. Napoléon was not king, but as Potentate of all Europe he was a more credible ruler than the Virginia farmer and American President, Thomas Jefferson. Don Carlos was certain that Napoléon had sold Louisiana to the most ineffectual bidder, the United States, to facilitate its immediate retrieval. Now Don Carlos would strive to advance Napoléon's lawful claims in the New World and, in the process, reap a hefty monetary reward and lands enough to restore his family's noble prominence. He heaved a satisfied sigh. "And now, *Señor* Bourgeron, if you will permit *Señor* Clamorgan and me one moment alone."

Bourgeron stood his ground stubbornly. Dreams of wealth had made him bold. But a muscular black slave motioned him out.

Don Carlos leaned back, sipped his drink, and, swinging his feet onto the desk, slouched to a more comfortable position. "You are sure of him, Clamorgan? He is French with a good dose of Indian, not Spanish."

"No matter, Carlos, he is a prickly little man. When he holds a grudge, he will find the jugular, sink in his knife, and hang on like a mad dog. With due respect, Your Excellency, the French are an obstinate race."

"And our peasants swarm and scurry like hungry rats. Take care that his vengeance does not implicate all of us. I do not trust this Frenchman, this Bourgeron. You'd best put Sandoval in charge. Have him keep an eye, but give the Frenchman a title to satisfy his pride." He added with a knowing leer: "And I would like to meet the sister, *Señora* Calderon." Don Carlos's wife was toothless and sallow. He had often sought his pleasure elsewhere. The leer evaporated as swiftly as it had come. "Your informants within the American camp, are they reliable?"

"Of course, Carlos. How do you think I have outsmarted my competitors? It is why I am a rich man and ship five times their number of beaver pelts." Clamorgan, too, was proud. "There are three men within the American camp. They have already provoked fights and pilfered stores. The Americans suspect nothing. They have not even sniffed the scent."

31

"Your spies must do nothing to reveal their true loyalties."

"They know their mission, Carlos . . . to stay in contact with Sandoval and warn the tribes away from the treacherous American landlords. Sandoval is a strong leader. He will lay hazards in the river, sew discord among their troops, and hold the expedition to a tortoise's pace. We have already supplied them inferior maps. Our soldiers from Santa Fé will overtake and destroy them." He snapped his fingers. "It will not be difficult. Even pesky Bourgeron could have stopped them. The Americans are innocents, ripe for plucking." He laughed at that.

Don Carlos smiled wryly and poured more wine. He liked the wily little Creole.

Clamorgan raised his cup. "A toast! To Americans! To bumpkins! They know not with whom they joust. If we don't catch them, the British will head them off in the north." Clamorgan smacked his lips. "The British still think the thirteen colonies belong to them and that the northwest rivers will remain forever within their realm." He raised his glass and proposed a toast. *"A la gloria eterna y victoria de España y Francia!"*

Their goblets clinked loudly, and they drank to the dregs. Don Carlos leaned back contentedly and closed his eyes.

Clamorgan lowered his to see what remained in the bottom of his goblet. Bits of cork floated like tea leaves in the last few drops, and he twisted the stem to let the sunlight penetrate and reveal their pattern. Tiny red blots like blood dripping from a sword adhered to the brass interior of the vessel. The little Creole frowned momentarily. It was a bad omen. A Gypsy woman at the docks had warned him. The old hag had declared that he must follow the direction of the sun, that turning aside from his fated path would wring the blood from the marrow of his bones. It had sounded like Biblical ranting at the time, but now he was not so sure. He exhibited a smiling face to Don Carlos Delassus, while in the depth of his brain he was afraid. He determined to ingratiate himself, also, with the new American rulers. He didn't like Meriwether Lewis, an implacable, tenacious, nervous but intelligent competitor, very like himself. William Clark, the military man, was more predictable. But James Wilkinson was rumored to be the newly appointed American governor, and Wilkinson was Catholic, a man of the world and a friend of Spain. Perhaps Wilkinson could be of use. Perhaps he, Clamorgan, could befriend Wilkinson. His hands were shaking as he got up to go.

Don Carlos stopped him just before he was to take his leave. "There is a man . . . he is old, the cousin of a friend. He has requested to go along with Sandoval and to join the Santa Fé battalion on its return. He has a brother there. His name is Botero. I trust you and Sandoval can provide for him."

"With pleasure, Carlos." Clamorgan rose and bowed.

Chapter Three

The sweet pleasure of female companionship had escaped John Collins. He followed Georges Drouillard with some reluctance. He was slightly drunk and very tired. They were a striking pair, the dark Frenchman and the fair-haired Celt. Both were dead shots. Both stood nearly six feet tall. Both carried the weapons of their trade: rifle with powder horn and bullet mold, hunting knives, and tomahawk. One was domestically bred, but intelligent and impetuous; the other, weaned with bears and wolves, had learned prudence and watchfulness in the wilds.

Drouillard had sharp, round eyes that flicked constantly in all directions. His cheekbones were high and seemed to emphasize the intense, dark fire of his eyes. His most prominent feature was his nose which had been broken and covered the center of his lean face with broad rubbery nostrils that sniffed constantly. His lips were soft and sensuous, but they rarely changed expression within his black tangled beard. A long, black braid extended like an animal's tail between the blades of his shoulders and twitched with every movement of his head. He wore a buckskin shirt that hung loosely over his lean, athletic frame. His leggings and breechcloth were Indian, and he had belted a red Hudson's Bay blanket around his waist which expanded his mid-section considerably. Moccasins covered his feet, and a 'coonskin hat anchored wisps of black hair behind his ears. He spoke excellent English with the punchy accent of the French and Indian languages. His voice, when he chose to speak, was soft, except on the rare occasion when he became excited, and then it exploded like the blast of a cannon. His movements were quick and always premeditated. At times, he seemed more feral than human because he could detect danger unerringly and because he hardly ever smiled.

Collins had come from the civilized East, had tended crops and husbanded animals. He, too, wore a shirt of buckskin, tucked at his slim waist beneath a thick strap of leather that held up a pair of stained leather britches. His boots of scuffed brown cowhide were hobnailed and laced up to the knee. His hat was Quaker plain, square, faded black, and floppy from frequent use. He carried his weapons with a careless bravado that made Drouillard shudder. His speech echoed with the easy drawl of the southern colonies and tones of sweet music. His eyes were blue, his nose straight, his lips full and pink, and his teeth white and straight. He took pride in his looks, especially his thick shock of yellow curls which he brushed daily. He kept his beard neatly trimmed. The symmetry of his handsome face was agreeable to all, especially women, but he was not always prudent in his choice of companions.

The two men complemented each other well. Where Collins was impetuous and naïve, Drouillard was careful and discreet. Where Collins tended to overindulge, Drouillard enforced a limit. And where Drouillard appeared disinterested and unapproachable, Collins was always friendly and cheerful.

The meeting with Louise Bourgeron had angered Drouillard. His dark stare hovered like heavy smoke, but he did not vent the full force of his wrath. The track leveled out as he walked stubbornly on, leading the horse and wagon, head hunched between his shoulders, choosing to avoid controversy, and chewing his frustration to a digestible mush.

Collins followed silently, pushing where needed, when the wagon struck rock or sank into soft sand, half expecting scalding criticism each time Drouillard glanced backward. In the end, Drouillard offered solution, not punishment. "You come with me, you will not have to marry Louise and Bourgeron will not draw your blood. I owe you that much for your help and for the horse. Together we'll fend off the agents of Spain who pilfer everything we lay aside for the American exploration . . . but first to the ferry and the other side."

It began to rain. Heavy drops tortured the brown surface of the river like the pricks of a thousand needles. Masses of weed, stumps, rocks, and mud rolled in the powerful flow. John Collins shuddered when he saw the ferry. It was no more than a raft of unhewn logs, lashed together with rawhide thongs and rimmed around with thin boards to a height of a few feet. A crude rudder grated against the stern where a tarp covered a makeshift cabin. A mast rose from the center like a lone tree in the desert. The halyard slapped against it with the eerie rhythm of the tossing waves. The sail was furled because a high wind ripped the air and sent muddy water surging over the deck.

The ferry looked to Collins like a teacup in a tempest as it tugged at the frazzled hawsers that held it tentatively to the rickety pier. The lines squeaked under the strain. He un-hitched the horse and led it to the edge of the gangplank. The animal snorted. Eyes rolling in its head, it touched a hoof to the planks and reared back. The boatman laughed. Collins clipped the shank over its nose and pulled harder. The horse shied again from the bobbing surface of the craft and pulled Collins back up the embankment. The impatient boatman yelled testily: "Hobble the god-damned beast and carry 'im aboard!"

John Collins cursed. The frightened animal pranced and

whirled, but he held tight to its lead and shouted back: "I've paid double my fare! You have no other passengers!"

The boatman countered over the pounding rain: "With every minute it rains harder, *monsieur!* The river, she does not wait!"

Drouillard's bass bellowed suddenly from behind. "How much did they bribe you, Henri, to see that the supplies I carry do not arrive?" He turned to Collins. "Henri is hungry for dry clothes, his pot of *ragoût,* and the caresses of his plump wife and he is in the pay of Clamorgan. Pay him no heed, Johnny Collins. He is lazy as a tortoise, and lends his meager labors to the highest bidder." There was cynicism in his voice and accusation in the whites of his eyes. He drew out coins from his pocket and threw them clattering across the deck. The boatman, Henri, swept them up like a starving wolf and cringed. Drouillard upbraided the stubborn boatman. "I have casks to load, Henri. The rain is warm like the kiss of a woman. You can wait one moment for me while I help young Collins with his animal and he helps me with my wagon."

The dried beef, sugar, flour, and dry soup came from the best suppliers in St. Louis. The casks filled with black powder had to be handled with utmost care. Collins saw several larger barrels that contained sailors' rum. The unwieldy cargo had to be carried down the slippery bank, rolled aboard, and lashed down. It meant another hour, at least, of hard, wet, physical work. And then there was the wagon. It was longer than the raft was wide and had to be run up onto planks that the boatman extended like fragile wings on either side of his raft.

A litany of curses spouted from the boatman's lips. He set out the planks, sat stubbornly in the only dry place, under a tarpaulin in the stern, and lit his pipe.

Drouillard prodded the man. "You could help us, Henri,

and set sail more quickly, or have I only bought your resistance and your stubborn silence?"

The boatman pretended he had not heard. Collins and Drouillard loaded their cargo and ran the wagon up on the boards. Drouillard smacked the horse in the tail with the wide stock of his rifle, and the terrified animal lunged aboard. The boatman let loose the thick cable, and the raft lurched out and away, into the powerful stream. A wave crashed broadside. The panicky horse kicked as water slapped against his legs. His hoofs clambered like a drum roll on the deck. Collins held the rein tightly while Drouillard leaped after loose barrels, and John Collins felt his stomach heave.

"Steady that beast or I'll make 'im swim." The boatman leaned his full weight against the tiller, and the boat came about. "Hobble 'im. Twitch 'is nose afore he jumps overboard." Collins fashioned the simple device of thong and stick. Drouillard held the head while Collins tightened the twitch over the soft tissue of the animal's upper lip. It was enough to distract him while Drouillard hobbled the forelegs. They swirled into the midstream where the eddies tossed them like a drowning insect, a mindless speck on the seething flood, and propelled them swiftly downstream.

John Collins bit back his fear. He was a landsman, not used to the power of flood. Frederick, Maryland, his home, was level country watered by gentle rills and runs, not wide and surging rivers. His trip west from Pittsburgh on the Ohio was quiet by comparison. He had traveled in the dry season, when the sweat ran down his cheeks and a good soaking was a welcome respite in the summer heat. Now the river was cold, and the air spit splinters of ice that whipped his face cruelly. Water slogged in his boots. Whitecaps lapped mercilessly over the deck, soaking men and baggage and chilling them to the bone.

The raft seemed to career out of control. The surly boatman did not care. John Collins looked to Drouillard for reassurance. The older man stood stoically propped against the base of the mast, rifle propped under an arm, with his dark eyes closed, his head lolling. He was humming to himself a sad song that sounded to Collins like a dirge.

Drouillard sensed the tension in his young companion, opened his eyes, and spoke with the confidence of a prophet. "He thinks he can scare us, *mon ami* . . . make us cower at the might of the river, because he is in the pay of Clamorgan, the Creole. This is the Mississippi, the mother of all rivers, ruled by the power of God. I have prayed. Do not fear, because God will not allow the boat to founder. Neither will Henri. He would go down with us and land himself in hell." He winked suggestively. "The help of my God is what makes me brave." Collins swallowed hard and thought to himself: *Who is your God, Georges Drouillard?*

Gradually they approached the eastern shore. It had been sheathed in mist. Now it defined itself more sharply as they drew closer. They sailed under a great cliff which expanded in height and breadth, looming like a huge symbol of the impenetrable unknown. Collins felt suddenly belittled, like a speck of humanity in a cosmos of water. Was there a landing there under that weight of rock or would the great rock rear a solid wall, push him back into the river or crash down on him and bury him under the waves? His muscles contracted, and his heart pounded with apprehension. He tightened his hold on the horse's twitch with hands that trembled.

Drouillard had stopped singing and had slumped to a sitting position. He cradled his musket in both arms across his knees. His head rested on his arms, and he had fallen asleep. The boat swung around suddenly and sent Drouillard careening sideways. He awakened as the boat hit the dock with a loud thud, and shouldered his rifle. The boatman shouted a stream of curses, threw a bowline loop over a piling, leaped ashore, and ran downstream to tie the stern that spun around in the current parallel to the shore. The lines snapped tight and held, and the boat settled snugly against the pilings. The rain had not let up. Collins and Drouillard led the frightened horse first onto dry land and then pushed the wagon up the narrow beach. It sank in mud up to the axles. They hitched the horse that scrambled to his knees, trying to pull its weight. "The beast cannot," Drouillard said. "Tomorrow will be time enough, if it is still here and Clamorgan's raiders have not looted it." They loaded what they could onto the horse's back and their own tired shoulders, and left the wagon in the mire. They would return when the road was dry.

A narrow switchback led up the steep cliff. Collins muttered inquisitively: "Who is this Clamorgan, and why must the Spaniards contest us? There is country enough for all."

Drouillard nodded. "It is all for power and treasure. Clamorgan and his cohorts think the seventeen American states divided and weak. Our provisions have value. We must deliver them to Captain Clark whose partner, Captain Lewis, is *ami* to Tom Jefferson, and that is the difficulty. It is rumored that Tom Jefferson is the new ruler of Louisiana. The Spaniards do not easily part with their lands or any of their possessions. They extract the gold and silver and precious gems. They covet the rich furs. They hold all close to the chest." He glanced back through the blur of raindrops at his friend. "But you have already met Captain Clark, Johnny, and he is an honest man."

Collins shook his head. "Clark? I don't remember."

"You pulled him by the red hair of his head from the rapids of the Ohio when the current had seized him. . . . You are a fine swimmer, Johnny Collins! Who taught you how?"

John Collins shrugged. Swimming came as naturally as riding a horse, firing a musket, or dancing.

Drouillard continued: "The captains are looking for strong young men who can swim and shoot and are unmarried and will brave the new wilderness. You are one such, Johnny. You should come with us to the far horizon."

Collins hesitated a minute and wiped his wet face on the sleeve of his shirt. "This river is the boundary of my country."

Drouillard lifted his face to the rain. "The land stretches farther than we know. You cannot see how far? Look!" He stretched his arm into the storm, out over the river toward the gray bank of clouds that walled off the western horizon. "That was all the realm of the French King Louis when my father was born. It became the property of Spain. Now Emperor Napoléon commands it. It has been the pawn of kings and princes who bartered it back and forth like coins in a market. And now, if Mister Jefferson and the captains are successful, it will belong not to a tyrant from across an ocean but to us who people it. The land is greater than you can imagine. I will show you, tomorrow, when the air is clear." Drouillard spoke of the land lyrically, like a poet. He loved the land, and the attraction was infectious. "It is a promised land of milk and honey, like Moses saw, and there is no end to it." He fell silent and bowed his head reverently, then resumed: "Captain Clark will pass to the western sea, by the Missouri, and down the distant Columbia. He will find a Northwest Passage. I will go with him." Drouillard's conviction and enthusiasm electrified Collins. "But there is danger and risk, and I may not return."

Collins squinted and looked away into the gray wetness. He pictured the expanse of the land behind the mist, inhaled, and swallowed a hesitancy that blocked the back of his throat, but his heart swelled. Drouillard would return, and he would, too, if he elected to go. He had hacked his way through uncharted wilderness along the Ohio, carving away massive snags, hauling canoes over eroding bars, bracing the current while rough cables burned furrows in his shoulders and strained every vertebrae in his back. He was proud of his endurance and strength. He was not proud of a latent fear that he buried deep in his chest.

Drouillard sensed the uncertainty of youth, and tempted further: "We go upstream to the Shining Mountains, where no American has set foot before?"

To be the first, to discover wonders unheard of, Scottish Indians and lost tribes of Israel, mountains of glass, the Fountain of Youth! John Collins had laughed at the incredible reports, but now he could taste their excitement on the tip of his tongue. The Missouri River was a wide and powerful force, especially in the spring when melting snow from off the Shining Mountains spilled over its banks. No one had penetrated to its source. The unknown beckoned like the bed of a maiden, but he held his voice to a glib monotone and questioned: "When will Captain Clark leave?"

"When he and Captain Lewis have assembled supplies and men at Cahokia, sometime next spring." Black fire shot from Drouillard's eyes like an arrow straight to the heart of his young companion, and he waved his hand casually. "The supplies you see here are part of the provisioning." John Collins sealed his lips, pulled up his collar, tucked his head into the rain, and marched on up the trail.

Drouillard slogged behind him and talked to his back. "You are strong. You can shoot. You can swim. The captains will pay well for your services." Still, John Collins did not answer. Doggedly, he wrenched up each foot from the sucking mire and placed it down again. Drouillard's voice bounced off his back like the ticklish raindrops. "A young man can make his fortune in skins of the beaver and meat of the bison. Have you ever hunted the bison?"

It seemed to Collins an impossible dream. He loved to hunt. He loved the chase and the kill and the arrival home with food for the feast. His mind raced in spite of himself, and he tried to silence it.

Drouillard waited. Finally he spoke: "I hear the Frenchmen talk. They say there are furs and gold for the taking. There is also the wonder of beholding God's makings. There is a good fortune for a young man."

John Collins tried to define the word—*fortune*. Was it something ephemeral like peace or happiness, or was it physical like comfort and warmth and fresh, dry clothing? He had left that all behind when he left home in Frederick, Maryland. His family had grown too large for the farm. There was no viable plot for him. Ten surviving Collins children, his brothers and sisters who had grown and formed families of their own, barely scraped by. His brother, Henry, had also left to seek his life elsewhere. Others would follow. He wrenched his mind from the nostalgia of loss, the home that was, his parents' persistent struggle to feed their children, and dreamed of empty prairies and the possibilities of new and varied relationships. The seeking and the finding condensed the inspiration that consumed the young man's soul.

Dusk was falling. The gray light was fading, the raindrops becoming colder. He was wet to the bone, but the sweat of exertion kept him warm. They marched on by a forest trail over a hill, to a faint light in a clearing. Dogs barked. Drouillard called out. "Bertrand, *attention! C'est moi*, Drouillard!" He used the French pronunciation of his name. The settler did not speak English. Drouillard looked back at Collins with a warning. "You keep quiet. I will speak for you. Bertrand is cousin to Jacques Bourgeron."

Cousin. They were all cousins. Cousin did not mean friend or even blood relation. It referred to a vast web of familial relations who inhabited the bottoms of the rivers. Bertrand the settler came forward, a short round man with a long rifle that stood taller than himself. Drouillard jabbered a flood of choppy syllables, while Bertrand stepped back and welcomed them into his home. It was little more than a shed with a lean-to for two cows and space for a horse. But rows of dry cornstalks blanketed a vegetable garden, and the smell of bread baking and meat roasting wafted across the yard. This Bertrand was a happy, humble dirt farmer with a bouncy wife and an infant son. Collins thought of his brothers and his sisters who lived much like Bertrand, then of Louise Bourgeron. Louise did not resemble motherly Madame Bertrand.

When Drouillard introduced him, Collins smiled obediently and went to tend the horse. When he returned, Madame Bertrand had heaped plates with bread, cheese, pink juicy ham, and mounds of yellow squash. He ate ravenously like a starving mongrel and downed the thick red wine. It warmed his insides and lulled his brain, and, when he rolled up in his blanket on the hard dirt floor, he fell immediately asleep and dreamed of the western ocean, crystal rivers, and glittering mountains streaked with gold.

Chapter Four

He awakened to the insistent cry of a hungry infant. Madame Bertrand carried the child, Indian-style, upon her back while she ladled steaming porridge into a bowl and smothered it with dried apples, honey, cream, and fresh-churned butter. Collins hadn't tasted butter since he left home. It melted in a pool on the surface of his tongue, and Collins savored the taste. It was smooth and sweet, and the hole in his stomach expanded accordingly. He and Drouillard stuffed themselves. Drouillard reached for his cup and washed the breakfast down with stale wine, sat back, and lit his pipe. Madame Bertrand took the child to her breast to nurse. Collins left to pack the horse.

His stomach settled in the open air. A heavy mist hovered after yesterday's rain, and the black earth smelled like mother's milk. The sun broke through the film of clouds when a light wind picked up from the west. It blew away the mist and blew in delicious scents of wood and prairie from the vastness across the river. Drouillard came out and led away.

They had climbed a headland when Drouillard stopped. He squinted, turned his back to the sunrise, and pointed: "Now, look! You see it in the sun's brilliance." The slant rays of the morning shed a pink light across a panorama of snaking river, wide plain, and distant wooded hills. "There is an empire."

John Collins blinked. The vastness was spellbinding. He felt a spontaneous rush of energy, as if he could leap from the precipice, out over the river into the abyss, and let the wilderness engulf and nourish him like a newborn in the womb. Drouillard waited. The horse fell to cropping the weeds. Finally Collins inhaled deeply as if to draw the expanse within himself, picked up the animal's lead, turned, and nodded to his French friend. "Beautiful! How much farther?"

"We're almost there."

Cahokia was a fair-size settlement. The fort, with its earthworks and stockade, commanded the crest of a hill. Hovels of settlers spilled down its flanks. The dwellings were a mixed group of tents and log cabins, varied as the people who inhabited them: Anglos, Spaniards, French, and Indians. And there was a grouping of strange mounds. Drouillard explained: "The Indians say they were the foundation of an ancient city."

Collins gawked. A scattering of mounds covered many acres of land. It was a larger city than any he had known, and it had vanished like ancient Jericho. Where were they now? It seemed a vision from out of a myth.

"They were a powerful people. Some believe their ghosts still roam." But Drouillard was not impressed. He rambled on: "When I report to the captain, you come with me, Johnny, to learn if he has a place for you . . . and bring the brown horse. The captain is your kind, from the East, from Virginia. Like the Indians, like many Virginians, he loves a good horse."

John Collins was not listening. He looked back in awe at the fantastic conical shapes, and his mind conjured images of costumed natives, colorful rituals, homes, and tilled fields.

Drouillard pushed him forward. "You wonder at these mounds? We will see many more wonders than these in the western lands." They passed huddles of frontier humanity, trappers and hunters and Indians with their squaws, dressed in pieces of skins or old Army issue. Shaggy horses and oxen stood munching dry hay. Campfires smoldered, and cooking utensils lay strewn over the ground. Cahokia was a bustling settlement.

There was no sentry at the entrance to the tent that Drouillard entered unannounced. Captain Clark was seated at a rough table on a camp stool, studying his maps. A huge black man stood by his side. Clark himself was a big man with broad muscular shoulders and powerful arms. He wore buckskin britches and knee-high boots whose leather was cracked and muddied. His red hair spilled over the collar of a standard blue military coat that bore the insignia of a lieutenant. A sword hung on the back of his chair. He looked up when the two men entered, blotted his quill, and lay it on the rough table before him. His blue eyes twinkled. When he recognized Drouillard, he rose to his full six feet, grinned, and extended a hand. "Georges, I'm so glad you're back."

"*Moi aussi,* my captain, but I had to leave the *charette* and supplies bogged in the mud at the landing. It will take several men and horses to pull it out."

Clark clapped twice, and another man entered. "Sergeant, take McNeal, Goodrich, Warner, and York and a horse and collect the wagon that Drouillard left at the landing. Go quickly before thieves strip it clean. If the road is too soft, leave the wagon and pack in the supplies." Sergeant Ordway saluted and turned briskly on his heel. The black man, York, followed.

Clark turned back to Drouillard. "The men that you sent from Fort Massac all arrived except two."

Drouillard's black eyes danced gleefully as he mumbled a reply. "I've brought you another. This one is impetuous but worth two of those, my captain. He can swim, he brings a horse, and he gapes at new and wonderful sights."

Clark lifted an eyebrow. "We will pay him for the horse." He looked up and appraised Collins from the wide soles of his boots to the thatch of blond curls beneath the black hat on his head. "Do I know your face?" A glint of recognition crossed his brow.

Collins opened his mouth as if to speak, thought better of it, then offered sheepishly: "At Clarksville, at the falls of the Ohio, sir."

Comprehension spread like a wave across William Clark's face. "You pulled me from the whirlpool!"

"I held you up, sir. Other men pulled the rope that saved us both."

Clark's face opened in a wide grin. "And I never learned your name."

"John Collins, sir, from Frederick, Maryland."

"Far from home like the rest of us." Clark waited for the young man to explain himself.

Collins grinned back like an eager schoolboy.

Drouillard interrupted. "He is young. He is not married. He can cook and shoot and swim"—he hesitated before mumbling—"and fight like a demon for the attentions of a woman. He cannot read or write, but he can learn." He smacked his lips, rocked back on his heels, and lifted his gaze. "At times, sir, my captain, he lacks control, but so do many others here."

Clark turned to Collins. "That is high praise from Drouillard. You do know why he brought you here?"

"For employment, sir, for discovery, for adventure, because he needed help crossing the river, and to escape from an embarrassment in the French settlements." He was not afraid of the truth.

Drouillard explained: "A woman, my captain, a witch who

tempted two men to blows. The river people do not easily yield their women."

Clark flashed a glance at Drouillard. "You French are jealous folk."

"We defend our own like a lion on its den, sometimes without cause, where the affairs of the heart are concerned."

William Clark laughed. "So you run from the clutches of Eve, Mister Collins. There are no women where we are going, but I will not tolerate fighting for any reason among my men."

"I was challenged, sir. I did not begin the fight."

William Clark grunted. He appreciated ladies, too, and smiled knowingly up at Collins. It was an electrifying expression that anchored allegiance and respect. Clark's voice, too, had the force of command with a mellow admixture of human understanding. He was a true leader of men. John Collins hung on his every word.

"I will give you a trial, Collins, on Drouillard's recommendation." Clark's gaze was riveting. "And I trust you to keep the knowledge I tell you secret, lest the British or the Spanish or another competitor try to waylay us. . . . Myself and Captain Meriwether Lewis are organizing a Corps of Discovery on behalf of the United States of America. President Jefferson has directed us 'to explore the Missouri river . . . by its course and communication with the waters of the Pacific Ocean.' " Those are President Jefferson's own words. We are to cross the continent of North America and find a passage to the Pacific Ocean. It is an enterprise not without danger, from wild beasts and the forces of nature, from the Spanish whose lands we must cross and who do not want to yield one inch of territory, from the British Hudson's Bay and North West Companies who want to exclude us from lucrative trading opportunities with the native peoples and cause myriad other hazards we cannot predict." He paused and added somberly: "The Spanish do not recognize American sovereignty and will throw any obstacle in our way. We need men, horses, supplies. You will be paid the same as a private in the Army of these seventeen United States . . . five dollars each month and warrants for three hundred acres of prime land upon completion of the expedition." He grinned suddenly. "I can offer you provisional appointment until we assess your ability to contribute to the success of our enterprise." He added slyly: "But I cannot promise you the attentions of beautiful young ladies."

Georges Drouillard frowned. Collins swallowed his embarrassment and stood silently, trying to digest Clark's implications. In the end, he stammered: "I accept, sir. Thank you, sir." His voice was overly eager, almost naïve.

Drouillard interrupted. "My horse cracked a hoof. Collins's is a serviceable beast."

Clark shuffled his papers. "I will pay thirty guineas now for the horse."

It was a fair price. John Collins hesitated, shifting his weight nervously from one foot to the other. He had not anticipated selling the horse. He didn't need the money. He had his winnings from the fight and the faithful animal that had carried him safely all the way from Maryland.

Drouillard slapped his shoulder and volunteered. "He will be well fed, and you can still tend the beast. It is a chance to carve footprints in history, Johnny."

Adventure tempted John Collins, but the memory of Louise Bourgeron and an unwillingness to part with the animal lingered.

William Clark's mellow voice echoed definitively: "Join the encampment, talk to the other recruits. Drouillard here can introduce you. Then decide." Drouillard steered him out of the tent. Collins led the horse to a rude corral, patted the soft muzzle, and turned him loose.

The men huddled around the blazing campfire were much like Collins himself, young, uneducated, rough but friendly. They exuded an infectious energy. One strummed his fiddle. Others were singing raucously. Three more were arguing over a card game. A man standing on his hands, upside down, was one of the ugliest men Collins had ever seen. They fell silent when he and Drouillard walked up. The fiddler was George Gibson. The singers were Hugh Hall, a sandy-colored box of a man, and George Shannon whose youthful tenor carried the others. John Colter, whose name followed Collins on the muster rolls, nodded a greeting. Joe Whitehouse, who still retained the fresh pink newness of a farm boy, moved over to make a place for Collins near the fire. Two brothers who looked almost like twins offered to share their meat.

The ugly man still standing on his hands shouted: "Yet another devil's rogue you bring us, Drouillard, *mon frère?*" François Labiche, Frenchman and acquaintance of Drouillard, flipped upright and turned to the companion at his side. "Three minutes I held it, Leakins, you owe me your whiskey!"

Labiche's dark neighbor passed him his cup and bellowed at Drouillard: "Can he heft an axe and shoot a deer or must we strain 'is milk and cut 'is meat like he was a babe?" Amos Leakins was a surly, unpredictable man.

One of the apparent twins rebuked him roundly: "Give the man a chance, Leakins. He's a tolerable lookin' lad."

Leakins did not drop his eyes at the rebuke but stared back menacingly, first at Labiche, then at Collins, the newcomer. John Collins read challenge in the surly glare. Leakins was a sore loser. Collins would have to prove himself to Leakins,

51

but he was grateful to the man who had spoken up for him. Joe Fields was that one's name. He and Reuben were not really twins, but brothers separated in age by two years. In manners and looks, they were very alike. Joe Fields's monotone rolled over Collins now like warm soothing water. "Set man, and tell us of yourself and of your doin's." Later, Drouillard introduced him to two sergeants named Floyd and Pryor, and disappeared into the enveloping darkness. Collins made his bed in a crowded tent with Sergeant Pryor, Joe Whitehouse, and young Shannon, because they made a welcome place for him, as they had around the crowded campfire.

There was another group of men that Collins did not meet that first night. They had built their fire on the opposite side of the fort and held to their own counsels. Amos Leakins belonged to this contingent of a few regulars and hangers-on. The two groups came together when the entire company gathered with Captain Clark to move the encampment upriver, across from St. Louis, closer to the mouth of the Missouri and the point of their embarkation. Leakins's men worked less than the others. They never put forth an effort unless William Clark or Sergeant John Ordway were watching. From sawing wood to target shooting, they performed adequately but minimally, never brilliantly. Collins won shooting matches and foot races. Howard was the best swimmer and Joe Fields, a good man with a horse. John Potts, the short German, could chop wood at dizzying speed, and Labiche, the hand-walker, was the best man with a knife. At the end of the day, Collins and his new friends ate and collapsed, but Leakins's men were ready to laugh and sing.

They moved upriver to a fertile bottomland near the mouth of a river named Wood. They rowed and sailed and pulled the heavy boats against the stream by the brawn of their backs. They slipped and bogged down and helped each other up. The skin of their fingers blistered and cracked. No one criticized Collins now. His muscles were strong; he never complained; he brought the horse that pulled triple a man's share; and he could cook, a talent that endeared him to constantly hungry frontiersmen. Still he felt the eyes of Leakins, like stinging insects on his neck, as he hoisted his oar or hefted his axe, or suffered the burn of the tow rope on the peak of his shoulder. Drouillard's words about Spanish threats returned to haunt him. Leakins ridiculed any man who worked his hardest. It seemed as if he did not want to succeed, as if he possessed a prescience of disaster. He curried favor and planted seeds of doubt. Unconsciously, Collins sensed subtle subversion but could not define the fearful suspicion that gnawed at the back of his brain. Drouillard would have exposed Leakins. Drouillard would have known what to do. But Drouillard had been absent these last few weeks, translating for Meriwether Lewis and making last minute preparations in St. Louis. Captain Clark was in charge in camp, but he was preoccupied with his maps and stores. Clark, too, was frequently absent. Sergeant Ordway, the stern New Englander who was left in charge, had little insight into the disputes of enlisted men.

At the wintering place, on a triangle of land where the Wood River spills into the Mississippi, the rivalries flared. Camp discipline reverted to Sergeants Ordway, Pryor, and Floyd. The work did not fall evenly on the shoulders of the men. They nailed together sheds, split wood, hunted and dried meat, and collected stores for the duration of winter and the journey ahead. Everyday they marched and drilled. Evenings, Cruzatte or Gibson plunked his fiddle, and everyone danced. But Amos Leakins lost his wager when John Collins chopped more wood than Reuben Fields. Leakins stalked off like a plucked rooster. From that day, his treatment of Collins deteriorated from indifference to open antagonism. John Collins missed his stoic mentor, Drouillard. There was no longer a mediator when a fight threatened, no encouraging voice when his young confidence flagged.

But life in camp was not unpleasant. There were shooting matches, horse and canoe races, tests of speed and strength with axe and pick, or skill with a paddle and sail. They hunted and fished. They learned the Indian ways of preserving meat and grinding corn. Food was plentiful if not tasty. The whiskey was bourbon from Kentucky and wine from St. Charles, and there was rum from the port of New Orleans. Howard brewed his own corn whiskey that he sold against regulations, behind righteous Sergeant Ordway's back.

William Clark had ordered a strict military regimen which Ordway, the officer in charge, followed to the letter. He was a strict disciplinarian and stickler for detail and Clark's chosen second in command. The dour New Englander retained his Puritan work ethic. No minute in the day lay idle. The men awakened at dawn, marched and mustered and drilled again. Collins enjoyed the physical effort, but the strict, unwavering routine galled him. There were times when he was tempted to join the shirkers who melted into the forest when the work became burdensome or substituted a visit to the grog shop for a day of hunting. At times like these, Collins would remember his friend, Drouillard, and the confident face of William Clark. But Leakins, Moses Reed, and others grated like burrs in his blankets.

Both Lewis and Clark arrived to celebrate Christmas. A happier holiday for Collins came at the New Year, when Drouillard returned with a keg of Tennessee bourbon. "God's brew. Better than Kentucky bourbon. Makes

Howard's potion taste like yesterday's piss." Drouillard laughed without cracking a smile.

The New Year's games were loud, the dancing lively, the betting furious, and the melodies strident with drink. The German, Potts, tapped out a rousing tune from his native land with the heel of his boot on the deck of the boat, drowning out the sweeter melody of Shannon's tenor and Cruzatte's furious strumming. John Collins won a dollar in a tug of war. Labiche won five at cards. Captain Lewis, who came only lately from the salons of Washington and Philadelphia, did not party with the men. He preferred more cultured, orderly festivities. But William Clark, the youngest member of a large, boisterous family, who had campaigned on the frontier with his older brother, joined the revelry with enthusiasm.

On New Year's Day, the captains summoned Collins to their tent. It was a frosty, gray day. An icy, sobering wind swept in from the west and blew cold moisture in pricks of sleet from off the river. Collins rose from his place at the mess, handed his bowl to Shannon, and wrapped himself in his blanket for the cold walk across the camp. His boots crunched on the hard, frozen ground. The warmth was welcome when he stepped under the flap and into the captains' hut where a fire burned in a brazier. His face flushed from the sudden heat as he let his eyes adjust to the dimness. Sergeant Ordway stood at attention, immovable as a stump. Meri- wether Lewis sat at a camp desk and hunched his head over scrolls of maps that shone under the uncertain light of a row of candles. Collins shuffled in and snapped to attention.

William Clark stepped from behind Lewis and walked forward with hand outstretched. "Mister Collins, Captain Lewis here has left the manning of our expedition to me as I have left the politics and diplomacy to him." Clark hesitated as if he harbored some doubt. Lewis's head snapped up. He shot a stern look at Collins. Clark continued: "Collins, what Drouillard said about you is true. You are strong. You are a good marksman. You do not shy from hard and dirty work, and I believe you get on well with most men. I am happy to offer you a permanent position in our corps." He smiled and his face broadened visibly. "Understand that it is I who make the offer to you on my own inclination and the recommendation of Georges Drouillard whose opinion I respect. Captain Lewis and Sergeant Ordway are not as convinced as I that you will become a responsible member of the company. You have been impetuous, mildly disobedient, but never to the point of endangerment. They think you a philanderer, but then there are no women here, and no one doubts that you are brave or that you have the skills and strength required for the journey." He stopped and exhaled. His breath blew out like a shower of steam in the frosty air.

Meriwether Lewis spoke up. His speech was slow, his voice soft. "Your troubles, Collins, have all been libidinous. I trust you can exercise some self-control."

Libidinous? John Collins had never heard the word, but he recognized Lewis's admonishing frown.

The final caution shifted back to Clark. His lips drew back into a thin pencil line. His blue eyes turned cold and held Collins like powerful magnets. "Your final disposition will depend on your behavior during the next few months prior to departure. For now, Captain Lewis and I appoint you to the rank of private in the Army of the seventeen United States. We expect you to conduct yourself with discretion and prudence. You will receive your pay according to your rank, and we have added your name to the muster rolls starting January First, today." Clark's eyes held Collins attention, eye to eye.

That he would tolerate no transgressions from the stated code, Collins did not doubt.

Collins shifted his weight tentatively from one foot to another. His eyes flicked from the serious visage of Meriwether Lewis to the stony grimace of John Ordway, to his own restless feet. He raised them again as William Clark's broad palm extended toward him, and he grasped it and sealed the covenant. Clark's grip was sure and hard.

Collins swelled his chest. He pulled himself to his full height as if to prove himself worthy of his new position. A youthful grin spread over his face like syrup on a pancake, and his voice echoed his enthusiasm: "Thank you, sir. I will do my best to honor the trust that you place in me." He thought suddenly of Louise Bourgeron, of the pleasures he was leaving behind, and his lips twitched slightly. But those thoughts paled now before this formidable man with the iron handshake. William Clark would lead John Collins like a pilgrim through the sloughs, up rivers, across plains, and over mountains. John Collins, faithful apostle, would follow. Before he left, he asked one question. "Mister Drouillard, sir, I presume he will he be coming with us?"

Captain Lewis answered: "We could not proceed without him." Lewis, too, held out his hand. It was softer to the touch than Clark's, without the calluses of one who labored. But Lewis had a light, ethereal smile. He added: "Welcome, Private Collins, and good luck." And he was sincere. Collins left with a new faith in his heart and fire in his eye. His shoulders seemed wider, his back straighter, his chin higher.

Drouillard was leaning against a tree, holding Collins's dinner plate and licking his fingers. He handed the plate back now, empty. "Cold venison gives the flux." Collins was too excited to care if his stomach were empty or full. The certainty of a decision made marked the swing in his step. His imagination had leaped ahead to the wonders he would experience. Drouillard raised a shaggy brow. "You are coming with us, *mon ami?* You like the Captains Clark and Lewis? They have just hired Tom Howard and Alex Willard, and now you."

Collins nodded and took a deep breath. His grin was his assent.

Drouillard lay a gnarled hand on the young recruit's shoulder. "You will forget Louise Bourgeron. The native girls, upriver, are very beautiful." He touched the tips of all five fingers to his lips and kissed them in a typically Gallic gesture, and he added philosophically: "My mother was such a beauty, and kind and patient, with black flowing hair like the river at night. The beauty that runs deep is more desirable than the flaunted charms of Louise Bourgeron. But we have not finished with Jacques, the *frère*." Drouillard gave no further explanation.

Collins blinked. He had not followed Drouillard's reasoning. Enthusiasm charged his voice. "We are going against the flow, the hard way, Georges, but I like it. I'm ready." He dropped his eyes, then settled their slate blue fire on the sun's own reflection in the river. "I am not a weak man, Georges. Captain Clark is a fine leader, and you are a good teacher. I will deal with Jacques Bourgeron. If I am man enough for Captain Clark's corps, I am man enough to defend my name. I have already whipped the brother once."

"Will you whip him again, if he buys the services of villains, if the Spaniards discover he is a useful tool, or if he returns in the night behind your back while we sleep? Then, *mon ami,* it will be necessary for all of us to deal with Jacques Bourgeron."

The possibility of subterfuge had not occurred to John Collins. He did not answer. He shook his head, annoyed that

Drouillard could so easily plant doubt, and that he himself might allow the uncertainty to take root and grow. From now on he would grip his rifle more tightly. He walked off to water and feed the brown horse.

Chapter Five

In February, three dugout canoes crunched onto the shore at Wood River camp. A dozen French rivermen heaved them up onto the narrow beach. Hall and Goodrich, who were on the shore fishing, nodded suspiciously. The Frenchmen marched in a tight knot toward the camp. The tramping feet, the sharp cry of their leader, and the bark of Lewis's dog announced their arrival. Sergeant John Ordway stepped from the captains' hut to collar the dog. Gibson and the vociferous German, Potts, ran for their rifles. The Field brothers, Collins, young Shannon, and Colter, who were chopping wood, dropped their axes and grabbed their guns.

Georges Drouillard was butchering a deer. He jumped up shouting. "Lay down the arms! They are friends . . . *amis!*" He alone had understood the jargon of Spanish, French, and Indian that the newcomers spouted and that grated on the ears of the company like a knife on a whetstone.

The rivermen were short like Potts and dark like Drouillard, with shoulders made massive by transporting game and paddling canoes against the strong currents of rivers. To a man, their hair was black, their noses hawk-like, and their skin tanned. All but two of their faces were scarred. One was missing an ear, another the tip of his nose and two fingers of his left hand. Some wore flat, felt hats, others hats made from skins. One wrapped his head in a bandanna that held his black hair back from his predatory eyes in the manner of marauding pirates. Pouches, powder horns, muskets, tomahawks, and blades of every sort hung from loops in their belts or thongs slung over their shoulders. They dressed in a combination of skins and homespun, in wide, loose shirts hanging halfway to their knees. They tucked ragged pantaloons into laced, knee-high moccasins. The teeth and tails of animals, bright-colored beads, and shells adorned clothing, the lobes of their ears, and the tresses of their hair. Each carried a large hide pack. Broad, colorful belts cinched their shirts at the waist. Some of their belts were quilled in the Indian fashion, and the quillwork gleamed with oily brilliance in the cold winter sunlight, like satin ribbons in a maiden's hair.

There was no mistaking their leader. He was built like a box, wide as he was tall. He wore a quilled belt of blazing orange and cobalt blue. The colors wove snake-like around scrolls of intricate flowers and emphasized the considerable breath of his paunch. Most of the men of the company had never seen such fine handiwork, and they looked with envy at the heavy man with the black lion's mane who wore it. The man sensed their desires and glared back aggressively from under corniced brows that locked together over the bridge of his nose. He spoke in a voice that roared up from the depths of his paunch. "Baptiste Deschamps is here! Your patron, *Capitaine* Clark, where is he?" It was not a request but a command, harshly spoken, devoid of trust and respect.

"Captain Clark ain't here." Hugh Hall grumbled the answer with strict attention to rank. Collins, Shannon, the Field brothers, and John Colter stood by warily, but Gibson and Potts marched squarely into the rivermen's path. Potts's raucous voice flung insulting comments back over his shoulder. "Savages are here! Grab your weapons! Mind the whiskey and powder!"

Deschamps heard the insult and scowled. The rivermen

stood in a circle, heels dug into the soil, shaggy heads facing outward like buffalo in a stand. Their black eyes scanned the company and halted at the stocky form of Potts. Deschamps's voice boomed: "We are not savages, *monsieur*." He spat, and the saliva landed inches from Potts's feet. "We sail the rivers for our wage. We make our own drink, *monsieur,* from the sweet red blood of the vine. It does not dull our wits or inflame our tempers like your pale yellow water of the grain."

Drouillard stepped in front of Gibson. "Why do you challenge us, Deschamps? We have no quarrel with you." He turned on Potts. "Put the gun away."

Potts lowered the rifle as Deschamps scanned the faces of the company and alighted on John Collins. "So it is here you hide, seducer of maidens." His hand fell to the hilt of his knife. "Calderon is my uncle. Now he will find you."

Collins rose to the challenge. "I bear Calderon no grudge. Louise is not so young as to be without blame. I have no claim on her nor she on me."

"Louise has run away. Bourgeron, the brother, says she has eloped." His fierce eyes narrowed to angry slits. "Eloped with you!"

"Georges Drouillard is my witness. I have not seen Louise since December last, and there are no women in this camp."

"You left her after you took your pleasure."

Collins's voice jumped an octave. "I took no pleasure. You have my word." The Frenchman's blind assumptions angered him. He felt his blood gush through his veins. To be falsely accused, now, when he had just been accepted here, when the captains had placed great confidence in him, was a test of his own honor. He sensed himself reaching for his knife, shouting his own accusation. "You have no right. The woman toys with truth."

An iron hand descended like a vise on his biceps and

twirled him around. Drouillard thrust himself between the two contestants. "Deschamps, the boy is telling the truth." He repeated it in French for the others to hear. "*C'est un innocent!* You come here spouting fire like a dragon, begging to fight. Where is your courtesy?"

"I came to see your *capitaine.*"

"You can see him without your knife."

Sergeant John Ordway pushed into the mêlée. "I am in command here!"

Frowning, with eyes glued to Collins, Deschamps handed a scrolled parchment to the sergeant who unfurled it officiously and began to read, stumbling over the foreign pronunciation. Deschamps grumbled angrily, extended a gnarled finger, and pointed directly at John Collins. "Your patrons have employed a devil."

Silas Goodrich and Moses Reed sauntered up. Like wolves, they could sniff a fight. Goodrich called to Collins: "The river rats snappin' at yer heels, Johnny? I'll stand behind you." He had just come from fishing and stood with a string of trout slung over his square shoulder. He let go the fish and balled his fists. The Frenchmen grouped more tightly. Drouillard pinned Collins's arms and yelled at Deschamps: "Call off your men or blood will flow!"

Deschamps lifted a fat finger to point at Ordway. "When your sergeant atones for this man's insult"—pointing at Collins—"and that man's lust!"

Meriwether Lewis stepped from his hut. He deliberately ignored the commotion and walked forward with arms extended wide, unarmed, vulnerable. "Baptiste, my friend. . . . what's this? A fight when we would make you welcome?" He turned up both his hands. Deschamps shoved his fingers beneath his belt. Lewis continued calmly in perfect French: "*Bonjour mes amis et bienvenue. . . .*" The French language rolled easily off his tongue, like soft rain after drought. Lewis smiled affably motioning to Collins. "This man's word is true, Baptiste. I give you my word and the word of Captain Clark and of your countryman, Georges Drouillard, that he has resided here for the last month. . . ." He turned to John Collins. "Private Collins, step forward." He placed his palm on Collins's shoulder and whispered privately: "Come easily man, do not enrage them." And again to Deschamps in liquid Gallic syllables: "Collins is a valued member of our company. We have placed our faith in him. You are a God-fearing man, Baptiste. We will swear by the Holy Book, as God is our witness, that John Collins, here, is an honorable man. Will that satisfy you?"

Deschamps nodded darkly. "He must swear to the truth."

"Sergeant, bring the Bible!"

Ordway left and returned with the sacred book. He stood before Collins while Lewis delivered the oath. "Private John Collins, do you swear before the Christian God and these good gentlemen, here present, that you have not seduced this young lady Deschamps speaks of, and that you have been here with us, celibate and alone, since December last?"

"I do so swear, sir, as God is my witness." Collins's voice was clear and loud. He stood proudly under the hawk-like glare of the Frenchman.

Now Meriwether Lewis faced the threatening stare and repeated the oath. "And I swear before God and before you, Baptiste Deschamps, that Private John Collins, here present, has resided with us, without company of woman, since the first day of December." He took a deep breath and scanned his audience. Deschamps's eyes clouded. Open animosity diminished, but suspicion still smoldered.

Lewis stepped back, smiled affably, and addressed his own company. "Gentlemen, eight of these boatmen will be joining us to assist on the first lap of our journey. They are accomplished in their trade and know the whims of the river and the inhabitants of her shores. They have made such trips before, and they will help transport our trade goods and supplies." There was grumbling in the background. Lewis pulled himself to his full height and scanned his audience with an elegant tilt of the head. His mild blue eyes narrowed. His lips pulled back, and his jaw tightened. He waited for silence, then continued: "It is time to put aside petty dislikes for the sake of the greater good of the unity and proficiency of this company. Work together, learn together. Prejudice and distrust must not crush the hard kernel of our strength. Captain Clark and I will not tolerate fighting or dissension within these ranks." His sharp glare withered his listeners. He stood tall and spare with knees locked. With patrician grace, he made his pronouncement. "On behalf of all of us here present, I welcome our French friends." He bowed elegantly in front of Deschamps, backed away, and extended his arm, inviting the hefty boatmen to the campfire.

Lewis had not raised his voice, had not threatened or cajoled. With unflappable composure, he had thrown cold water on the flames. The Frenchmen came forward to set up their camp. Collins, Hall, Colter, and Drouillard returned to the wood pile and shouldered their axes. Lewis himself and the stalwart Field brothers helped the Frenchmen unload their canoes. But Leakins and Moses Reed lingered in the background. Reed backed into the shadow of the stockade and sat heavily on a log. Gibson and Newman followed. Drouillard tracked them with his eyes and counseled: "Avoid them, *mon ami*. They want war. They want to see blood flow."

Next day, Deschamps and his crew had drawn the large keelboat on log rollers up onto the muddy shore. They pulled it higher by brute strength. Dark sweat soaked through the fabric of their shirts. Its stale smell permeated the humid air with the scent of man's labors. Finally, they tilted the heavy boat on its side. The huge keel spread out on the beach like the wing of a dead bird, and they set to scraping the sharp crust of mollusk and weed from the boat's bottom.

The Field brothers, John Colter, and John Potts were assigned to scrape the red *pirogue*. They were not as co-ordinated in their efforts as their French counterparts. The *pirogue* wobbled sideways, slipped off the rollers, nearly crushing Potts's foot, and sank back heavily into the mud. Collins and Colter jumped in to help. It was a massive, embarrassing effort. The lines creaked and strained and rubbed their hands raw. The red *pirogue* tottered and slid back again. Finally, like Atlas supporting the world on his shoulders, Collins and Potts wedged their backs beneath the vessel, and raised it up. When it threatened to crush them, a Frenchman shoved in a heavy pole to hold the sinking weight. His countrymen followed with more poles to winch the boat higher. French and American crowded to the task, and the boat rose one inch at a time. Together, they lay the *pirogue* on its side and set to scraping. Knives flashed and polishing stones rasped. Deschamps came to inspect the work. Collins was so absorbed that he did not notice the surly Frenchman at first. He stiffened suddenly when he spied the large shadow at his back. But Deschamps did not criticize and passed on by. No more was said, and the convergence of effort was the first fine thread of co-operation between French and American.

When the boats were clean of weed and growth, they repaired the rigging, shook out the sails, and replaced the boats in the river. It was grueling work. Captain Lewis emerged periodically to watch and encourage. He smiled down on his men with pride, with a luminous, all-enveloping sign of approval, and the men worked harder.

But it was William Clark who came out to congratulate the men at the morning muster. Clark's pleasure beamed in his dancing eyes and florid face. He promised them each an extra gill at the evening mess, and ended with a laugh and a cheerful order. "Clean yourselves up tonight, boys. We go to the city tomorrow for the ceremony. His Excellency Don Carlos Dehault Delassus, Lieutenant Governor of Upper Louisiana, will officially hand over the territory to our United States. Captain Amos Stoddard will accept the Territorial Charter on behalf of Thomas Jefferson, your President. And we have not forgotten our French friends who made it all possible. Their flag will fly for one day over the city, March Tenth, mark the date well! It will live in history! The day after, we will raise our own seventeen stars. You all will be witness to the event. It means that the lands and rivers we are about to explore are the free and self-determining territories of the United States."

Comprehension dawned gradually. The men stared for a moment, then broke loose. But William Clark was not finished, and his face turned grave. "The transfer ceremonies imply strict responsibilities. I expect each one to conduct himself with grace and decorum. There will be drinking and dancing. You represent your country to these, our new citizens. I insist on spotless uniforms, polished boots, and, above all, exemplary behavior." He paused for emphasis. "There are those in Saint Louis who will not be pleased with the transfer. They may jeer and harass you. You must restrain any youthful enthusiasm, any urge to retaliate." He turned on his heel and retreated to his hut.

After Clark was gone, the men burst out in loud cheers, backslaps, and shouts. Collins threw his hat high in the air, then like a mischievous child hefted a fistful of mud and lobbed it at Potts. Potts scooped up his own slug, heaved it back, and the frolic began. Amid hollers and whoops, chaos broke loose. Shannon and the two Field brothers, Hall, Goodrich, and Reed, who had come in from fishing, joined the mêlée. William Clark ignored the revelry of his young and feisty troops. Tomorrow was time enough for discipline. Today, they ended by stripping off their shirts and jumping into the ice-cold water of the river to wash off the slime. The cold water was slap enough of future reality.

When John Collins calmed, Captain Clark's last words echoed ominously in the back of his brain. He had heard similar warnings from Drouillard. A premonition came over him and engulfed him like a thick fog. He realized, all at once, that this journey that they would attempt was more than some playful adventure. It was a struggle against incredible odds, for land, for dominion, for liberty. It was an affirmation of the existence of his infant country. It seemed such an easy trek to his boisterous companions. He watched them and shuddered.

William Clark himself served the whiskey that evening. Each man received an extra gill. The Americans danced and sang far into the night. But the Frenchmen downed their drink and sat morosely around a separate fire. They had lost Louisiana twice, once in 1763, to the greedy Spaniards, and now in 1804, to the bumbling Americans, who could not even pull a *pirogue* out of the river onto the beach. Napoléon had sold their soil, the beaver and fish in their rivers, and the trees in their forests. They yearned for the days of their grandfathers' songs, when France was supreme and King Louis XV ruled the territory like the good St. Louis for whom the vast territory was named.

Chapter Six

The day appointed for the official transfer dawned sunny and cold. It was still dark when the bugle sounded. Collins jumped from his bunk into the frosty air, ran to the river, and splashed his face. He'd been dreaming, a recurring vision of Maryland and a home that he couldn't precisely remember. It shook his young confidence like the petals of a wilting flower. Was he in his right mind to be heading farther west? He was here on the shores of the mighty Mississippi, the end of the English-speaking world. Today, he would sail with his troop to the other side.

He shoved his self-doubt deep beneath the surface of his soul and wiped the cold drops from his face. How foolish he looked, standing like a beanpole, clapping his hands, rubbing his half-naked body to stir the warmth, barefoot with his blanket dangling down around his hips. Hughie Hall saw him and laughed. Collins uttered a hoarse croak, pulled the blanket tightly around him, and walked over to stir the fire. It sputtered and came alive. Humiliated, he retreated to the safety of his tent.

Nat Pryor was up, groping sleepily for his shirt. George Shannon was blinking sleep from his eyes. He was a likable boy, enthusiastic, inexperienced, but good company. Now, young Shannon had lost a boot and was feeling his way around the floor on all fours. Collins tripped over him and kicked the errant boot into Pryor. In the Army, a man's feet were his transport, and his boots protected that transport in the dead of winter when snow and ice covered the ground and the earth was frozen hard as pig iron. Shannon could have been reprimanded severely for carelessness, but Nat Pryor, like William Clark, was a patient man who possessed a particular sensitivity to the foibles of young men. He knew when to blame and when to look away. He did the same for Collins and all the young recruits. He understood that the men of his corps were like frisky colts in their first snow, careless of the slippery ground, eager to jump and buck.

Clark and Lewis had deliberately chosen spirited young men, many still in their teens, without family attachments, spawned on the frontier, independent, enterprising, vigorous, and active. Some were illiterate. All possessed the practical intelligence necessary for survival in a strange land. Some had learned a trade, like Shields the smithy, and Gass the carpenter. All could shoot a rifle and butcher a cow, and all could find their way by the stars in the wilderness. Some were irresponsible with their possessions, like young Shannon who was always losing things: flints, a blanket, his knife. Everyone knew never to lend him anything. There were the pranksters in the group like Hall and Warner, fun-loving and indiscreet but never malicious. Some had annoying habits like Joe Whitehouse, the fourth man in the tent with Collins. Whitehouse rarely spoke but was always scribbling notes on bark, leather, anything that would absorb ink. At first Collins took him for a mute. But when Whitehouse finally spoke, he reddened and stuttered. There was Potts the blusterer, McNeal the dreamer, ugly Labiche, the hand-walker, with his set of dice and deck of cards, the perennial gambler. Howard was a tough boatman who drank whiskey, not water, and brewed his own. Cruzatte, an old, scarred voyageur, wanted to reform every man in the troop in the name of God.

Collins, like many, was blind to his own quirks. He liked the company of men and was eager to be liked by his fellows. He was careless of danger, brave to the point of imperiling himself, impatient to substitute the excitement of discovery for the boredom of life in camp. Men befriended him easily, and women fawned over his boyish good looks. But he was too quick to use brawn before brain, and too eager to jump to the defense of those he called friend.

Now, in the early dawn, on the morning of the territorial transfer, Collins shrugged into his blue uniform coat. It stretched tightly across his broad shoulders whose muscles had filled out and hardened from the daily exertions of the winter camp. He squeezed his feet into his boots. They were too tight and cramped his toes. His old ones had worn through. He longed for soft moccasins. For a hat, he pulled on his black felt that drooped awkwardly over his ears from days in the rain. But uniform dress did not usually matter much to Captain Clark. Young Shannon still wore his Quaker felt, and Drouillard, who was left-handed, always slung his powder horn over the wrong shoulder. John Potts couldn't button his coat over his barrel chest without splitting a seam, and Moses Reed squirmed uncomfortably like a monk in a hairshirt. Collins was sure he had lice. Reed's wiggling was distracting. So were his eyes that always seemed to be looking elsewhere, preoccupied with periphery instead of core. But Reed could read and write and dismissed Collins and any man who could not as inconsequential.

Today they fell out for muster in a cold early mist. When Captain Clark passed in review, he usually overlooked all except the most glaring faults. But this morning was different. He stopped when he came to Potts, tugged the two facings of the coat close together, and exclaimed: "Potts, stop eating!"

Potts reddened and protested: "With due respect, sir, it's

71

muscle, not fat. Only Howard can live on drink, sir."

To Collins, Windsor, and McNeal, Clark presented new hats and watched as Drouillard shifted his powder horn to the opposite shoulder. A drum rolled, and they practiced simple parade formations. In the end, Clark ordered the incorrigible Potts to attach himself to the Frenchmen, who would attend the ceremonies in the capacity of civilian contractors, without uniforms.

They marched uphill to the city below the stockade in the late morning and lined up behind troops of Lieutenant Stephen Worrell in front of the Government House. Meriwether Lewis and Captain Amos Stoddard would accept the charter of Louisiana from Spain, who would cede it first to France and then to the United States. The dignitaries stood resplendent in new uniforms on a small stage erected for the purpose. The spectacle was fit more for a palace court-yard than for this rough outpost of barely two hundred hovels that lay like a doormat beneath the timbered fort.

A roar of cannon split the air, the first of several loud salutes. The young men of the company stiffened under the scrutiny of the precise, immaculate, Spanish ranks. The Americans sensed a slight, drew back their shoulders, swelled their chests, and maintained perfect formation for the first time in their lives.

Salvos continued at regular intervals. A Spanish drum corps and honor guard accompanied the coach of the Spanish lieutenant governor. Don Carlos Dehault Delassus de Luzière stepped out, posed, waved, and ascended the plat-form with a pomposity that made John Collins recoil. The drums fell silent, and Delassus began in fluid Spanish. His proclamation was not brief. "The flag under which you have been protected for thirty-six years is to be withdrawn." He was a haughty nobleman, bedecked in plumed hat, lace cuffs,

and ribbons of rank. A gold-hilted sword hung at his side, and
the medallion of his rank adorned his chest. He spoke of the
glory of Spain, a glory he exhibited in himself, and a glory that
the infant United States could not match. Delassus's voice
thundered. Finally he raised a white-gloved hand the length
of his arm high above his head, and brought it down in a
broad sweep. This was the signal. The coat of arms of Spain
and of His Catholic Majesty slowly began to descend from
the flagpole on the heights of the fort. It was Delassus's
farewell, the same Delassus who had refused permission for
the Corps of Discovery to pass upriver into His Majesty's do-
mains; who had denied Captain Meriwether Lewis a Spanish
passport and who had caused the Corps of Discovery to
winter in the U. S. Territory of Illinois, and not in Louisiana
Territory; Delassus, the nobleman who had fled the Revolu-
tionary Terror in France, who represented the stubborn
course of a failing empire. Now Delassus bowed obsequiously before Captains Stoddard and Lewis. He congratulated
them on their country's purchase of his rich territory. He did
not mention the United States by name, as if he did not really
believe the events unfolding before his eyes were real, and he
need only wait a few days for a more stable, conventional
power, Spain or France or England, to assert her sovereignty.

Stoddard saluted formally and expressed his country's
and Mr. Jefferson's gratitude. He stated his sincere hope that
Louisianans would place their loyalty and confidence in the
United States of America. It was a confidence that Delassus
and his Spanish overlords would try to undermine, a confidence that would be hard-won.

The two men stepped forward to sign the documents,
Delassus with a dramatic flourish for Spain, Stoddard with
stiff, impersonal precision for France and the United States.
Meriwether Lewis and two French merchants of the city,

Antoine Soulard and Charles Gratiot, signed as witnesses.

Delassus clasped hands with Stoddard and Lewis, then Soulard and Gratiot, and withdrew. John Collins and the detachment watched in awe as the haughty Spaniard took his country's flag, threw it over his shoulder like a cloak, and wrapped it around himself. He exited like a lord, the way he had come. The Spanish soldiery filed silently out of the fort and joined him at the wharf.

For one day the French flag flew. The Corps of Discovery marched again the next day, this time to the fort on the hill above the city, where Amos Stoddard personally lowered the French flag and hoisted the American. Another salvo, another salute, and Louisiana belonged to the new republic. Captain Clark dismissed his men for the round of celebrations that would fill the night. Cannons boomed. Drums beat. Cheers and huzzahs split the air, and the wine and whiskey flowed.

At Meriwether Lewis's request, Delassus made one last effort before departing finally for Mexico. He called a council of Indians to confirm the transfer of the Territory and their allegiance to their new Father. Delawares, Abanakis, Shawnees, Sauks gathered together to hear him. Delassus ended with a promise: "You will live as happily as if we Spaniards were still here." It was not a deliberate lie. He knew that Spain would do all in her power to incite the tribes to resist the authority of the United States. He knew that in Mexico, the Marquis de Casa Calvo and Brigadier Don Nemesio Salcedo y Salcedo had ordered the arrest of Captain Meriwether Lewis and the detention of the explorers. He knew that the Englishmen of the Hudson's Bay and the North West Companies would abet the Spanish efforts and urge the natives to resist American rule. But word traveled slowly on the rivers, and the order to stop the Lewis and Clark expedition with military force did not arrive back in New Orleans before Delassus's departure for Mexico, and the departure of the explorers from Wood River camp for the Mandan villages and parts unknown.

Chapter Seven

Preparations for departure accelerated during the month of April. Captain Lewis collected every shred of knowledge he could about the tribes on the Missouri. He befriended Pierre Choteau, John Hay, and other men whom he trusted and who had traveled upriver. He entertained Kickapoo and Osage chiefs. He studied Indian vocabularies, read maps and diaries. But of what lay beyond the great bend in the river, beyond the Teton Sioux, where the stream turns from north to west toward the Shining Mountains, he learned very little. The Spanish overlords withheld the information.

Provisions were easier to obtain. Barrels of flour, sacks of corn, salt, sugar, biscuit, peas, and gallons of whiskey swelled the commissary stores. Major Rumsey of the U. S. Army furnished bullet molds, sheet lead, and black powder sealed in leaden kegs which could be melted down for bullets. But merchandise ordered from St. Louis traders of Spanish persuasion did not arrive. This included the necessary items for trade with the Indians—guns, knives, mirrors, and glass beads. The captains suspected that Spanish subterfuge caused the delays but did not dare state the belief openly. They harbored deep concern within. Would the agents of Spain try openly to stop the expedition, incite and arm the tribes for attack? And what of the British in the north? Would they stand by complacently and let the expedition pass? Apprehensive, the captains purchased two swivel guns and installed them in the stern. They requisitioned a cannon for the bow.

Finally, Meriwether Lewis went in search of goods ordered but not delivered. Postponement, error, loss, and denial impeded many of his inquiries. He trudged though the muddy streets of St. Louis in the dogged effort to procure what he needed. He paid for it out of his own pocket because he had no other recourse. Spanish authorities snubbed him. Clamorgan voiced their concerns, and his comments were always negative. The little Creole was one of the wealthiest Spanish traders on the Mississippi, a powerful man in St. Louis and New Orleans. He received Lewis cordially, in the manner of a grandee, waving away Lewis's complaints like so many gnats over French brandy and rum cake.

Rumors of Lewis's difficulties spread among his men. They worried that they would be denied guns and ammunition in the treacherous wilderness. Infiltrators exaggerated the dangers. Leakins, Reed, and a new man, Robertson, related accounts of vicious savages who lay in wait at every bend in the river, ferocious beasts with claws and fangs like daggers, and traders who would steal a man naked. Resentment and fear spread like a miasma among the men. They ridiculed young Shannon for his eagerness, and John Shields for his steadiness, calling it boorishness. Because of his handsome face, John Collins bore the brunt of lewd gestures and crude sexual innuendo. He suppressed his anger because of Georges Drouillard and because of his growing admiration for William Clark. They had all heard of George Rogers, William's brother, brave and hardy hero of the revolution, who had seized the Northwest Territories for the United States. George Rogers had inspired tremendous devotion from his men, led them through treacherous swamps and virgin forests. Some of his charisma had worn off, not without merit, on William.

William Clark was neither too lenient nor too strict. He exerted a humane but disciplined leadership that young men like Collins could readily accept. Sometimes Collins objected to the regulations. Sometimes he accepted them. Clark did his best to explain their necessity and earn the willing obedience of Collins and others, but he did not always succeed. Frequently, the exuberant young men refused to listen.

They persisted in testing the limits. Like every young man, Collins dared to chase his desires beyond the limits of safety and prudence. He knew the expedition was military, regulated by strict military discipline. Gradually, he learned to restrain himself. That was why, now, when Leakins's comments turned vicious, he would fold his arms, hold them tightly to his chest, and bite down hard until his teeth ached. The effort strained. He could feel his muscles twitch and the blood pulse at his temples. And there were times when the effort failed and his temper exploded. He was impatient to be on the way, to escape the petty grudges of civilization, and release the torrent of energy building within him.

Leakins's heckling intensified. It wrapped its slimy tentacles around every member of the expedition, squeezing out the vigor and ambition and injecting prejudice, jealousy, and anger. The two captains were absent from the camp much of the time and were powerless to stop it. The sergeants did not know how. When suspicions grew, they exonerated the guilty and denounced the innocent. Leakins took care always to appear innocent. He slithered about the camp, looking over shoulders, poking his beak-like nose where he did not belong, suggesting faster, easier ways to cut corners and finish early and steal a gill of whiskey. He was busy as a mouse in a granary, except when Charles Floyd, his commander, made the rounds. Then he oozed compliance like a widow shedding tears.

John Collins felt a visceral repulsion toward the man and complained to Drouillard. The dark man's reply was ominous and guarded. "He's a shirker. He may be copping Spanish pay, but I've no authority to stop him."

"Working for the Spaniards is treasonous. Why do they allow him to stay?"

Drouillard's black eyes flashed; his frown deepened. "Treason? We are not at war with Spain, *mon ami*. The Spaniards administer Louisiana. We need their guidance and cooperation. . . . And then he is a measure of each man's worth Do your job well and you have nothing to fear. Patience. The captain will unmask the truth."

"The captain is never here!"

Drouillard's lips parted, a dark crack in the rutted creases of his face. Collins credited Drouillard with great wisdom, but it was hidden like a nugget of gold at bedrock beneath the swirling sands of a deep river, and Collins was often too tired or too careless to scratch it out. He spent most of his days laboring harder than he ever had in his life. His muscles ached. Calluses formed over blisters on hands and feet. He envied Drouillard, the best of the hunters, who rode out each day on a horse. Drouillard could see like a hawk and track like a cat. When he was successful, he would summon Collins to help butcher and pack in the meat. The younger man looked forward to these outings that were a happy respite from the tensions of camp life. And he was also learning how to search out wild herbs and berries that add flavor and nourishment.

Sergeant Ordway supervised the frantic packing and repacking. The French boatmen fussed like cackling fowl about weight distribution in the keelboat. Too much weight in the bow would slow progress against a strong current. Too little and the boat would run up on every sand bank that barred its way. They packed and repacked. Finally, Ordway ordered the task completed, and summoned every man to complete the loading. No one was exempt. It was repetitive, boring work, and it continued implacably from dawn to dusk. Tons of cargo had to be moved up the gangplank onto the boats, lowered into the hold, positioned, and lashed down. Captain Clark, when he was in camp, worked alongside the men, but the captain was usually absent.

Clark was in St. Louis the day Collins fell in the river. Collins was glad the popular captain did not witness his embarrassment. He was walking up the gangplank to the keelboat, balancing a crate of spare flints on his shoulder. Reed, who preceded him, stopped suddenly, tottered backward, and fell into him. Collins started to right himself when he felt a slam on his shoulder. The crate slipped, and Collins fell head first into the river. The wood cracked as it hit the water and split open, showering the sparkling flints across the muddy surface. They disappeared in a flash and sank to the weedy bottom. Miraculously, Collins sustained only a gash on his chin and no one was hurt.

Reed stood on the gangplank with Leakins, staring down contemptuously and laughing derisively. "Watch yer flat feet, Johnny boy! Dumpin' the cargo to lighten the load won't earn yer pay!"

Collins didn't hear the gibe. The cold water sloshed about his ears and stung every pore like shards of sharp mica. He surfaced, gulped mouthfuls of air, and shook his head to clear the water from ears and eyes. Then the impact of the tumble hit him: muskets were useless without flints to trigger the spark. Flints were as necessary as powder for survival. He dove to retrieve them from the inky, weed-choked bottom, but he could not see through the murk. He came up, choking and shivering from the cold water that penetrated his clothing like thick oil. He heard Reed's taunting voice, reacted angrily, and spat out his resentment like a bitter pit from unripened fruit. "You pushed me, Reed! You wobbled the plank like a waddling goose and knocked me down. You been pilfering from the whiskey barrel." Collins stood knee-deep in the river. He wiped a glob of weed from his cheek with the back of his hand and flung it at Reed.

Reed ducked. A cynical leer split his black whiskers as he countered with a veiled threat. "Missed yer step an' yer spit, Johnny-boy. Don't lay yer clumsiness onto me." He turned away brusquely and launched a final barb. "And you lost yer hat."

Collins's restraint cracked. His compressed fury erupted. He lunged for Reed's ankles, but Reed jumped back. Hugh Hall splashed into the water between them to stave off a fight. The hat floated downstream.

Suddenly Leakins's voice blasted like a bugle from the shore. "The young blackguard's been throwin' provisions overboard, despoilin' our livelihood, losin' good flints an' a fine hat. There's the wasteful fool." A bony index finger pointed straight at Collins.

Sergeant Ordway arrived, bellowing orders. "We'll have no fighting, Private Collins. Explain yourself."

Collins was not quick enough. Leakins blurted accusations as Reed stood back. "You seen it with yer own eyes, Sergeant. The young blackguard slipped with a crate of flints that's sunk straightway to the bottom of the river, an' he's blaming Moses Reed for pushin' 'im in. Wants to cover his drunkenness, stick 'is thumb in yer eye by shamin' an innocent man."

Head hunched like an angry bull, nostrils flaring, Collins looked very guilty. He had been caught as firmly as a beaver in a trap, and like a beaver he dove deep for cover. There were no witnesses to confirm his version of events except Hall, who was chasing downstream to rescue the hat. Frustrated, Collins remembered Drouillard's cautions and breathed deeply, but it was a moment before he spoke. "I'm sorry, sir. It was an accident." The apology required an angry effort of will. He would even the score with Reed later, in his own time, far from the righteous eyes of Sergeant Ordway. He could feel the sinews in his neck strangle his upwelling rage.

Ordway blinked and blustered: "See that you take greater care in the future, Collins, where you place your feet. And thank you, Private Reed, Mister Leakins. Carry on here." The incident was at an end. Reed picked up his sack, and Leakins backed away. Collins dug his heels into the muddy bank.

Hugh Hall came up with the hat in hand. Hall could sniff the truth. "'Twarn't no accident, Johnny. I know. Reed tried the same yesterday, on George Shannon, but Georgie righted himself in time. Reed's a snake, and he knows how to coil and squeeze our prim Yankee sergeant. You stay clear o' him, you hear. And don't dry the hat by placin' it too near the fire or it will shrink." The hat shrank anyway, and Collins let his anger harden like a brick in the sun. It lay like an indigestible weight in his chest, baking to impenetrable, durable bedrock.

William Clark returned to the camp shortly after the incident and summoned John Collins. "I have a report here, from Sergeant Ordway, that states you threatened Moses Reed."

"Yes, sir. I did that." Collins did not lie.

"Do you have an explanation, Private Collins?"

Collins hesitated a moment and bit back his lip. Reed and Ordway would contradict any explanation he could offer. In reply, he muttered softly: "I had good reason, sir. I have no witnesses. My word is good. I am not a tattler, sir."

Clark knew the code among the men. An honorable man did not shift blame, did not betray a fellow. He could prompt, but he could not demand. "I cannot judge fairly, Private Collins, without knowledge."

Collins nodded ambiguously. "I trust you are a just man, sir."

It was a flattering remark, but it shed no light on the divisions that engulfed the corps, divisions that William Clark did not yet fully comprehend. The refusal to turn in a comrade could be an asset or a flaw. Clark noted the straight clamp of Collins's jaw, the unblinking, stony stare. Anger? Rectitude? Defiance? Sympathy for the mistakes of another or dogged struggle to control strong emotion? Clark shuffled his papers. He was a patient man. He would consult Drouillard about the incident, when Drouillard returned from the hunt. Clark had no time for petty quarrels. He had an expedition to launch.

Meriwether Lewis was in St. Louis when he received the final word from Clark. Clark was moving the expedition upstream, beyond St. Louis—too many Spanish there, too much opportunity for subversion. He would meet Lewis at St. Charles. All was ready. Each man was healthy, armed with a good rifle, powder and one hundred balls, clothed, booted, and eager. The packing was complete. The spring season was advancing. It was time to go.

Chapter Eight

On Monday, May 14th, at four in the afternoon, William Clark led three boats out into the mainstream of the Mississippi. The men rotated positions that first day, manning an oar, hoisting the sail, setting the pole, tugging the tow rope. They entered the Missouri at its mouth and sailed west, four miles upstream in the waning evening light. It was an easy effort. The wind was favorable. They camped for the night on an island in the river and ate and slept with their squads. Clark had chosen the lonely isle deliberately, so his men could not depend on the crutches of civilization, so they would have to rely only on each other for help. It was a place where a man's faults became gremlins that taunted the patience of his neighbor and loneliness stared down like a cold moon. Clark studied the reactions of each man: who ate, joked, and worked well together; whose talents complemented another's, whose duplicated another's; whose habits were best applied alone; who was content and who constantly sought justification. Antagonisms were obvious from the first. So were friendships. William Clark noted it all, but he made no corrections. It was too soon. And he did not comprehend, that first day, how deeply divisions had penetrated his corps.

It rained the first night on the island. Collins chose to sleep alone on hard, high bedground. Exhausted, others had collapsed carelessly on the first soft sand they found. They awoke wet and uncomfortable, with water puddling in their blankets.

All the next day it rained. Captain Clark sent Shannon out

with Drouillard to hunt. Each man would have his round with Drouillard who taught woodcraft and tracking and survival in the wild. Clark assigned Collins to a larboard oar next to Hall. Fog covered the river, and three times the boat ran up on snags. The Frenchman, Deschamps, insisted that the fog was not the cause. The keelboat needed more weight in the bow if it was to buck the current and push aside débris. Sergeant Ordway, who had directed the loading, protested, but Deschamps insisted, and Clark issued another order to repack.

The 16th dawned fiery red, and they sailed on to St. Charles. Meriwether Lewis was not waiting for them on the pier as planned, but the village elders were there with a bevy of curious villagers. They were a jabbering, gesticulating mass of unkempt humanity. They all professed their undying allegiance to the United States, and they had prepared a feast to wish the corps Godspeed. Word of the feast swept like prairie wind over the camp.

John Collins smiled and shipped his oar as the boat struck the landing. He wiped the sweat from his brow. A sharp pain stabbed at the back of his neck and radiated down the length of his arms to his wrists. He could feel stiffness in his spine. His mouth was cotton dry. He stood up, stretched, and walked to the water barrel.

Drouillard was dipping his cup as he came up. He rinsed his mouth, spit a stream into the river, and almost smiled. "I marched your horse twenty-six miles today. That's a good horse, *mon ami*. He's fit and knows his job." He waited for Collins's reaction.

Collins winced. He hadn't wanted to part with the animal and muttered: "I know. Captain Clark feeds better grain than I could afford. I would have lost him anyway betting against Labiche."

"Always bet with Labiche, not against him. He's as sharp a pirate in a game of dice as I have ever known. Your horse will probably end up chasing buffalo with a red man on his back."

"It was a card game." Collins didn't mention the horse.

Drouillard mumbled through his beard: "Horses are gold to an Indian. He will be well cared for." Collins felt good about that, smiled weakly, and turned to go ashore, but Drouillard called him back. "Johnny, Calderon is here!"

"The same Calderon who married Louise?"

Drouillard nodded once. "*If* he married Louise." Drouillard left the thought hanging like an empty noose.

There was no time to talk further. At that moment, Ordway summoned all hands for evening muster. His shrill voice echoed over Collins's head. "This night, Captain Clark will dine with Mister Duquette, mayor of Saint Charles. The good people of Saint Charles welcome you all, wish you safe voyage, and invite you to a feast. The captains give permission for each man present, except the posted guard, to attend at seven o'clock on the public square on the hill in front of Saint Charles Borromeo Church. The captain expresses his desire that each man act in keeping with proper respect for his hosts, for the prestige of this corps, and for his own personal honor. He has left me in charge of proceedings here. The order of guard is posted on the masthead. The captains and I wish you all a pleasant evening."

John Collins hardly heard. Drouillard's news preoccupied him. Calderon! Why now? Why here? He trudged to the masthead where Whitehouse read aloud the daily posting. Collins's spirits sank. He was assigned the first shore watch with Leakins who drew the watch on deck. There was a sour taste on his tongue when he went for his rifle and took his position at the end of the gangplank.

The river front was unusually empty. Music and laughter

filtered eerily downhill from the busy town. Collins turned once to look for Leakins, didn't see him, and concluded that he was dozing while on guard, hiding behind the cabin. He didn't care. He detested the man.

He watched the road. He watched the waves lap steadily against the planking of the boats. No one approached. He saw a plover peck a snail from the mud. A night heron called. A fish jumped. A rodent slithered down the riverbank, its hairless tail carving a thin track in the mud. The hours ticked by slowly. Dusk was falling when Hugh Hall and Billy Warner arrived to relieve him. Leakins did not appear.

Collins turned over his musket to Hall, and trudged wearily up the hill. Red-faced John Colter met him halfway with a jug of whiskey under his arm. Colter was already mildly drunk. "She's there, Johnny, an' you're in luck! She's married! To a Spanish don. Drouillard said to tell you. And these are good folks, give us whiskey free for the takin'. Know how to keep a man happy. A whole jug's waitin' with Sergeant Floyd to oil your dancin' legs and warm your belly."

"Did you see Leakins?"

"Aye. Twirlin' the *señora*. High and mighty that one, no prettier filly to behold. Stumblin' over 'er toes, he is. He'll fall deader than a stuffed pigeon before you get there."

"Or dig in for a fight." Collins's worried look startled his friend. "Leakins didn't stand his watch. Warner or Hall will probably report him."

Colter's good humor could not be suppressed. "Be glad it ain't you or me that's turnin' him in. Leakins is short on forgiveness, long on revenge." He flung back his head, took a long swallow, and held out a jug to Collins. The hand holding the jug jerked suddenly splattering whiskey over them both. "Would you look at that!" Colter pointed to two buxom maids running up the hill, breasts round as pumpkins, bouncing nearly out of their blouses. "Chug down, friend. We've ladies to woo." He took off at a bounding run.

The scene on the square was one of wild revelry. The residents of St. Charles danced vigorously on the flat ground in front of their church. A statue of St. Charles stared out stoically from a niche above the door, oblivious to the excesses below. There was music, drums, fifes, and fiddles. Roasted pig, a whole deer, puddings, and pies covered rude boards set on blankets spread over the church steps. More food spilled out of the backs of carts parked haphazardly about. Barrels of whiskey and bottles of wine dripped their bounty carelessly into the dirt. John Collins recognized more that one of his comrades weaving through the dancers or stuffing his pockets with sweetmeats. Potts was gnawing a bone and belching grotesquely. George Gibson and Pierre Cruzatte stood with the fiddlers, plunking dizzily. Georges Drouillard stomped and clapped while young Shannon twirled like a dervish.

Collins shouldered his way to a table piled high with the food—beef stew, thick soup with potatoes, onions, and leeks. He was hungry. He heaped his plate, collected a jug from Sergeant Floyd, and sat down cross-legged on an empty patch of spring grass. The food was delicious. He filled a second plate. French matrons smiled approval.

Baptiste Deschamps walked up and cast a massive shadow over John Collins. Collins tensed. He wasn't sure that the Frenchman hadn't come to fight, and he didn't invite the huge boatman to sit. Deschamps moved his lips as if chewing on a fish bone. "*Monsieur Collins,* I come to repent." *Repent,* the word rang hollow to Collins's ear but this was to be a confession, and the man was proud. "Louise is here and married to the *ancien Español,* Calderon. He is rich, and she is a willful, scheming woman. She has lied to me. Now that she is

married, I am below her station. She does not speak to me.
. . . Please take this." He leaned down and placed another
bottle of whiskey at John Collins's feet. "And accept my re-
grets."

Collins did not smile. He blinked stupidly, took the bottle,
and held out his hand. The Frenchman took it. The huge
palm was rough and his fingers gnarled, but the grip was
strong. Collins wondered if this man could ever be his friend.
Finally he forced a smile and muttered: "It is over." He
croaked reluctantly: "Thank you."

Deschamps lingered a moment and repeated: "Over.
Terminé. Je suis content." He sauntered off.

John Collins took a long swallow as Colter came up with a
girl on each arm and prodded: "Make us four, Johnny. Ber-
nadette wants to dance with you."

"Ask her first if she's married or promised."

The girl laughed coyly. "You think I am *folle, monsieur,* to
settle for one when there are so many."

Collins danced with several girls, but always held a
watchful eye out for Louise. When the music stopped, he left
both girls with Colter, slumped down again with his jug
against the trunk of a giant elm, and let his mind drift. The
whiskey made him sleepy. He was dreaming contentedly,
when someone kicked his shins. It was Louise Calderon, *née*
Bourgeron, and she had awakened him deliberately.

She stood over him, dressed in an elegant, fringed Spanish
shawl, smiling haughtily. "*Monsieur* Collins, you have not yet
met my husband." The shriveled husband stood like an
adoring spaniel at her side. Collins jumped to his feet. She
continued slowly for effect, lengthening every syllable of her
husband's illustrious name. "Don Jaime María Gustavo
Calderon de Ruiz, may I present Private John Collins. Private
Collins is a former acquaintance of my brother." She enjoyed

emphasizing his lowly rank. Collins recoiled from her sting.

Calderon stepped forward. He was dressed entirely in faded black and leaned on a stubby cane. He was short from the shrinking of age, but his back was ramrod straight. His dry, wrinkled lips pulled stiffly back under a pointed nose and exposed black, decaying teeth. His skin was yellow, his beard stark white and trimmed in a neat point against the stained white bib of his shirt. Sharp brown eyes flicked points of light from under snowy brows, and a rim of wispy white hair crowned his bald head. He reminded Collins of a sorcerer.

His English was heavily accented, sprinkled with Spanish, and blasted from his chest like air from a bellows. "Eet ees my pleasure to *conocerle, señor.*"

Collins thought how the little man could live to be one hundred. He struggled to keep a straight face.

The little man screeched on. "I bring you a bottle, good *Señor* Collins, for you to celebrate our felicity and your own fine luck as member of *esta expedition maravillosa. Pero primero,* drink with us." He uncorked two bottles, passed out three cups, filled them to the brim, and raised his high. "To *mi esposa hermosissima.* To Louise, *mi amor y mi vida.* And to you *Señor* Collins, that *un día,* you may be so blessed *como yo.*"

The overblown toast made John Collins squirm, but he lifted his cup and replied simply: "To your happiness, Louise." There was a prickly cynicism in his voice, like a dull knife cutting stale bread, but Louise chose not to notice.

The little man emptied the first bottle into their cups and uncorked a second. He gestured grandly once more. "To your *gran viaje peligroso.*" Calderon had not completed a single sentence in English and seemed to harbor an aversion to the language.

Collins downed his drink. They drank a third toast to

Spain and a fourth to Napoléon. Collins proposed a fifth, but he had stopped counting. "To Thomas Jefferson and the new republic." His head swam, his vision blurred, and he swayed on his feet. Calderon sputtered, but he drank to Jefferson. When the Calderons left, Collins's knees gave way.

The night progressed. Blazing torches lit the square. Collins's head pounded. He knew he'd drunk too much. He stashed his remaining bottle in the hollow of a tree, curled up on the ground, and, holding his aching head, closed his eyes.

Warner and Hall, who had stood the second watch, roused him. They had another jug between them, and they added his to theirs, pulled him up by the armpits, and marched him to the banquet. "Eat, Johnny, it will revive you."

Collins shook his head to clear the fog from his brain. Now that the business of Louise was over, his head no longer ached but his stomach growled. He devoured venison with mushrooms, onions, leeks, and wild greens, roast pork with raisins and walnuts, fresh trout from the river. The French inhabitants refilled the jug to wash it all down. He vomited and passed out. Hughie Hall and Billy Warner tried to sober him enough to return to camp, but they could not support his weight. The sky was lightening with the first suggestion of dawn when Leakins and Reed came up to help.

"He'll not make it back to the boat in time for morning muster." Leakins held out a bottle. "Give 'im this. The smell of it will wake the damned. An' you might take a swig yerselves to wash yer stinkin' breath."

Hall held his nose when he uncorked the bottle and lifted Collins's head while Billy Warner poured the liquid down his throat. Then Warner tilted his own head back and gulped and handed the bottle to Hall.

Leakins watched with approval. "You'll feel its punch in the head first and in the muscles a moment later. You'll not be needin' me an' Reed any more." He clapped Reed on the shoulder, and the two sauntered away.

Hall crinkled his nose and sniffed. "Foul tasting. Foul smelling. Leakins didn't stand 'is watch. He owes a trick to you and me and to Johnny here for not reporting 'im."

Warner looked down from his standing position. Suddenly he stopped breathing. His hand went to his mouth. He wheeled and ran into the brush. Hugh Hall rubbed his red-streaked eyes and poked the unconscious John Collins. "A fine help they are, all of them, and you, Johnny, who can't walk like a grown man on the two long legs God gave you. I've a mind to let you grovel like a snake in the grass for all the trouble you bring us." But Hughie Hall felt a sharp pain in his middle and instantly folded in two. He gagged once and collapsed on top of his friend.

Captain Clark had ordered the morning muster delayed by two hours to allow the men to recuperate from the partying of the night before. But he had remained in St. Charles at the house of François Duquette, and Sergeant Ordway was in charge again. There was more repacking to do. The bugle sounded, and the men hurried to their posts. John Colter, next on the muster roll to Collins, was the first to notice his absence. Two more places were empty next to Goodrich and Weiser, for Hall and Warner. Ordway immediately called out a patrol to find the deserters and bring them to justice. Leakins volunteered and elected Reed and impressionable young Shannon to go with him.

John Collins, Hugh Hall, and Billy Warner were barely alert when the patrol found them. Collins sat cross-legged, holding his aching head. Hall had rolled over on his back to ease a lingering cramp in his groin and let the morning sun warm his face. Billy Warner had crawled out of the brush on his hands and knees and now hung his weary head over the red face of Hughie Hall. All three were groggy and incoherent.

Moses Reed grasped Billy Warner by the collar, hauled him to his feet, and tied his hands behind his back. Leakins did the same to John Collins, then tied Collins to Warner and both to himself, and set a rapid pace down the hill. The two prisoners, who did not yet have full control of their limbs and who could not right themselves with bound hands, tripped and rolled the length of the main street down the hill to the dock.

Young George Shannon watched the humiliating procession in shock. It was contrary to the captains' direct orders. Leakins and Reed, who could have borne their charges quietly, had disgraced the entire company. Shannon bent over the limp Hugh Hall, shaking him like a doll, pleading with him to get up. Hall finally came to and blinked stupidly. "What time is it?"

"Late morning, Hughie, past muster, running on to midday."

Hall jerked to a sitting position. "Midday?" His mouth hung open as he tried to focus. "Can't remember midnight." He fell back when he tried to stand. Shannon anchored his arm under Hall's armpits, and they began the descent. With the increased activity, Hugh Hall's mind began to clear, but he still had no recollection of what had occurred. "How did you know where to find me?"

"You missed muster. Sergeant Ordway sent us to look for you and Warner and Collins."

"We were together. Where are they?"

"They took them on ahead." Shannon could not speak of the deliberate brutality. He was embarrassed for the older man and turned away from Hall's bloodshot stare.

"Leakins?" Hugh Hall's brain was slow to comprehend,

but he smelled trouble like a coon hound. "He's the one who gave me the drink!"

Shannon nodded. "Reed was with him. We found the three of you lying in a drunken heap."

"Goddammit!" The curse came like a blast from a cannon. Shannon drew back, shocked by the intensity. Hall gasped. "We're in the soup, ain't we?"

Shannon confirmed it. "Absent without leave."

"I've almost a mind to head back downriver and forget the whole mess, but I can't be runnin' and leavin' my friends to cop our punishment without me, like leavin' a man wounded in the desert. Got to stand with 'em."

Chapter Nine

Ordway was waiting in the captains' tent when the patrol returned. Leakins and Reed herded their prisoners in front of the implacable sergeant. The sergeant's voice was sharp, the syllables like splinters of ice. "You're late, Privates Collins and Warner. Where have you been?"

Billy Warner tried to speak. "At the ball, sir." His speech was slurred. Collins remained stoically silent.

"Orders were to maintain respectable conduct at all costs. You are overdue, so late that I had to send these men to root you out like beasts from your lairs, and beasts you are from the stink of you. And Private Collins, I have a report that you were absent from guard duty last night."

John Collins's jaw dropped. He blinked wildly and shook his curly head. He had not fully recovered, and he shouted back in protest. "That's not true, sir! I stood my watch! I was here!" Unbelieving, he glared hatefully at the smug form of Leakins who stood behind Ordway and who toed a loose pebble, eyes down.

Ordway bristled. "Are you calling me a liar, Collins? Two witnesses, Mister Leakins and Private Reed, have both reported you absent."

John Collins struggled to free his hands. His darting eyes flashed fire at Amos Leakins. "There's the liar. Colter, ask Colter. He was there." In a burst of angry strength, Collins broke free from his guards and, hands still bound, lunged at Leakins like a horned bull. Leakins jumped back behind

Ordway to protect himself, and Collins tumbled headlong into the dirt. He rose up seething with rage.

Ordway hardly raised his voice and commanded: "Restrain that man."

It took three men to brace Collins by his two arms and the hair of his head, tie his hands, and haul him back before Ordway whose jaw moved up and down with the mechanical rhythm of a machine. "Private Colter is not here. He has been assigned to hunt with Mister Drouillard. Have you anyone else who can speak on your behalf to exonerate you?"

Leakins had moved up to the sergeant's side, a pillar of assumed innocence. The thong cut into the flesh of Collins's wrists. His captors pinned his arms to his ribs. He forgot the careful restraint that Drouillard had so patiently instilled. He arched his neck, gathered saliva on the end of his tongue, took aim, and spat. At the same moment, Ordway ducked forward to brush a mosquito from the back of his neck. It was a small movement, no more than a few inches, but it was enough to shield Leakins's scruffy face and place Orway's cheek in the direct path of Collins's spit. The viscous glob landed squarely on the rosy cheek of Sergeant John Ordway.

Stunned silence fell like a shroud. Ordway paled in shock. Leakins's lips rose in a half smile as he broke into a flood of accusations. "He's by the devil possessed, sir. Thinks he's God Almighty with his airs. Shows no respect for 'is betters, sir! Acts no better than a pig in 'is sty or a pissin' wolf."

"Confine that man! Mister Leakins, control your tongue!" Ordway's command was loud and sharp.

John Collins pulled back. He wanted to smash Leakins's smug nose, drive his smirk back down his throat, and take him by the hair and smother him in the muck of the river. He felt the fingers of his captors like a vise on his arms, squeezing the blood from his veins. Someone pulled his head back and shoved a fist into the small of his back. Struggle was useless. The reality of his position suddenly overcame him, and he let his muscles go limp. Too late he tried to think, and his thoughts rained down in confusion. He could not sort out the ramblings of his addled brain as they swept frustration, anger, and recrimination before them like flotsam in a spring flood. Drouillard would know what to do, how to stay sober, how to think, how to redeem himself, how to unwind the deception that enveloped him like bindweed . . . if Drouillard were here. He dug the heels of his boots deeply into the dirt, tensing the long muscles of his legs. They had to carry him to the St. Charles jail.

He sat listlessly on the damp clay floor of the jail, when Nat Pryor lay a hand on his shoulder and whispered in his ear: "You don't help yourself, Johnny, by spitting at Ordway, shouting, resisting. They think you unruly as a wild stallion or a rabid dog." Pryor, also a sergeant, had some authority, and Collins yielded to his gentle touch. Pryor loosened the thong binding Collins's wrists and prompted: "Work your hands . . . your fingers are blue. You only draw the knot tighter with your stubbornness. Tell me what happened."

John Collins did not immediately respond. His lips quivered as he rubbed the circulation back in to his hands. For one who could spit so forcefully, now he could not summon saliva enough to work his tongue and speak. Never before in his young life had he been so wrongly accused. Never before had he needed to defend himself against utter falsehood. Never before had he been met with such stark disbelief, and never before had he so completely lost his temper. Tears welled up in his eyes. He blinked, dug his teeth into his tongue to contain the liquid until the blood flowed, and turned away from Pryor to hide his shame. When he spoke, he masked his embarrassment with cynicism. "They lied, but you are right, sir. Who would believe a mad dog?"

Pryor waited. Collins did not speak more. Pryor sighed and shook his head. "What would you have me believe, man?"

Hughie Hall and Billy Warner were ushered forward. Neither could answer any questions about their absence. They did not remember. But Hall's brain had cleared enough to speak in his own defense and the defense of his friend. " 'Twas not Collins missed his guard duty, sir, 'twas Leakins there. Collins was at the gangplank, on shore watch, awake and in position, when we came to replace 'im."

"Answer only when questioned Private Hall . . . and only when the question concerns yourself." Ordway's jaw locked tightly, and his mouth contracted to a bloodless line. He asked the same questions of Billy Warner with the same result, then signaled to Newman and McNeal. "Hold these men. Place them under guard and convoke a jury for the court-martial."

An hour later, at eleven in the morning of May 17th, the jury convened. Ordway headed it himself with Reuben Fields, Richard Windsor, Joseph Whitehouse, and John Potts for members. Drouillard and Colter had still not returned.

They sat at the captains' table, before the captains' tent, on camp stools set on the trampled grass by the wharf where the keelboat was tied. Sergeant Ordway adhered strictly to the rules and articles of war. He sat in the center with two jury members to his right, two to his left. The prisoners marched up, one at a time, to hear the charges against them and plead their cause, guilty or not guilty. All the men of the company crowded around.

First to appear was Hughie Hall who pleaded guilty to the charge of absence without leave this morning early, contrary to orders. But Hall could not erase the injustice of the last hours from his mind and protested loudly.

Ordway persisted doggedly. "Answer yes or no, Private."

"Yes, sir, this morning, but last night. . . ."

"Yes or no, Private!" The rebuke was sharp.

Hall looked to the four members of the jury. Quiet Joe Whitehouse and the German, Potts, were not unreasonable men, and they, too, had suffered from Leakins's barbs. Potts sat in a lump, arms folded across his barrel chest, feet tucked up under his stool, frowning. Whitehouse's face was white. He sat, eyes down, lanky legs stretched straight before him. Reuben Fields fumbled with the buckle of his belt, clearly ill at ease, and Windsor was cleaning the dirt from under his fingernails with the point of his knife.

Hall turned back to Ordway's granite face and muttered: "With due respect, sir, ask Gibson, ask Shannon, here, or Howard, about Collins. Ask Johnny Colter, when he comes back, and Drouillard. Sir, please! We all saw Leakins dancin' at the ball, early, while Johnny Collins was standin' at his proper station, on the watch."

But Reed stepped forward to contradict Hall with what sounded like an eye-witness account. "They was drinkin', Sergeant, all o' them, leanin' on each other like tumble-down posts . . . this here Collins, Hall, and Billy Warner. No way any one of 'em could stand a proper watch or recognize what they was lookin' at, if they could. I don't like to think of drunks like them protectin' our belongings with thievin' savages paddin' the wilderness all around. We won't have nothin' left, not even our lives."

In the end, a unanimous court voted both Hall and Warner guilty, and sentenced them to twenty-five lashes each on the naked back. But the court commuted the sentence in consideration of their prior good conduct.

John Collins stepped forward with renewed confidence. But the charges against him were more serious and more numerous: absence without leave; disgraceful conduct at the ball; disrespect for the orders of the commanding officer upon his return; and, worst of all, failure to stand his assigned watch.

Sergeant Nathaniel Pryor stood by Collins as they led him before the jury. Ordway read the charges, lifted his eyebrows, and demanded icily: "Private Collins, how do you plead?"

John Collins stared at the faces of his jury. None would look him in the eye. Reuben Fields seemed asleep. John Potts studied the calluses on his hands. Joe Whitehouse, the member of the jury that Collins knew best, was milk pale and had anchored his gaze on the signal flag that whipped proudly in the wind at the top of the mast. Feelings of anger, frustration, and utter loneliness encompassed Collins. Sergeant Pryor nudged his shoulder. "They want to know how you plead, Johnny."

John Collins was completely sober now. He held his voice to a restrained whisper and began: "Sergeant, sir, I was late getting back, but the rest is all lies. Amos Leakins lies willfully to cover his own guilt. He knows I'm innocent."

"Private Collins, Mister Leakins is not on trial. You are." He cleared his throat. "Again, how do you plead?" The words were clipped and measured.

Collins looked around frantically for a trace of sympathy. Whitehouse's cheek quivered slightly. The others sat morbidly like carvings in a mausoleum. "I got drunk with the others, sir, and we were late reporting, but I am not guilty of the dishonorable conduct described. I stood my watch. I'll not plead guilty to the crimes of another man."

Ordway reached up to wipe his cheek. He had not forgotten where Collins's spit had landed.

"And I apologize for the spitting, sir." As soon as the words were out, Collins realized that he should have withheld them.

Pryor whispered in his ear. "We all saw you do it. It was a foolish, crass thing to do. Ordway will abide by the rules, and the others will vote on what they saw. They have no choice."

John Collins dropped his eyes. Not until now had he fully understood what was happening to him.

Pryor registered his plea. "He pleads *guilty*, Sergeant, to the first charge. He admits he was late with Warner and Hall, but he pleads *not guilty* to the rest."

Ordway lifted an eyebrow. "Do you have witnesses, Private Collins, to support your plea? Do you have proof thereof that will exonerate your conduct toward the officer in charge?"

"Drouillard and Colter, sir. They know. I was excited, sir. I lost my head."

"Drouillard and Colter very conveniently have not yet returned from hunting."

A spark of anger suddenly ignited Collins, and he snapped defiantly: "Every defender I have is not here. Leakins, sir, he knows, and the Calderons spoke with me at the ball early, sir. They know the truth."

"Who are the Calderons?"

Again Pryor interjected: "*Señora* Louise Calderon. Deschamps knows them. Missus Calderon is his niece."

"Please, sir, *Señora* Calderon is here." The announcement came like a trumpet blast from the outer rim of the gathering. Heads turned. "She came to wish her uncle Godspeed and successful voyage." It was François Rivet who spoke, a Frenchman.

Ordway stiffened. "A woman has no place in this camp . . . at a military trial. Regulations forbid it."

Nat Pryor objected firmly. "Begging you pardon, sir, but I issued permission for the Frenchmen to accept visitors, to say their good byes. Many have relatives who reside here in Saint Charles."

"They were to visit in their own homes and meeting places, Sergeant, not in this camp."

"Perhaps I was not specific enough, sir. Captain Clark did not specify."

"Captain Lewis did."

"I acted on my own discretion, sir. The lady is here. She is intelligent and literate and can testify on behalf of Private Collins."

Ordway scowled at Pryor who equaled him in rank, and muttered: "Send for the woman."

Louise arrived shortly, seated beside her husband, in a handsome phaeton, driven by her brother, Jacques Bourgeron. He jumped from the box seat to help her down. A way opened through the throng of men to let her pass. She stood like an angel of innocence before the stolid members of the jury, while Calderon remained in the coach.

When he saw Louise, John Collins's hopes rose. Every man in the company trained his eyes on her. Even accused, John Collins straightened his shoulders and swelled his chest. A warm pride coursed through his veins that this vital woman would come to help him. But there was a slant to her eye and a stiffness to her bearing. Her lip bent to a subtle curve, not quite a smile. When Collins realized why, he drew back in alarm. She was acting her new rôle of Doña Calderon, a diva playing to a captive audience. She would state whatever favored her new position. She would not be interested in the plebeian truth.

Ordway began cordially: "Thank you, Mister Calderon and Missus Calderon, for coming forward in this disagreeable matter." He was as true to protocol as any diplomat from Europe.

"We are only too happy to *ayudarle,* Sergeant." It was Calderon who squawked from his perch atop the open coach. His raucous voice jarred.

Ordway directed his questions at Louise. "Missus Calderon, you are acquainted with Private Collins?"

"I am, Sergeant."

"And you saw Private Collins at the ball early last night? Do you recall what time that was?"

"No, Sergeant." She giggled. "I wouldn't call it a proper ball. It was more a carnival, a *Mardi Gras*. I saw so many people." Her voice had a lilt like the sweet music of a lute, and the men of the jury hung on her every word.

"You have no recollection of the time?"

"I have no recollection of the time or the man, sir. I saw so many men, and there was excellent wine." She giggled lightly and covered her mouth coyly with her handkerchief. Jeweled rings flashed from her fingers and reflected the brilliant sunlight.

Fool! Collins's brain rang with self-recrimination. The woman had tricked him. Her denials were damning.

It took Ordway a moment to digest the import of her words. He repeated: "You have no recollection of seeing Private Collins last night?"

Louise pursed her lips in a pout and shook her head. The movement was calculated to tease. "The wine was so smooth. It went straight to my head, Sergeant. My memory fails me." She held her hand to her temple and sighed. Bourgeron smirked from beside the coach.

John Collins cringed. She had gulled him and the jury. Bourgeron was behind it, and the fawning husband who had acted so friendly. He studied the two of them now. Calderon had shrunk back into his cushions like a rodent in his hole. He was barely visible. Louise stood languidly on one hip in front of Ordway, who deliberately diverted his eyes from her ample cleavage. Potts and Fields ogled like toads. Whitehouse blushed and averted his eyes. Drouillard and Deschamps had warned him. He had paid little attention. Would Louise lie for the gold that glittered from the fingers of her hand. Or was her lying payment for his rejection and her brother's defeat? Was he, Collins, the victim of a scheming, vindictive woman or some pawn in a Spanish plot? No matter now. Like her brother who had called him out to fight, this was her revenge, an eye for an eye. Money, marriage, position, power, and the feeble pretense she called honor ruled the court. He would suffer for it, and she would gloat.

There were more questions and more testimony, but John Collins no longer listened. His eyes scanned the crowd for Drouillard, for Colter, for Deschamps, for anyone who might have something good to say for him. The proceedings ran swiftly ahead, gathering force with every damning word. They asked him to speak. What could he say? The words would not come. Then it was over. The four jurors scribbled their verdicts on scraps of paper, and Ordway unfolded and read them one by one. "Guilty!" The verdict echoed like a volley of musket fire. "The court is of one opinion that the prisoner is guilty of all charges . . . and sentence him to receive fifty lashes on his naked back, punishment to take place this evening at sunset."

"No!" Collins's denial melted softly into empty space. His heart sank, and he shook his head. Nathaniel Pryor led him away. The prisoner collapsed in a heap on the cold stone floor of the St. Charles jail where he could hear the sweep of the scythe cutting the weeds from around the whipping tree.

Leakins's voice echoed nearby as he lay out the nine ugly

thongs of the whip. It was a brutal weapon, called the cat because its nine barbs, like cat's claws, could skin a man's spine. Leakins jabbered loudly as he practiced the strike. "The sharper the bite, the quicker they jump." Collins heard the bark rip from the tree as Leakins repeated the taunt. "The sharper the bite, the higher they jump, the louder they scream."

Collins grit his teeth. He would never give Amos Leakins the satisfaction of a scream, not even a murmur. He heard the thump and swish as the whip struck the tree. His muscles twitched, and the skin on his back contracted over each nub of vertebra.

Worse than the cat was the ostracism of his fellows, the men whom John Collins called friends. No one dared come near him, except Nat Pryor who offered him a drink and Hugh Hall who called bravely through the walls. "I'm with you, Johnny. The rascal hoodwinked us, all three." Hall could be reprimanded for even speaking, and his sentence increased, and John Collins was grateful. As the hours passed, his hope waned. He prayed that Drouillard would return in time.

Drouillard did not return, nor did Colter, but William Clark did. He summoned Sergeant Ordway immediately for a review of events. As the story unfolded, Clark's face elongated, and he looked away into vacant space, deep in anguished thought, examining the dregs of his conscience. "I have been too much absent, Sergeant, too heedless of the subtleties of managing young and vigorous men." He took a deep breath and turned to look Ordway straight in the eye. "I have never used the barbed cat even on York, my slave, and I never will! I will not have such a barbarous tool employed under my command." He stopped trembling, lowered his bellowing voice, then continued: "Bear in mind that what I say, I do not direct personally to you, Sergeant Ordway. The prisoner has been adjudged guilty by a jury of his peers, and the sentence must be carried out. But you will use a green rush from the river to administer the punishment, not the cat-o-nine-tails."

John Collins could see the sun through the barred window of the jail where he was held. It moved in a wide arc from near the zenith in the early afternoon toward the western horizon and the appointed hour of sunset. He turned his face toward its warmth and castigated himself for trusting the woman and vowed never to believe any woman again. On a sudden impulse, he uttered a prayer. He was not usually a religious man. He prayed for the courage not to cry out; he prayed that Drouillard and Colter would return soon to prove him innocent. Prayer fortified his will. He thought of more dreadful evils that men had endured—famines and plagues and maiming—and the dread of his own pain diminished. He remembered a lesson he had learned as a boy, in church. God had blessed a man whom evil persons reviled. That man's name was Job, and he had survived horrors here on earth before reaping his heavenly reward. Collins felt the warmth of the sun on his face as the fiery ball descended toward the horizon, like a brush of divine sympathy, and he felt better, but Drouillard did not come.

Minutes before sunset, Gibson and Howard came for him and led him out to the tree. The entire corps was drawn up in two lines to witness the punishment. William Clark stood at the head. Collins walked the gauntlet to his fate. He looked stoically ahead. They stripped the shirt from his back, stretched his arms around the trunk, bound his hands, and shoved a pine knot between his teeth. Ordway, not Leakins, administered the lashes. Reed kept the count. John Collins bit down hard and did not utter a sound. William Clark noted his perseverance and whispered to Pryor: "The man bears up without complaint. He will endure hardship."

The reed raised welts in the skin that broke open and oozed blood, but did not cut deeply. When they untied him, Nat Pryor covered his bloody back with his blanket and led him to the river where he bathed the stripes and covered them with lard and moss from the bank. During the night, they crusted over, and John Collins went back to work in the morning.

Drouillard and Colter arrived the next day, Friday, at noon. They reported immediately to Captain Clark and verified that John Collins had, indeed, stood his watch, Wednesday night, the 16th of May, 1804. William Clark summoned Collins to his tent. Collins came reluctantly, expecting to be permanently dismissed.

But Clark began by shaking his head and shoving his hands deeply within his pockets. He trembled physically as his eyes locked on Collins, and he began: "Private Collins, I owe you an apology. Georges Drouillard and John Colter have returned and confirmed that you did, in fact, stand your watch. I exonerate you of the most serious charge. Sergeant Ordway was precipitous in his decisions. A jury of your peers was not correct in its judgment. I am disheartened and saddened by the whole affair. I must add that I hope you will not resign your position, and that I was impressed by the honorable manner in which you endured your punishment. You are a brave man." He held out his hand.

Collins barely muttered: "Thank you, sir." Numbly, he shook the hand.

"But understand, Collins, that you are not without fault. You did report late for duty at which time you accosted Sergeant Ordway, and you drank too heavily. That was imprudent and unpardonable. But I will lay that behind us because you have served your sentence honorably." A slim smile crossed the captain's lips. "Now, Collins, Private Shannon came to me this morning to complain of Mister Leakins. This is not a trivial matter. The integrity of this corps could depend on what you have to say." He paused and swallowed his obvious anguish. "This was not the first time you have suffered at the hands of Amos Leakins, was it?"

"No, sir."

"And I am notified that others also have suffered his taunts."

Collins nodded.

Vertical lines pulled at the points of Clark's eyes and mouth. He slumped into his camp chair as his voice fell, and he closed his eyes. Thumb and index finger pressed hard against the bridge of his nose. "Thank you. Dismissed, Private Collins."

Chapter Ten

William Clark sat for a long while alone in the semi-darkness of his tent and only aroused when his friend, old Matthew Lyon from Kentucky, arrived with two large boats loaded with tobacco, whiskey, and knives. He sent Ordway to supervise the transfer to the keelboat. A Frenchman named Lorimer arrived from a Kickapoo village, and reported rumors spreading rapidly among the tribes of treacherous, cruel, and greedy Americans. Clark's sad face turned angry when he heard the news. He summoned Drouillard.

Drouillard entered so quietly that Clark jumped when he saw the tall thin form standing at ease before him. Drouillard's stealth was an ability that contributed greatly to his talent in the hunt, an ability inherited from his Shawnee ancestry, but it annoyed some of his white acquaintances because it enabled him to observe the goings on in camp, undetected. But he did not know who was defaming Americans in the Kickapoo villages.

Clark pinched the bridge of his nose. His eyes were bloodshot, circled with dark rings of worry. "Sit down, Georges. Light your pipe." He motioned Drouillard to a camp stool. "Captain Lewis is not here . . . I need advice, and I do not know if I can trust my own sergeants. I cannot believe Ordway is at fault. He is a capable and obedient officer. He has supervised the provisioning and packing with utmost patience and great care. His record with Captain Bissell's infantry is impeccable. . . ."

"Ordway does not penetrate the hearts of his men. He smells the flower, but never waters the root." Drouillard's black brows connected in a deep frown.

"Speak plainly, Georges."

"My captain, Ordway is a good housekeeper. Water in the hold, a torn sail, wet powder, an extra pound fore or aft, these consume his thinking. To that extent, he is very effective. But he does not perceive the souls of men. It is not a fault, only a limitation. Others are more threatening."

"Collins?"

Drouillard waved a hand, no. "Impetuous, sometimes a blow-hard, Collins has a temper when provoked, but he is young and not malicious."

"Who, then?"

"You will not reveal that I told you, sir?" The question was unexpected and seemed an indication of a latent apprehension even on the part of Drouillard.

Clark prompted: "I will keep your secret from the men, but not from Captain Lewis."

"There are men abroad who do not want this expedition to succeed . . . Spaniards, and a sprinkling of English traders. I believe they have planted spies within this camp."

William Clark absorbed the words in silence. He leveled piercing eyes on Drouillard, breathed in deeply, sank back, and frowned. "The Spanish have been slow and uncooperative, but now the United States has purchased Louisiana. Spanish dominion is at an end."

Drouillard shrugged. "The territory is boundless, sir. The Spanish mind does not know where it begins or ends. You do not know. Mister Jefferson does not know. The Spanish think that they can retrieve what they have lost, or reserve a portion for themselves by maneuvering and subterfuge."

Deep furrows carved into William Clark's smooth brow,

and he questioned: "Spies, here with us, in this camp?"

Drouillard's mouth barely opened. "Amos Leakins, sir. Others, too, but he is the leader. Leakins gave Collins, Hall, and Warner drink that caused their sleep."

"Drugged them?" The revelation pained. Clark wrenched words from deep within.

"Recruiters do it regularly to the unsuspecting in the ports, unscrupulous naval captains, pirates . . . when desertions increase, and they need crewmen. Labiche can tell you. He was a seaman."

A long silence intervened in which neither man spoke. Drouillard sat back and puffed his pipe. William Clark rubbed the stubble on his chin and stared gloomily at a shadowy corner of his tent. Finally, he took up his quill and dipped it in ink. "I want you to deliver a message, Georges, into the hands of Captain Lewis at Saint Louis." Clark drew up a sheet of paper and began to write:

Lewis, a situation has arisen here which will require the dismissal of one or more of our corps. The problem is urgent. I do not want to act without your full assent. I believe that the problem should ease greatly once we are finally on our way. Please return at the earliest.

Sincerely, William Clark

He folded, sealed, and handed the letter to Drouillard. "To Lewis and no one else, as fast as you can."

Drouillard repeated: "To Captain Lewis, sir." It was near evening on May 18th. Drouillard took the dispatch, shoved it down the front of his shirt, and left immediately.

The wind came up during the night. It began to rain hard. Near noon of the next day, lightning split the sky in the south-east over St. Louis. William Clark feared for Georges Drouillard. He remained alone in his tent and reviewed the enlistments of every man, especially Collins, Hall, and Warner. Hugh Hall was a solid soldier who was fond of his drink, but an Army man whose allegiance was never in doubt, brave and older in years than many. William Warner was young and easily led, but diligent with no demerits against him. Collins was also young, headstrong, and handsome, physically strong, a good hunter, capable of great endurance. His conduct with Ordway was rash. But Ordway tended to draw his world in black and white, to jump to conclusions, and not paint in the color of reality. And Collins's antics offended Ordway's strict Puritanical ethics. The spitting was a terrible affront and could not go unpunished.

William Clark rubbed his chin, stretched out on his cot, and decided to separate Collins from Ordway for the near future. Collins or Hall would do better under Pryor or Floyd—or Drouillard. He worried about Drouillard. He had sent Drouillard on a dangerous mission, and he had not returned. But then he had not made public his suspicions: a spy would have no reason to pursue and intercept Georges Drouillard, or would he?

William Clark sighed with relief when Lewis and Georges Drouillard arrived the following evening, Sunday, in heavy rain. Drouillard had forced a speedy march. He had covered the twenty-one miles to the city of St. Louis and back in twenty-four hours in the rain, and, like a good Frenchman, he had probably gone to Mass.

But he did not arrive alone. He brought a bevy of important visitors: U. S. Army Captain Amos Stoddard, Messrs A. Chouteau and C. Gratiot, and Dr. A. Saugrain and one Charles Tayon, the former Spanish commandant of St. Charles. They were wet and hungry, and William Clark duti-

fully invited them to dinner. The meal was meager because the wood was wet and cooking difficult, but the company was warm except for the Spaniard who sniffed at every corner like a nosy mouse. The group departed in the evening for dryer accommodations in St. Charles.

It was still raining on Monday, the 21st. William Clark and Meriwether Lewis sat behind a table in the gray interior of the officers' tent. They faced a depressing task. Sergeant Ordway stood to one side. Drouillard sat on an overturned bucket in a corner. Amos Leakins strutted in as Clark leaned forward ponderously on his elbows.

Leakins spoke up aggressively: "Only dry piece of ground, sirs, is right here under this canvas. We've all been wringin' out wet stockings and bailin' boats." He shook the drops from his coat and lowered himself, uninvited, onto a stool with a self-important grin.

Meriwether Lewis stiffened. He spoke softly and slowly. The words sliced thinly between his teeth. "Stand at attention, if you please, Mister Leakins."

Leakins's eyes retracted, and his grin melted like fat in a fire. He rose awkwardly and braced his shoulders.

William Clark looked up. "Mister Leakins, you have lied to Sergeant Ordway and by extension to us. You failed to report for guard duty last Wednesday, May the Sixteenth. Worse, you allowed one of your fellows to suffer punishment that should have been yours. Amos Leakins, you are herewith to collect your belongings and depart this camp. Sergeant Ordway will escort you to the perimeter."

Leakins's tongue lashed out for one last reprieve. "If I may explain, sir. I'm not an Army man. I'm a civilian, like Drouillard. He serves no guard duty."

Meriwether Lewis's usually mild face purpled in anger. "The veracity of any explanation you could offer, Mister

Leakins, is suspect. Mister Drouillard serves in a capacity vastly different from your own. If you were a duly enlisted member of the United States Army, your punishment would be much more severe. The decision is final." He clapped his hands. "Sergeant, see Mister Leakins out."

Leakins's black stare hardened visibly. "If I may wait until the weather clears, sir, until the roads dry out?"

Again Lewis snapped back icily. "You would do well, Mister Leakins, to care less for the mud on your boots and more for the mire that smears you name." He turned his face away. It was a deliberate snub. Leakins backed away like a cur that had been kicked. Sergeant Ordway stepped forward with the same dogged adherence to regulations that had so plagued John Collins, and escorted Leakins away.

When Leakins had gone, Drouillard spoke up: "I think there are others, sir."

William Clark's voice quaked. "I know there are, Georges. Señor Tayon was here. We must all act with great care and circumspection." Clark was an open man. Deception and stealth saddened and appalled him.

The expedition made good progress during the next few days, past Tavern Rock to the Devil's Race Grounds. On the 24th, as they passed an island, the larboard bank began to crumble. There were twenty-four men on the heavy tow rope that the French called a *cordelle*. Collins, Whitehouse, Potts, and Bratton pulled like mules on a freight wagon. Potts could not swim.

Potts slipped, lost his footing, and sank suddenly beneath the water's surface. Joe Whitehouse jumped in after him. The tow rope slackened. Twenty men braced against the swift current to counter the pull of the heavy vessel as the rope twanged tight. Now Collins watched in horror as the em-

bankment above them fell away. The wet strands of hemp
stretched and snapped. The flying end flew back, striking
Bratton across the chest and knocking him into Gibson. Men
lost their grip or were pulled underwater as the boat swirled
and the frothing current struck it broadside. The vessel
heeled dangerously to starboard. William Clark screamed an
order from the deck that sent the oarsmen over the side to
hold the boat upright. They clung like leeches to the gun-
wales to keep the keelboat from capsizing.

The gang on the severed rope dove and swam out into the
river to save themselves and escape the crashing riverbank. In
the mêlée, Whitehouse lost his grip on Potts who was floating
fast downstream, flailing helplessly. Collins reacted, threw a
log to Whitehouse, and ran and dove to save Potts. He came
up under the choking man, buoyed him with a forearm under
the chin, and swam with the flow. They floated aimlessly on
the surface until the waters calmed, and Collins pulled Potts
to shore.

It was Deschamps and the French boatmen who saved the
day. They collected by instinct, grabbed the frayed end of the
tow, and pulled toward the deep water of the channel as
Deschamps bellowed furious orders from the bank. They
took to the water like geese, swimming powerfully, downstream, ahead of the boat.

At the helm, William Clark was shouting over the din.
"Keep 'er pointed downriver till you find a solid footing!" He
was powerless, standing in the stern as the rudder slapped
wildly and the tiller spun loose. He threw cables to the swimmers who paddled until their shoulders ached, swallowed
water, blinked the mud from their eyes, and finally slogged
ashore when they touched solid footing. They wrapped the
cables around a massive oak and prayed its roots would hold.
When the ropes twanged tight, the keelboat came to rest, but

they had retreated downriver two miles.

They made camp that night near a lonely farm, one of the last on the river. John Collins could not remember ever having been so exhausted. He had struggled in deep water for over an hour. The soles of his feet were bruised and torn. A coating of muck had penetrated every pore. The scabs from his whipping had peeled, leaving the skin beneath pink and tender. Worse, the coarse rope had rubbed new sores. But others had worse injuries. Potts had almost drowned and could not stop coughing up water. He could not hold down food, even the thin broth that Thompson prepared. He kept calling for whiskey to wash out the mud in his gut and running to the forest until he heaved up air.

Drouillard and Reuben Fields came in from the hunt that evening with four deer that the exhausted men consumed ravenously. Drouillard's dark face hardened when he heard of the day's mishaps. After the camp had fallen asleep, when privacy and silence were possible, Drouillard shuffled to the captains' tent and lit his pipe. Clark had fallen asleep over his table of maps. A short candle dripped wax.

Drouillard pressed his shoulder. "A word, my captain, I think it important."

Clark nodded distractedly. Drouillard turned his back to the brazier and pulled up a stool. "I think, my captain, that the cable was weakened deliberately before it snapped."

Clark's head snapped up. The awful thought swiped like the flat edge of a sword. "You mean someone, here within the corps, broke it? But Leakins is gone!"

"Only just gone, sir. Joe Fields and I saw roots cut, loosened dirt, stakes driven upright into the ground where the earth overhangs the river, at the spot where the bank caved in. Deschamps says that cables do not fray like this one . . . that it was cut."

Clark seemed to fold and wither, then whispered: "Captain Lewis needs to hear." He summoned Lewis from his cot.

Meriwether Lewis stood pale-faced and rigid as he listened to Drouillard's report. He lips barely parted when he replied in stoic monotone: "The Spanish do not want us here. Post more guards, and send out scouts to survey the river ahead. And keep the *pirogues* forward of the keelboat, forward by one hundred yards or more, enough to give fair warning. They can take soundings, and they can be easily replaced. Man them with Frenchmen who are experienced in the caprices of the river. And purchase more strong cable from the farmer."

Drouillard's deep voice interrupted: "Tomorrow, my captains, we will arrive at the village of La Charette, the little cart. It is home to five families, the last whites who live on the river, the very last who can supply us more rope or any other material of civilization." Drouillard's back was turned to the light. They could not see the creases of his face, only the steely points of light that were his eyes. They watched the swift movement of his arm as he leaned forward and banged the table with his fist. His action punctuated their fears. He squared his broad shoulders and uttered: "Reward them well, the men who saved the keelboat. Their loyalty is proven. This man Collins I brought you, he swims like a fish and he is strong. Do not doubt him." In the darkness, a rare smile crossed Georges Drouillard's lips, and he continued: "After tomorrow, there will be no more purchases, no more white man's help, only what the tribes will offer or allow."

William Clark met his gaze. "And there will be no more white man's treachery."

Meriwether Lewis lifted his head. There was a cynical lift of an eye, but his voice trembled. "We carry the treachery with us, Will, like poison in our veins, and there are red men on the river who will exact tribute and will allow us passage only after the granting of gifts."

Drouillard nodded knowingly. "In your cities, you call it bribery, my captains, and we will pay. With hope, the greedy ones will have already gone off to hunt before we arrive."

Chapter Eleven

The following days on the river settled into routine. The three sergeants rotated posts every day. One at the helm steered; one at the bow scanned the river for obstructions; one in the center managed the sail and commanded the guard. This last allotted food and drink, reconnoitered a stopping place, and posted sentinels. Each sergeant commanded a squad of eight or nine men, while Baptiste Deschamps headed the French *engagés* who manned the red *pirogue*, and Richard Warfington captained his Army detachment in the white *pirogue*. Thomas Howard, François Labiche, and Pierre Cruzatte, the three most experienced boatmen, remained on the keelboat at all times. One of the other privates was assigned to aid the crews of the *pirogues*. Sergeants Ordway, Pryor, and Floyd, Deschamps, Captain Warfington, and the scout, Georges Drouillard, were exempt from guard duty. Orders were posted every evening for the following day. All food was cooked at night and a portion reserved for breakfast and lunch. Sergeant Ordway distributed commissary provisions.

On good days, when the wind blew directly from the stern, the corps hoisted the sail and rowed up the main channel of the river where insects were few. But good days were rare. The wind was capricious, and, even when it steadied, the river curved and the channel wandered. On bad days, when the wind blew head-on, they towed. Horses were no help because they could not find solid footing and their sharp hoofs accelerated the crumbling of the banks. It was hard labor for the strongest of men. They sank to their knees in the heavy bottom muck. Their toes stubbed hard rocks and sharp sawyers that lay like invisible snares beneath the surface of the water. Swarming mosquitoes and black flies landed on any exposed surface of a man's skin to suck his life's juices. Ticks were the worst because they burrowed holes in man and beast. Their bite left raised red sores that rubbed open and festered into boils. The dog scratched until he bled. So did the men. On bad days, when the wind blew hardest from the northwest, they proceeded only a few enervating miles. On the worst days, they made no progress at all, and there were dreadful, disheartening days, when they regressed.

William Clark realigned the squads on May 26th, and separated Collins from Hugh Hall and Billy Warner. He assigned Collins to Sergeant Pryor's squad of older, experienced men, and Hall and Warner to Ordway's. Clark wisely placed the impetuous Collins and the youngest man, George Shannon, under the mature influence of John Shields, Pierre Cruzatte, François Labiche, and quiet, unassuming Joe Whitehouse.

Ugly Labiche was the first to approach Collins since the whipping. "It was not the cat-o-nine-tails or it would have ripped the flesh from your spine." He flicked a deck of cards casually. They snapped like popping corn. "Resentment is a worm that will eat out your heart, Johnny. Come, we have a game. I play you for the scabs on your back or the lice in your hair." Collins couldn't help laughing.

Whitehouse was the next, and he spoke to Collins in the evening before dinner. It had been a hard day with little progress made. Collins had collapsed against a tree to examine his underarms for ticks. Whitehouse held out a gift. It was a pair of moccasins that he had cut and sewn himself from skins that he had cured. Whitehouse muttered an awkward: "For you."

Collins was as unaccustomed to receiving gifts as White-house was to giving them. He was equally taciturn. "I'm obliged."

Whitehouse countered softly: "No, I'm the indebted one, John Collins. You helped me the day the tow rope broke, when you threw me a log. I would have drowned without it." The compliment washed out and drained away, but Whitehouse remained. "I could examine the stripes on your back for maggots. It would make you feel better." It was not an appetizing task. Collins looked up, surprised. "It would at that. Thank you." He grinned, and Joe Whitehouse grinned back.

Another man who befriended Collins was John Shields. He was an older, experienced man, blacksmith, gunsmith, boat-builder, and a man familiar with womenfolk—he was married with one daughter. Shields kept to himself during his first few days, then positioned himself at mealtime between Collins and Shannon. He owned an old musket that he oiled meticulously every night. He would mumble impishly at the younger men and declare: "Here's my Nancy." Then he would stroke the barrel, dip his ramrod in oil, and shove it down with a mischievous gleam in his eye—Nancy was the name of his wife. Gradually the young men realized that the musket was his vicarious way of satisfying physical desire and banishing the loneliness. They were all lonely for the company of females. But Shields's nightly ritual reminded Collins of his last encounter with Louise Calderon, and the image generated resentment and anger. But his imagination yielded quickly to utter physical exhaustion, and he usually fell asleep.

The Frenchman, Pierre Cruzatte, was not so friendly. He was half Omaha, a mixed-blood like Georges Drouillard, but short and wiry. He spoke Omaha and was one of the men who played a fiddle. Gibson was the other. He was too old to attract a woman, and he knew it. He thanked God nightly for being alive. A blow from a tomahawk had left him with a red scar down the left side of his face and the use of only one myopic, color-blind eye. A streak of white hair like a brush of paint rimmed the top of the scar. The rest of his hair was black despite his age. He was a staunch Catholic—most called him papist—strongly attached to the symbols of his faith. When danger threatened, he invariably signed himself with the Roman cross. On a leather thong around his neck, he wore a piece of human bone with flesh still attached, enclosed in glass, and rimmed with pure gold. It looked more like blackened, year-old meat, but Cruzatte, who couldn't see clearly, declared it a holy relic, more necessary to his well-being than a medicine bundle to an Indian. He claimed it was the fingertip of Saint Luke, the doctor of the Christian Gospel, whose powerful intercession had healed his hideous wound.

John Collins was also a papist, but, to Cruzatte, a guilty one in need of repentance. Collins kept his conviction private, unlike the outspoken, judgmental Cruzatte. Collins and Gibby Gibson delighted in playing crude tricks on the old man. Cruzatte tolerated their antics and waited patiently to hatch his revenge. He trapped a nestful of beetles, ground the soft bodies to a paste, spread it over dry biscuit, and served it to the younger men. "Cures the ague. Served it to King Louis in the court of France. *Pâté* . . . paste in English. Sounds better in French." They ate and gagged and retched, and Cruzatte laughed until his scar turned purple.

François Labiche also spoke Omaha and a smattering of Oto and Pawnee, as well as French and English. He had an angular, asymmetrical face. The nose was off center, the mouth crooked, but his black eyes masked the eyesight of a

122

hawk and a quick, incisive intelligence. No one played tricks on Labiche. They tried it once, calling him "ugly bitch" which was English for *biche*. Labiche countered with a knife throw that whisked between the prankster's legs. He was an expert butcher. He carried two knives in scabbards attached to his belt, and a longer one strapped against the calf of his leg. Some said he had killed a bear with that very knife. He explained that it was only a cub, and that was why he bore no scars to prove the encounter, but the younger men were not so sure because he never took off his shirt. When the rest of the men were oiling their muskets, Labiche honed his knives. He had the long, graceful fingers of a sculptor, and he used his knives as their nimble, pointed extension. His hands were never at rest. With a knife he ate, dug roots, trapped, cut firewood, leveled the ground where he laid out his bed, slaughtered and butchered game. He slept with his knives at his side. For hunting, he preferred a lance or a bow and arrow to a gun, because these instruments could be replaced easily in the wilds and needed only sharpening, not reloading with powder that had to be bought. He was also an expert boatman. Some said he had sailed the seas in great square-rigged ships.

Labiche liked to gamble, and frequently organized trials of strength and skill. There were tugs of war, arm-wrestling, and paddling and shooting competitions. He owned a pair of dice and wore them in a pouch tightly secured around his neck. Collins wagered frequently to break the boredom. He could outshoot and outrun Labiche, but Labiche could outswim and outpaddle Collins. Personal items were constantly changing hands between them. But Labiche taught John Collins the delicate art of aiming and throwing a knife. Collins learned to prepare fresh meat for the pot, and to extract skeletons from the unknown specimens that Captain Lewis wanted preserved and shipped back to President Jefferson.

John Collins's relationship with his fellows was not unlike that with Georges Drouillard. Friendships were not forced. The older men deliberately let the young men founder because of stubbornness or ignorance or the youthful exuberance of their own rash designs. The younger men responded willingly or unwillingly. Experience was an exacting master.

Some lessons came hard. Collins was fond of strong drink. Others were fonder, like Tom Howard who bragged that he never drank water, and Hugh Hall who wobbled frequently on his stumpy legs after stealing an extra gill of whiskey from the barrel. No one reported him because of his perennial good humor, and, besides, whiskey supplies were plentiful.

They had been gone from St. Charles a little over one month. June 26th, dawned bloody red. The wind blew from the southwest, and they hoisted the square sail. Beneath a high protruding rock, a large rattlesnake lay coiled in the sun. At the mouth of the Blue River silt collected, and the conflicting waters converged into violent eddies. The waters, like the omen snake, circled back upon themselves. The lead men staggered in the swift current, and the tow rope fell slack. Collins heard a twang. He knew the sound. The tow rope had snapped again. The sail emptied, and the boat veered. The oarsman rowed madly to hold their course. Collins dove to retrieve the end. He fastened the two ends together, but they did not hold. Howard grabbed the anchor cable, swam out to Collins. The two men swam faster than the current downstream, until they held enough slack to wrap around a hefty oak that stopped the boat's retreat, while all hands pulled for the shore.

John Collins dragged himself onto the beach and threw himself down, exhausted. His lungs ached from the intake of water. Every muscle cramped. He had closed his eyes when he heard his name. Sergeant Pryor was standing over him. "Collins, the captains want you, now, on the double!"

He met Howard on the run. Trailing mud and water, they stumbled to meet their captain. Meriwether Lewis looked no better, and waited in the shade of a cottonwood tree with a reluctant smile. "Privates, we thank you. Our records and maps would have been destroyed, but for your quick and decisive action."

William Clark was equally grateful. "Well done, Collins, Howard! What can we do to commend you?"

Tom Howard was not shy. "A mite of whiskey, sir, to quench the thirst."

But Clark shook his head. "You want drink, Private, when you've swallowed half the river. I will assign you both to the hunting detail tomorrow."

"Thank you, sir," Collins groaned through cracked, sun-burned lips. He could still taste the mud of the river and the tang of whiskey would have washed it out.

But Tom Howard persisted: "A dram of whiskey, sir, would be a welcome reward."

William Clark refused again. "Whiskey will only distract you, Private. Get a good night's rest . . . the hunting will invigorate and inspire you." The men loved to hunt because it meant relief from the drudgery of unpacking, hanging out to dry, sorting, and repacking. It meant a chance to set foot on dry land. It meant dry clothes for fully twelve hours. It meant a day free from rules and an opportunity to ride rather than walk. Collins longed to throw a leg over a saddle and feel the sway of a horse between his legs. Later, at night, when Hugh Hall was on watch, he and Howard could sneak their reward from the whiskey barrel. Now he licked his dry lips.

He left early the next day with Drouillard and Howard. The hunting was poor, and Drouillard sent Howard back, then elected to stay out for an extra day. He assigned the brown mare to Collins and sent him into new terrain where he shot three deer. Fields had killed one, Drouillard two. No one had ever shot three animals in one day, except Drouillard himself. And John Collins saw a buffalo! William Clark and Meriwether Lewis personally congratulated him. Old Cruzatte slapped him on the back, and John Shields shared his allotted gill in a glowing toast. "To Johnny, may your eye be always bright and your aim true." When he raised his cup, all shouted—"Hear, hear!"—and old Cruzatte plunked his fiddle furiously. But he stopped abruptly and asked a prickly question. "You afraid of the buff? Why didn't you shoot him?"

"We were already carrying four deer."

Dinner that evening was a sumptuous feast. There was food in plenty. Everyone was curious, and questions buzzed louder than black flies. Collins obliged with lively descriptions of the shaggy bison. He talked so much he hardly ate, but then he could eat later. He would have to stay awake because he had drawn the first watch.

It was not hard duty after the exhilaration of days of hunting. The night was dark, the moon was new, and the air was warm and moist. Collins set his lantern carefully to one side, lowered himself to a rock, and leaned back against the hard staves of a whiskey barrel. The croaking frogs, the ripple of fish jumping, the eternal click and buzz of a thousand insects, the soft rustle of the wind in the trees on the bank, kept him awake. An owl hooted. A swish of wings descended, and a rodent squealed an instant death. It reminded Collins of his own perdition.

After most of the camp had fallen asleep, Hugh Hall crawled out of the blackness. "You're a big man in camp, Johnny. You can shoot and you can swim. You stopped the boat. Saved our dinner an' whiskey. I'd hated to see that floatin' down the stream. That's two times we owe you. I didn't see no captains swimmin' out in the river." Hall was jockeying for favor. He edged up beside his friend. "I brought you something to eat."

Collins was grateful, took the bowl, and shifted position to make room for Hall. "Come set, Hughie. Four eyes watch better than two."

But Hugh Hall had a purpose. "Captain didn't issue no more whiskey for celebratin', after all?"

"He's saving it for trading with redskins."

"I didn't see no redskin divin' after 'is bunch of roots an' bones an' moldy papers nor stoppin' 'is precious boat from runnin' all the way down to New Orleans. Barrel's right there. Lemme draw you a bitty dram!"

"Naw, Hughie, we get caught, we're trumped."

Hall shuffled his feet impatiently. "It's dark. I done it before and not got caught. You scared o' that skinny stick the cap'n calls a whip? That's a schoolmaster s switch. Ain't no real cat-o-nine-tails."

It sounded like a dare. Collins felt the saliva welling up under his tongue. He wore his cup on a thong tied around his neck and ran his fingers over the cool, slippery tin. "How'd you know I was thirsty, Hughie?"

"Cruzatte told me. Said you're a sinner. Frenchies have stomachs like wineskins. They shrivel and shrink, if you don't keep them wet. Cruzatte doesn't think the captain stocked enough whiskey fer us an' the redskins, too." Hall looked around at the barrels resting beside them. "We'd only be takin' our share. The bung's settin' right there in the hole, stickin' out like a cow's full titty, beggin' fer a pull. Who's to know if we milk 'er a mite?"

The entire camp was asleep. Hugh Hall pulled out the

cork bung. The whiskey spewed forth in a rush that knocked the cups from their hands and spattered the dusty ground where they stood.

"Now look what you've done."

"I'd never waste good whiskey, Johnny." He centered the bung on the hole to stop the flow, and the spray arched sideways, spattering their clothes and puddling on the bare ground at their feet.

"I can't see to cork it. Set the cups down. Bring the lantern here." He pounded the cork into the hole, but not before Hall had caught enough whiskey to fill both cups. "Here's yours, Johnny. Drink 'er down. Better you than them redskins."

Collins felt the liquid sloshing around his moccasined feet. "There's a whole puddle more, Hughie."

"No more mud in that puddle than in the water in the river, an' we been drinkin' that for weeks." Hugh Hall stooped to scoop up another cupful from the ground. Collins did the same. But the bunghole was still dripping and replenishing the puddle like a mountain spring. Finally, half the barrel had drained into the earth, and the two men were hiccuping loudly, dumb as two fat frogs in a pond. When William Bratton arrived for the second watch, they were thoroughly, uproariously drunk. They had started to sing a thumping, Gallic drinking song they had learned from the Frenchmen. *"Goûtons boire!"* The praise of drink began softy and grew in volume until the last line—*"Ici gît le roi des buveurs!"*—drew hoots from the groggy men.

Labiche understood every word and threw a boot at them. "There's a curse for your king of drinkers!" The whole camp awakened. Bratton didn't need to report them. Collins and Hall were still singing raucously as they were led off to the jail and confined, pending court-martial.

The jury consisted of Sergeant Pryor, Colter, Newman,

Gass, and Thompson. Potts was judge advocate. The verdict was predictable: the jurors "on the deliberation of evidence adduced are of the opinion that the prisoner is *guilty* of the charge exhibited against him and do therefore sentence him to receive *one hundred lashes on his bear back*."

Whitehouse who could read the posted sentence, snickered. "I spell better than Captain Clark. . . . Bears have fur, Johnny, but you'll be naked. Why'd you get drunk? Why'd you do it? Pryor's so disgusted, he won't speak to you." Collins's spree was not a laughing matter. Hughie Hall received a punishment of fifty lashes because he had not been assigned to guard duty at the time of the offense.

A sobered John Collins heard his own sentence in disbelief. He couldn't remember how much he had drunk. He couldn't remember the singing or conversation with Hugh Hall. He only reflected that he had suffered twice at the hands of these men whom he thought his comrades. Twice he had done nothing that the rough backwoods society in which he had grown up would consider sinful or criminal, nothing that others had not also done and escaped punishment. A lick of whiskey . . . what was that when the captains had whole barrels? At that instant, John Collins made up his mind to leave, to escape this niggardly, ungrateful expedition and strike out on his own.

Ordway administered the lashes when the corps paraded for inspection at 3:30 P.M. of the same day. Private Gass kept the count. Collins didn't hear their relentless rhythm. His face hardly twitched. He closed his eyes. He crunched his teeth deeply into the pine knot between them, while the taste of its sap lay bitter on his tongue.

Chapter Twelve

When they cut John Collins loose from the whipping tree and splashed a bucket of cold water over his back, Potts handed him his shirt and mumbled: "You stood yer penance like a man, Johnny."

It was meant as a compliment, but Collins glared back angrily. "You were my judge, Potts. You snubbed me to a post like a stubborn colt. Did you mean to break me, make me buck . . . after it was me who pulled your soggy butt out of the river?" His jaw twitched. The veins in his necks pulsed. The stripes on his shoulders and back dripped blood, but he ignored the pain. "I should've let you sink." He snapped the shirt rudely out of Potts's hands, and walked away in a defiant sulk.

Drouillard had sauntered into the camp with a fresh-killed buck over his shoulder and heard the exchange. He stood squarely in the young man's path. "Johnny, *mon ami,* what this time?"

Collins stopped in his tracks. He answered rudely. "*Ami,* friend? Where were you when a word from you could have stopped them? I don't want your sympathy." He moved to shoulder past, but Drouillard stepped in front of him.

Drouillard spoke softly. "They've not finished. . . . You want to stand here while Hall gets his? Has a little pain so numbed you that you have no feeling for the sufferings of your fellow man? I spoke to Pryor. You were wrong, *mon ami!* This time you were very wrong!" They glared at each other, shoulder to shoulder, eye to eye. Drouillard did not blink. Collins finally dropped his cold gaze and moved off toward the river. Drouillard called to his back. "There's blood on your back where you cannot reach. Let me wash it off."

Collins spat his next words back over his bloody shoulder. "Go away! One hundred lashes is too damn' many for a swig of whiskey. Pryor, my own sergeant, has done the same, and Potts, he's downed half a barrel himself alone. Who are they to judge me?"

"They were not on duty and they stole from the boatmen in Saint Charles, not the expedition stores, and no one reported them. Come, wash the stripes before they fester and the blow flies lay their eggs under your skin. . . . I'll share my meat with you." This time, Collins followed.

Drouillard walked to the shore where he sponged off Collins's blood, covered his cuts with cottonwood floss, and bound him up with the wide cotton sash that was his own belt. Neither man spoke, and Collins shoved his arms back into his shirt. The swish and thud of the lash sounded ominously as it sank into Hugh Hall's back and the count increased. Like Collins, Hall made no sound at all.

But at each stroke, Collins jerked involuntarily. "They treat us like the sand we grind underfoot. They treat York, the slave, better than me and Hughie Hall."

"York, the slave, would command a higher price on the block." It was bitter knowledge.

Collins sucked on the thought like a hard, impenetrable pit, then spit it out: "And I am worthless. I have not even the value of a slave! Leave me alone!"

But Drouillard would not go. He lowered himself casually onto the soft earth, like a dog at his master's feet and waited patiently.

The sounds of whipping stopped. Except for the rippling

of the river, an eerie silence enveloped the camp. Words stuck in Collins's throat. "I shouldn't have listened to you. I'm not wanted here. I should leave. Hughie Hall should come with me."

"And where will you go?"

"Downriver."

"In Saint Louis, they'll call you a deserter. The French say *poltron,* coward. It's an ugly word."

"In Saint Louis, they call the captains fools. Some call Jefferson a dreamer." Collins sat beside the Frenchman, staring morosely at the brown water as it coursed by.

"A fool is an honest man. So is a dreamer. A deserter has abandoned not only his friends, but his word and his loyalty. You are not a deserter, Johnny Collins, but you have been foolish." Drouillard picked up a flat stone and tossed it far out onto the surface of the water. The current seized it and seemed to float it on past. Gradually, it sank, and Drouillard continued: "Have you allowed others to lead you? Have you let whiskey fog your brain? Have you been like the pebbles in the river, tumbling in the prevailing current? If you go back alone, naked as that stone, you will sink, just like that." He snapped his fingers. "In the passing of one breath."

"I'll take my horse."

"You sold him. They paid you for the beast. Take the horse, and they brand you a thief."

"They paid me with a paper I cannot read."

"To be exchanged for good land and pay. It is a viable promise. The captains are honorable men, more honorable than you if you steal what you do not own, or desert when you have given your word. . . . And here you can learn the ways of the rivers and the mountains, and you can learn to read. What do you want, Johnny Collins?"

"Whiskey when I'm thirsty."

"And the respect and friendship of good men, no? A drunken man commands no respect and cannot be trusted as friend. The whiskey has made you foolish, and it is valuable, more so here, where we cannot buy more, than in Saint Louis. The whiskey is what will earn our passage upriver, when the Sioux and their British allies block the channel and exact their tolls. The whiskey will win us new friends and buy the fidelity of old. Yours was an instant's pleasure not a durable reward. . . .but I lecture and you do not listen."

Hugh Hall walked up, dabbing the blood on his cheek with the sleeve of his shirt. He hung his head, and he bit back his lips and mumbled an apology: "I'm sorry, Johnny. I never thought. . . ." Hall was not bitter.

John Collins's anger smoldered like a hidden fire in an underground root, ready to flare up when it found a vent and the oxygen to feed it. He hissed a reply. "Neither did I, and I'm not sorry."

When the order came to man the boats, Collins avoided his squad and asked Deschamps for an oar in the red *pirogue*. Deschamps agreed, and Sergeant Pryor let him go. At night, when they came ashore to make camp and cook dinner, George Shannon had assumed his place at the cook fire. He backed away into the anonymity of the forest, beyond the recriminating stares of his comrades. But Joe Whitehouse came after him and held out a bowl to him. Collins ignored him.

"Avoid me, Johnny Collins, or take it and eat and come to the fire light where you can see. Potts wants to give you a present."

"Potts has nothing for me. Potts was my judge."

"And you forget that punishment was exacted and justice wrought. It is over."

Collins was hungry. He went. Potts's hand stretched out

to him, holding what looked like the dark outline of a box. When he held it to the light, Collins saw it was a neatly folded leather belt, with a variety of loops and ties attached. Potts explained: "It's so you can carry your implements without slings and allow your shoulders to heal more quickly."

Joe Whitehouse stood by. He had a mild, disarming smile. Shields, the hefty smithy, growled: "We want you with us, Johnny." The soft words drifted. Shield's eyes were wet, and he turned away. Potts, the stoic, emotionless German, added reluctantly: "We didn't mean to drive you away. We will miss you, if you go, Johnny."

Drouillard was sitting on the opposite side of the fire. The smoke obscured his face as he called across to Collins: "See. They don't turn away. You turn yourself away."

John Collins couldn't sleep that night. The ground was hard, and the cuts on his back pulled open and oozed whenever he moved. He rolled on his stomach, then his side. No position was comfortable. His body, like his thoughts, felt like a million needles pricking. He liked Drouillard. He liked Whitehouse. He liked Hughie Hall. But some of the rest seemed doubtful friends, good only when friendship reflected favor upon themselves. He resented William Clark, and his dislike for righteous, unbending Sergeant Ordway was fast hardening into open aversion. But Leakins was gone, and he hated Leakins. He lay awake far into the night, weighing the advantages of remaining with the group or striking out on his own. St. Charles was only a quick run downriver. He would need a boat. He did not know how to hollow a tree trunk to make a sturdy dugout. Drouillard was right. He would be looked on as a shirker in St. Louis and in all the vast new territory west of the Mississippi, and in eastern states as well. He could not join the Spanish or the French because the Bourgeron affair had disgraced him. He could flee to one of the tribes, but his blond hair would stand out as a treasured trophy. He lay his head on the damp ground with the distasteful knowledge that, alone, his chances of survival were slim. All night long, he struggled with stubborn, resentful pride that prompted him to leave, and wiser, gentler prudence which dictated that he stay.

In the morning, his wounds were stiff and his eyes red from lack of sleep. It was very hot, and the salt of his sweat seeped into his open sores. They stung. They itched. Insects swarmed to the smell of fresh blood. Captain Clark assigned him to hunt and allotted one of the new Harpers Ferry rifles to him. It was a beautiful weapon, smooth and polished with a barrel half of steel. He slid the palm of his hand over its silky stock, raised it up, sighted, and exclaimed: "You trust me with this?"

Clark nodded and was silent. With such a weapon, Collins could retrace his steps to St. Louis alone on foot! Temptation stirred. Clark leveled his steely gaze straight at the soul of John Collins. He knew when to test the mettle of his men.

John Collins left quietly with Georges Drouillard, and they took the brown horse. Out of sight of the camp, they spotted deer in abundance. Every few leagues showed another animal cavorting in the sunlight. Collins was impatient to try the new gun, but Drouillard gave no signal to shoot. For an hour, they walked silently through the tall reeds bounding the river, using their rifles for staffs and leading the horse. They moved slowly. The sun was hot. The ground was soft. The bottomland rose gradually to a row of low treed hills, faint remnants of ancient bluffs when the river carved a different channel.

Drouillard stopped and pointed toward them. "Take the horse, *mon ami*. On the bluffs, will be spring water, game, and a cool breeze." Drouillard set his dark eyes directly on the brooding form of John Collins and added: "If you think the captains have treated you harshly, think of the *travail* they endure today on the river in this terrible heat. Today, they pass the Petite Platte with its shoals and eddies and rush of water." He removed his hat and wiped his dripping brow. "That is why you are here . . . to allow you to recover in body and in spirit." Drouillard held out the horse's lead.

Collins looked up darkly, took the lead, and brushed away a fly. "Stop calling me *mon ami*. I'm not your friend."

"As you wish. . . ." Drouillard tilted his head—it was his only hint of doubt—and started to walk away, when he stopped and called back: "I will be at the mouth of the Petite Platte one hour before sunset. Try to smile, Johnny. Hatred will devour your soul like a worm from the inside, but the Indian maidens will love you if you smile. So will your fellow man."

It was abrupt. Drouillard disappeared in a grove of willows. John Collins stood anchored to the ground, with the new Harpers rifle and the horse, the intent and the means of escape. Did Drouillard intend deliberately to chase him away? Did he want him to leave? He rubbed the soft flat patch of white between the animal's eyes. The mare had deep, brown, soulful eyes that seemed to penetrate the anguish in his heart, and he poured out his soul to the innocent beast. "They beat me like cruel men would beat you when they want you to pull harder." The horse nickered and nuzzled his shoulder. He removed the bridle to let the animal graze and found a spot of shade under a cottonwood sapling where he could sit and examine the gun. He stroked the Harpers, measured its smoothness and weight, and brought it level with his eye. It was lighter than he had anticipated. He would have to hold it more steadily and aim more carefully.

The brown mare broke out in glistening sweat, and Collins felt salt seep into his own wounds. The sweat soaked through his clothes and opened the sores on his back. Flies tormented them both. The bites stung. He picked up his gun and led the horse up into the hills where the breeze refreshed and blew the insects away. He found wild raspberries in a cool glade where he lay propped on his elbows, and hobbled the horse near a gurgling spring. In the heat of the day, he ate his fill and went for a swim. The berries were sweet and the water pure and cleansing, and, when he came out, he felt better. He let the air dry his back, propped the rifle on a log, lay out in the soft grass, and nearly fell asleep.

The horse's head came up suddenly at a rustling in the brush. Collins leaped up from his resting place as a dark silhouette appeared against the darker gray of a cottonwood trunk. The man was dressed entirely in greasy buckskin and camouflaged perfectly against the woody background. At first Collins thought he was an Indian, but there was a familiarity about the form. It was short and wiry with the swift, sly movements of a predator. One hand held the handle of an earthen jug, the other a Kentucky rifle. Collins jumped up.

The man's voice echoed with a strong French accent. "I thought I catch you without your weapons, and I find you also without a shirt. *Sans chemise,* you are a poor man, Private Johnny Collins." Loud laughter echoed blistering scorn.

Collins could not mistake the voice. "What are you doing here, Bourgeron?"

Jacques Bourgeron stepped into the sunlight. He staggered slightly. "I follow you. You leave a trail broad as an ox train." Whiskey had loosened his tongue. He laughed again, and his lips folded back over his teeth like a cat hissing. "I see they beat you? They will not mourn one whom they punish."

Collins's mind cleared, and he froze. He glared intently at the man and did not dare avert his eyes long enough to seize the new rifle that lay at his feet.

Bourgeron held out a jug. "Drink with me, my poor Private Collins, or you will die thirsty."

Collins ignored the offer, and Bourgeron lifted the jug to his own mouth. The liquid had already soaked his beard and soiled the front of his shirt. "To my sister and her ancient husband. Drink to woman, to Eve, to Louise, who makes an old man lust, who made you lust, my poor Private Collins. Drink to the old man's wealth and *à sa mort*, to his imminent death. Drink to me, Mister Johnny Collins, because I will inherit the power of his wealth. You see how it has made me brave?"

Bourgeron set down the jug, drew his knife from its scabbard, and ran his finger along the blade. His head weaved from side to side like a bull facing the cape, determining when to charge and where to gore. Bourgeron continued: "It is a *bon couteau*, sharp enough to carve more stripes in your back, or to gouge out your tongue or your heart." He tossed the knife up into the air, and let it fall point first to the earth, and stooped over to wrench it free. "It is well balanced, no? I use it to butcher the buffalo. I can throw it straight, plant it in the dirt at your feet, or throw it with the force to slice through your breastbone like the fowl I carve for dinner. I can throw it faster than you can aim and fire your gun."

A muscle twitched in Collins's jaw. Tension crept up from his groin, the length of his spine, out into the tips of his fingers. Bourgeron was drunk, he hoped drunk enough to skew his aim. A silence hovered.

Suddenly, the Frenchman moved. It was a diversionary ploy, a feint to the side to distract and confuse. He stumbled awkwardly and caught himself. Collins reached instantly for the rifle and brought it up to aim. It was too new and unfamiliar. He cocked, fired, and missed.

Laughing like a fiend, Bourgeron righted himself and lowered his head to charge. His red eyes blazed, and his nostrils flared. He thumped his belly with a fist, just below the center point of the rib cage. "The knife is more certain than the gun. Such a short gun for such a tall man. I make you fear, Private Collins, you who make a coward of Jacques Bourgeron in front of his countrymen. I make you dance and tremble until I see the soft point in the flesh where the knife will sink."

Collins's every sense tingled. He circled warily. "You're drunk, Bourgeron, or you're mad.

"Brave, not mad, not drunk, Private Collins. I even give you time to reload." Collins rammed another ball home as Bourgeron ranted on: "I will go back to my friends, the Otos, with your yellow scalp and the brown horse, and they will reward me with many pelts or the choice of a bride. Then I will return to my countrymen a rich and honorable man. I will be twice honored, and it will not be with Calderon's wealth and honor. It will be with my own."

A flash of insight stunned John Collins. Family and pride did not motivate this man. Talk of honor was a thin disguise for greed. Here was a little man who depended on an inflated reputation and material possessions for self-respect, on whiskey to make him bold, and on another man's riches to lend him prestige. Bourgeron was a dangerous, unpredictable man.

Collins placed his back to the horse. Bourgeron would not chance stabbing the horse.

But Bourgeron read his thoughts. "I will not miss, Private Johnny Collins. I will not pierce the horse." He laughed again, leaped sideways toward a streak of shade that covered the ground. Collins blinked at the speckled light. When he opened his eyes, he saw a glint of steel splitting the air. He ducked, sighted his rifle, and fired. The shot was true and caught Bourgeron just below the neck. Bourgeron went down, gasping for air.

Collins waited for his own knees to collapse. The pungent smell of powder pricked his nostrils. The crash of the explosion echoed in his ears. A ribbon of smoke rose from the barrel of the new gun. He felt his arms; he felt his legs; he took a breath; he took a step. The hilt of the knife protruded from the ground not two feet from where he stood. The long blade was completely buried in the soft soil. Bourgeron was coughing and writhing on the ground. The horse had broken its hobbles and run into the trees. Gradually the smoke settled, and silence fell slowly, like a veil, over the soft bed of wilderness and river, and John Collins stood unharmed.

He had never killed a man. His every muscle quaked. He stared at Bourgeron, his opponent of only a few moments ago. Bourgeron was smothering in his own blood, moving his lips as if to speak, pleading with his eyes, and twitching like a slaughtered fowl. John Collins knew instinctively what he wanted. He wrenched the knife from the ground and placed it in the hands of the dying man.

Bourgeron seemed to smile up at him blissfully. He signed himself, took the knife, held the point to his own breast, and, with his last effort, rolled onto the point of the blade. Collins heard the steel scrape bone, gasped, and turned away.

It seemed like hours that he stood there, eyes open but unseeing, ears still vibrating with the crash of the shot, horrified. He turned finally. The jug still stood where Bourgeron had placed it. Collins swiped it up and poured the dregs into the black earth. Slowly, he went to reload his gun and find the horse. The animal stood trembling nearby, wary of the scene and the scent of death.

Bourgeron's body rested in a round pool of blood, face down. John Collins spent the next hour digging with the best instrument available, Bourgeron's own knife. The blade was wider than his own, more suited to scooping and scraping the moist clay earth. He dug a shallow grave. When he finished, he lifted Bourgeron's body, lay it in the ground, and pushed the soil over it with his bare hands. He stuck the knife, like a grim marker, into the earth at the head of the grave. When he glared down at the mound, he reflected that it could have been his own body lying there, awaiting the beetles and the worms to work their decay, and he murmured a prayer. He signed himself and thanked his God for life, for the clarity of vision and stability of mind that made his aim true. He vowed never to let drink dull his wits and reflexes again. Because of drink, Bourgeron was rash and boastful. Because of drink, Bourgeron was not able to think. The reality suddenly congealed into determined intent. John Collins wanted to live. He wanted to survive the journey ahead. William Clark and Georges Drouillard were not so foolish or unjust, after all. It was drink that dulled a man, drink that made survival less certain, drink that killed, and finally Bourgeron's drink that absolved John Collins of remorse. For the expedition, Collins would need all his wits, finely tuned and alert.

The sunlight shimmered on the shiny metal blade that cast a long shadow over the grave. The knife was a good weapon, with a value of its own. No Indian, coming upon the mound, would leave such a knife to weather and corrode. In the end, Collins took it up and replaced it with a small pile of stones. Drouillard or his friends, Whitehouse, Potts, or Labiche, would have good use for the knife. He trudged to the river to bathe the blood from his hands and the earth from the knife.

He met Drouillard an hour before sunset at the mouth of the Petite Platte, about five miles upriver from Bourgeron's grave. Drouillard had shot three deer, butchered and laid them out for transport. Collins handed him the knife and the reins of the horse. His hand trembled slightly.

Drouillard recognized the change in him immediately. "So you are staying? He came after you, did he, Bourgeron, the demon with the knife?" He waited. Drouillard had known all along. So little came to pass in the wilderness that Drouillard did not know.

Collins answered nervously: "I shot him, but in the end he killed himself. He rolled over on his own knife." The image was still vivid and horrible in his mind.

Drouillard lay a steadying hand on his arm. "He did not have the courage to suffer. Captain Clark will be glad. The mosquitoes bite. Put on your shirt. Your lashes have scabbed over. They will itch, and you will want to scratch them open."

Collins didn't notice the mosquitoes or the flies. He did as he was told and followed obediently. He had learned this day that order and vigilance were necessary virtues to the cohesion and effectiveness of the whole. Bourgeron's fate had crystallized the reality. Clark and Drouillard had deliberately given him the opportunity to be absent without leave, to desert. He could have turned his steps south, and, by now, he would be meat on the point of a Spanish lance or a scalp dangling from an Indian shield, or worse, victim of Jacques Bourgeron, the shards of his bones scattered by wolves over the distant prairie or swallowed and drowned in the back pools of the river. He realized that he really did not want to leave the expedition, that he was like the river—rough, headstrong, crashing in around the edges, breaking out of its prescribed banks, with emotions and desires that eddied and swirled. He struggled daily with impulses that shifted like the grains of silt in the ruthless stream. But he vowed to control his own recklessness. He vowed to proceed with the expedition to its farthest point, the Pacific Ocean, across the

Shining Mountains, to fulfill his duties faithfully, to keep his word to his fellow man and abide by the wishes of his superiors. He vowed to swear off excessive drink as he followed his friend and mentor, Georges Drouillard, toward the waning light, westward, to the camp of Captains Lewis and Clark, around the bend in the river.

A huge buck suddenly crashed through the brush, and Drouillard shouted. "It's your shot, Johnny!"

Collins raised the Harpers, aimed, and fired. The ball hit the buck squarely beneath the point of the shoulder. The animal staggered, jumped a few steps, and fell. Drouillard nodded approval at his young apprentice, and Collins broke out in a radiant grin. "It's a beautiful gun."

"You're a good shot, Johnny."

The horse could not carry more. They butchered what they could load on their backs. It was growing dark. Night was falling. Drouillard took his bearing by the mosaic of stars, and they arrived late, to the cheers of their fellows, with pounds of fresh meat to fill the pot.

The men on the river had endured a trying day. At first, a strong wind had filled the sail. They manned the oars and made good progress until they rounded a blind bend. Sergeant Ordway manned a pole at the bow, eyes down, plumbing the depth. He spotted the cottonwood suspended over the stream. He dug in his pole to hold back the boat, but he had not the strength. Howard jumped to add his strength to Ordway's, then leaped to release the sail. He was too late. A sharp branch caught the canvas and ripped the length of the falling sail. The heavy weight of canvas severed the mast and pulled it loose from the deck, as the keelboat crunched into the thick, overhanging branches. The broken mast hovered dangerously over the deck, dripping sail and rigging like clothes on a line. Men shouted and jumped from the tangle into the muddy water. Gradually they pushed the broken mast overboard and cut their way out of the leafy morass while the relentless current hammered and heaved. The determined oarsmen had held her steady as Captain Clark shouted the order to beach immediately. Luck was with them. There were no injuries, and they salvaged all stores. But their forward progress came to a halt.

Late in the evening, by the dull light of the fire, Whitehouse and Potts sewed together the torn strips of sail. Cruzatte was scraping out a new oar. Thompson and Warner were counting their pots. Captain Lewis counted each tooth and bone of his precious specimens and lay out the pages of his journal to dry. All other able bodies cut and trimmed the new mast. Ordway castigated himself brutally, but he relaxed his stiff adherence to rules and worked alongside the struggling men.

Collins was tired, the skin on his back was stiff, but he picked up his axe and joined in the effort. In the flurry of activity, his transgressions were forgotten. He was asleep as soon as his head touched the earth that was his pillow. At five the next morning, they proceeded on.

Chapter Thirteen

Amos Leakins did not return to St. Louis nor did he float downriver. After the captains had banished him, he remained on the course of the river. He had friends there. A party of men in the pay of Clamorgan and the government of Spain lay in wait for the expedition. Their purpose was not to ambush, but to delay the Americans until an armed force of Spanish regulars from Santa Fé could arrive, cut them off, and arrest Captains Lewis and Clark. The assignment was not difficult, especially with so capricious a river and traders and tribes whose allegiance ebbed and flowed with the price of a beaver pelt and the supply of whiskey and muskets.

The Indians were astute traders and sold their loyalty to the highest bidder. England and Spain bid high. But now there was a third entry, an awkward, impoverished conglomeration of former colonies, with no visible king or strong military force. The Europeans were eager to squeeze out the United States from the lucrative fur trade and banish it forever from Louisiana Territory. Nor would their efforts stop there. Many with close ties to Europe wanted to erase the experiment of democracy from the slate of North America and the United States from the face of the earth.

On leaving the expedition, Leakins struck out overland to join Clamorgan's group of Spaniards. He knew their whereabouts—about four days out, far enough ahead to construct snares and set cave-ins and warn the tribes away from the unsuspecting Americans, and far enough away to prevent accidental contact. Most of the tribes were off hunting buffalo at this time of the year, so the Indian warnings were barely necessary. Leakins himself met with no Indians.

The men of the Spanish party were all seasoned mercenaries who sold their talents for good or ill. They preferred gold, the old pieces of eight of the Spanish Main. Loot was an added enticement, an expected part of payment for each man's services. Some were former soldiers of fortune and had fought in European wars. Some had fought Indians in the Southwest and Mexico. Some were sailors and pirates from the West Indies, or escaped slaves and prisoners who had found their way up the Mississippi and into the service of Spain. Some were renegade Indians. Lieutenant Governor Delassus supplied the gold. Clamorgan armed them, clothed them, fed them, paid them, and informed them of their mission, but he did not instruct them how they were to perform that mission. He did not care, and Lieutenant Governor Delassus did not want to know.

Clamorgan appointed as leader one Juan Sandoval, half Spanish, half French-Indian, along with Amos Leakins. Sandoval led the larger contingent of freebooters who would advance secretly ahead of the Americans and lay snares to slow their progress. Leakins had organized a smaller group to infiltrate the expedition itself.

Sandoval was a dark, big-bellied man, a former pirate from New Orleans, personally recommended for the task by Clamorgan. Highly intelligent, he spoke Spanish and English as well as a smattering of Indian tongues. Some said his Indian blood was of a fierce southern tribe, from the backwaters of the alligator swamps, that the tribe had driven him off for heinous crimes whose description was lost in the maze of geography and time, and that he had fled to the coast and signed on to a Spanish galley. From the ship, he had escaped to the bayous of the lower Mississippi, then worked his way upriver to trade in furs. That was the rumor. No one dared question its truth.

He was a cruel master. He drove his men to the limit of their physical endurance and did not hesitate to discipline with the barbed whip, the cat-o-nine-tails. The men who followed him were accustomed to such treatment. They had endured a worse fate at the hands of African slavers, Spanish overseers, or the despotic captains of the British navy. For their fealty, Sandoval guaranteed their continued freedom, a small pittance, and whatever they could obtain from theft and pillage. He ruled them with an iron hand.

Leakins's men were fewer and more Anglo in appearance. They had penetrated the Corps of Discovery and worked like a worm inside the fruit to hinder its progress. They encouraged fights and disagreements and the pilfering of supplies that had led to John Collins's conviction. They lost and broke equipment and wasted stores. But their successes gave way to carelessness, then to the boldness that resulted in Leakins's discovery and dismissal.

Juan Sandoval had news of Leakins's banishment long before he reached the camp. His Indian scouts had spied on the expedition from the beginning. Now they shadowed Amos Leakins from the moment he left the Americans, until he sauntered into Sandoval's camp five days later. Juan Sandoval was not glad to see him.

He had seated himself on a log outside his brush shelter, his huge belly wrapped in a bright crimson sash, his knobby head swathed in a dirty kerchief. It poked out from double chins and massive shoulders, like the peak of a bald, craggy mountain. Sharp, intelligent, black eyes bulged from the folds of his face. As he waited for his visitor, he shaved a soft stick with his hunting knife. He seemed intent on his task and did not look up when Leakins arrived.

Leakins sauntered up brazenly. He did not reveal his failure. *"¿Amigo mio, qué pasa?"* The melodious Spanish rolled smoothly off his tongue.

Sandoval chewed a splinter of wood between his front teeth. He answered in measured, precise English without parting his teeth. "You come boldly, Amos Leakins. I told you never to approach this camp in daylight."

Leakins's eyes flashed at the dark, scowling face, then down at the raw slices of wood that lay like the ashes of sacrifice at Sandoval's feet. He hesitated, then blurted: "I need my pay. When will your Santa Fé soldiers arrive?"

"My soldiers!" Sandoval's harsh voice punched the possessive as his eyes narrowed and his lip curled. "Clamorgan's soldiers. They are not mine unless I pay them."

Leakins recoiled as Sandoval stared him down. He waited for the disagreeable welcome to settle like acid dust.

Sandoval spit out the splinter like a dart. "The troops will arrive soon with your wages and mine." It was a lie.

Leakins complained forcefully: "I cannot wait forever. My men are restless." Sandoval had dropped his eyes and gone back to shaving his stick. In an effort to regain his attention, Leakins blurted: "I'm not going back without my pay and the pay for my men."

Sandoval lifted his eyes, stopped the action of his knife, tilted his head, and waited.

Leakins coughed. He had rehearsed what he would tell Sandoval many times, practiced and perfected its delivery. Now he stammered a doubtful excuse: "Lewis and Clark are dismissing men. They tell us they need only half the number they hired . . . that the larger number is too unwieldy." He snickered lightly to relieve tension. "They want to line their own pockets. They'll sell the supplies that should have gone to feed the extra men." It sounded plausible.

Sandoval was not fooled. Stubbornly he forced the truth. "You are not going back where?"

Leakin's smile retracted to a tight clamp. He picked a yellow tooth with his fingernail, and declared: "I'm not going back to the expedition."

"Because they dismissed you!" Sandoval shouted the disagreeable fact.

"Yes, and others, as I told you." It was a hard admission. Leakins didn't mean to shout.

Sandoval frowned. "Where are these others? Did they come with you to collect their pay?"

"They went home by canoe, downriver. The Americans need money more than you, more than me. They've bought a territory, and they're scratchin' blood from the earth to pay for it."

"And you scratch money for men who have already deserted you?"

"For a mission they completed, yes."

Sandoval laid his trap subtly. "And have the Americans paid you?"

"No. They gave me a paper says I can collect from the governor in Saint Louis."

"Don Carlos Delassus?"

"The new American governor who I don't know, but the paper is worthless."

"Is it? You collect wages from the Americans, yet you charge Don Carlos, also. Now you want me to reimburse you for men who have disappeared. You have already been paid several times over. I am not a fool, Amos Leakins."

Leakins's face paled. He had heard of Sandoval's avarice. He ground his teeth and cracked his jaw.

Sandoval continued: "Don Carlos will pay only for time

you spent with the expedition, what you were hired to do, not for time with me. As for those who deserted you, they are here in this camp. *I* paid them." Sandoval watched Leakins squirm, and grinned. His jagged teeth came apart like the jaws of a trap. "You have an axe and a musket, Mister Leakins. You want to stay here, you work for your keep. Take your place beside Botero, and I will find a use for you."

Resentment gripped Amos Leakins like a snare tightening around his heart, but he did not dare object.

Botero was only one step above a slave. He was an old man, depleted in strength and effort. He performed menial, degrading tasks, cleaning slops and scrubbing pots. He scraped together what was left on other men's plates to fill his empty stomach. Now Amos Leakins stuffed his mouth with the same scraps. When Botero lay his blankets on the roughest ground at the edge of camp, Leakins lay there, too. When Botero heaved his axe into the wet soil of the riverbank or the tough bark of a tree, Amos Leakins followed suit and toiled harder than he ever had in his life. Anger flared with every twinge of his aching muscles. Clamorgan had chosen him to lead, not follow, but Clamorgan was in St. Louis and Sandoval ruled the rivermen like a fire-breathing dragon.

The day Leakins was assigned to chop wood, he and Botero pulled at the base of a huge elm by the river's edge. With his bare hands, Botero stooped down to scrape the dirt from the tentacled root the width of his fist. "I am not strong enough." He motioned to Leakins. "Chop here and she will fall." The noonday sun was hot. Botero's sweat had matted the black curls of his bare chest into balls of grime and plastered the hair of his head like lichens to a stone. His skin was gray; his mouth twitched. "I go for water."

Amos Leakins stepped back. "Bring some for me." He did not resume the work but leaned defiantly on the long handle of his axe while Botero collapsed by the edge of the stream.

"No water for you until after she falls!" Sandoval appeared, standing behind the old man, face to face with Amos Leakins. He ran the thongs of a whip between the palms of his hands and shouted through his teeth—"¡Adelante! Jaime! Fernando!"—and stepped over Botero. Leakins cringed and froze as a powerful bull of an Indian and a short-muscled Spaniard stepped forward and slammed their axes into the gnarled root. The tree shook but did not fall.

Sandoval's voice resounded sharply over the camp. "A jug of whiskey for the man who fells the giant!" He whirled to confront Amos Leakins. It was an agile move for a fat man. Leakins jumped back as Sandoval shouted: "They do your work, Amos Leakins. They earn their keep. You do not earn yours." He lowered his head and snorted. The Indian and the Spaniard straddled the root, accelerating their strokes in alternating thuds. Sandoval's nostrils flared, scenting danger. Leakins's head weaved in anticipation. The Indian swiped the decisive blow, but the Spaniard quickly swung his axe into the crack as the tree leaned and claimed the whiskey. Slowly, like the closing curtain in a play, the great trunk wrenched its roots from the ground, screeching and cracking in protest. It descended over the river, pulling at the bank where its tentacles still clung. The clay soil crumbled and dissolved in the water and splashed up circling waves. The trunk balanced perilously, propped by its maze of branches, stuck in the mud of the caved-in embankment about fifteen feet over the channel. Its limbs blocked effectively any craft that might try to ascend the river.

Sandoval and Leakins did not see the tree fall. Their eyes had locked on one another. The fat man circled, sniffing out advantage. He mouthed a relentless, degrading stream of invective. "Are you weak or lazy, Amos Leakins, or too proud to work? You think Sandoval will break like a dry stick? Or that you can shave off his followers like splinters, one by one?" His voice changed suddenly to a low growl. "I chew useless splinters and spit them out. You are a lazy man, Amos Leakins, and you are foolishly careless with your life." Sandoval drew in his huge bulk and inhaled deeply. He held his hunting knife at the ready. "Go back to work, or I flay you like the heathen you are."

Leakins did not answer. Trembling, he hesitated. Then in a burst of recklessness, he retorted: "You're a brute, Sandoval. Your men hate you. Maybe they choose to follow me."

Sandoval shrieked laughter. "They do not speak English. They cannot follow you. They cannot understand you. I have no use for a lazy fool." The hand that carved the wood flicked out, and Sandoval's knife flew. Amos Leakins tried to unsheathe his own knife. He feinted to the side. One hand went up as if to shield himself, but too late. The point of Sandoval's knife, aimed for Leakins's chest, struck him just below the waist. He stood a long moment glaring, not breathing, pulled the knife from his belly and tossed it aside. Slowly, he melted to his knees and fell. Sandoval retrieved his knife, sat back down on his log, picked up a splinter of wood, placed it between his teeth, and watched. He muttered to the dying man: "I am fat, but I am not slow." When he was sure Leakins had bled to unconsciousness, he carved enough shavings to cover the pool of blood, ordered the body dismembered, and thrown in the river. Sandoval moved his camp that afternoon away from the river.

Chapter Fourteen

The Americans had not missed Amos Leakins. Most had been glad to see him go. John Collins had returned to duty. July 4th came and went quietly with only a discharge of one shot from the swivel and an extra gill of whiskey for each man, to celebrate the founding of the new republic. The summer heat intensified. Sergeant Floyd, Silas Goodrich, and Reuben Fields fell sick, struck down, some said, by the hard glare of the scorching sun. A snake bit Joe Fields. Shannon and Colter suffered from boils on feet, hands, and shoulders where the braided tow rope rubbed. It was so hot, Collins felt the sweat run between his scarred shoulder blades even when he stood absolutely still. Tom Howard and Hugh Hall took off their hats to let what breeze there was dry their soggy hair, but the cruel sun burned and blistered their faces. Only Labiche seemed impervious to the heat and kept his shirt on.

The river was falling. Lower water meant more shallows and sandbars, more effort for the oarsmen. They hitched the horse to the towline, but the animal slid to its knees on the steep bank. They passed a deserted Indian village and a large island. A southerly wind picked up, and they greeted it with a cheer and hoisted the sail. But the Spaniards had laid their trap well. They had trimmed the branches that rose above the surface of the water and loosened the clay of the embankment. Sergeant Floyd was stationed in the bow. He had been sick and did not see the obstruction around the bend through his watery eyes. The boat scraped, groaned, and came to a halt. They spent the rest of the day disentangling the maze and repairing a deep gash in the hull. They camped that night on an island where every man collapsed from the enervating heat.

July 8th, Sergeant Pryor summoned John Collins, Billy Warner, and John Thompson to the captains' tent. Collins approached with some foreboding. The last time he was summoned had resulted in his court-martial and whipping. But this time was different. Clark met him with hands outstretched. Even Captain Lewis smiled acceptance if not open welcome. "We have much to thank you for, Private Collins."

This was high praise from Meriwether Lewis. Collins stood tongue-tied. He had never addressed one word to Meriwether Lewis. In fact, he had always felt uneasy in the presence of Lewis, the aristocratic secretary to the President, Lewis with all his books and instruments and specimens. Lewis was a learned man. Collins could hardly write his name.

Lewis continued: "Captain Clark and I have created a special position for which we think you well suited, Private Collins. You, Private Warner, and Private Thompson are to serve as superintendents of your respective messes. You shall be responsible for the preparation, consumption, and distribution of food for each squad. You are to ration the supply of corn, salt pork, biscuit, beef, etceteras with a view to each man's strength and health, and our projected future needs for the duration of this expedition." He hesitated and added gravely: "And you are charged with the rationing of spirits." He avoided the word whiskey. "Your responsibility is central to our survival and success. You shall be exempt from guard duty, but we would not want to curtail your ability to hunt. You are adept with a rifle, especially the new Harpers." He turned first to Collins. "Do you accept the appointment, Private Collins?"

John Collins jaw had dropped midway through Lewis's speech. He snapped it shut and looked wide-eyed to Captain Clark, who stood red-faced and beaming behind Lewis. Collins blurted: "Yes, sir. I'm to be a cook, in charge of the commissary. Thank you, sir."

"The health of the corps will depend on you. And do you accept also, Private Thompson . . . Private Warner?"

The two privates echoed Collins.

"Then it's settled. Sergeant Pryor will acquaint you all with your new duties."

The three men exited together. Pryor was waiting at the cook fire and took only a few moments. Warner and Thompson left to report to their own squads.

Nathaniel Pryor moved away from the heat and stinging smoke of the fire and fell to a prone position, propping himself on an elbow and closing his eyes. Collins had remained standing, watching the roasting meat drip hot fat into the coals. He sliced off a chunk, speared it on the point of his knife, and chewed it off.

The breeze shifted and blew hot smoke into Nathaniel Pryor's face. He jumped up, rubbing his stinging eyes. An annoying question hammered Collins's conscience. When Pryor opened his eyes, he asked: "Why me?"

"It was Clark's idea. Same reason he appointed Warner. You know all the tricks. You know what, where, and when to guard."

Early next morning, there was a new spring to Collins's step. Drouillard noticed it when they set off to hunt. He also noted fresh moccasin tracks. They toed out unlike the footfall of an Indian and led away from the river. He pointed them out to Collins with a casual nod. "Friend or foe, can you tell?" Collins could not.

There was a rustling in the brush as a whitetail deer poked his rack out from the greenery. Drouillard nudged the young hunter and nodded. Collins lifted the rifle, sighted, and fired. The deer jumped and disappeared. Drouillard ran forward. He was the first to find blood on the leaves. "You hit him, Johnny. You're a dead-eye with the Harpers. Come, follow until he breathes his last."

The thrashing was loud, and it came from the river. They ran in the direction of the sound and found the deer in its death throes, at the river's edge. Drouillard slit the soft throat for the final kill. "I do not do with the gun what I can do quietly with the knife." His dark eyes glared under drawn brows at some saplings farther upstream that parted where an animal trail cut into the embankment. He motioned Collins to follow as he went to investigate.

It started to rain, first a soft misting, then a heavier pelting that washed the sweat away. Collins took off his shirt and hat to let the welcome water slosh over his healing back. Drouillard approached the base of the trail silently as a cat stalking his next meal. He stooped down suddenly, ran his fingers in the wet soil, and brought them up to his nose. "Blood. And by the smell of it, human, not animal, but several days old. It has dried once, and the rain has moistened it again."

Collins rubbed his own palm over the wet earth and sniffed the salty, pungent odor of human blood. What had happened, accident, crime, or bloody natural death? The rain had washed away any evidence of wrong-doing. Collins moved back into the undergrowth where the soil was dry beneath the leaves. "Moccasin prints, here"—he pointed— "and not very far from camp." He remembered that an hour before dawn the sentry had called, but the captains had dismissed the alert as false, the result of rummagings of wild animals. "They're a man's prints, not an animal's." Drouillard left no room for doubt.

Slowly, in silence, the two men followed the trail. The footprints wove through a small wood to the wide, open prairie beyond, and lost themselves in the waist-high grasses. Drouillard stopped at the edge of the wood. "It's no use. The rain has dulled the trail, and, if we follow now, the wolves will steal our kill."

But he had piqued Collins's curiosity. "Who made the prints?"

"Maybe Indians. Maybe whites. Not Spanish regulars." He swept his hand over the panorama of waving grass. "I wear moccasins. So do Cruzatte and Deschamps. So do you."

"If not Indians . . . ?" Collins left the rest unspoken.

The black whiskers barely parted. "Traders who wonder what business we Americans conduct." His next words were more ominous. "Those who want to steal our goods . . . those who want to turn us back."

The words lingered in the younger man's consciousness. He declared stubbornly: "I'm not turning back." The possibility that others might force him to return rankled.

Drouillard countered solemnly: "Neither am I, *mon ami*."

They butchered the deer and packed the meat. It was a long walk back to camp in the rain. When they arrived, Collins dug a fire pit and put on a cauldron to boil, but the wood was wet and the flame weak. Drouillard sought out Captain Clark. It was late when the two men summoned John Collins.

Clark began by questioning: "Drouillard tells me you found tracks. Could you identify these prints again?"

The young man shrugged, and Drouillard interrupted. "He can identify a man by the smell of his blood."

Clark looked up surprised, and Collins denied the praise. "No, sir. Drouillard exaggerates."

157

Clark smiled and reverted to more serious agenda. "We have not met the tribes. We have not yet met any natives. Captain Lewis wants to go in search . . . ostensibly to hunt and procure his specimens. I want you and Drouillard to go with him."

They began by scouting the lower reaches of the Nemaha River, and, although they did not find men, they found a horse. It was a serviceable animal, muscular and healthy, used to the company of men and unharmed by wolves or cats. They used it to pack in six deer, but the feasting was marred by suspicion. Who had left the horse and why?

Sergeant Ordway had brought forward another man charged with "sleeping on his post whilst a sentinel," which under the Articles of War was punishable by death. The court was summoned, the prisoner, Alexander Willard, judged guilty and sentenced to "one hundred lashes on his bear back, at four different times in equal proportion." Again Ordway held the whip. Was Willard's offense so grave? Willard was young and inexperienced, like Collins, and the physical effort they all exerted cried out for precious sleep. The bile rose in Collins's throat when he heard the sentence. At the appointed hour, he and Hugh Hall moved several hundred yards into the wilds, far enough away so as not to hear Williard scream.

Georges Drouillard found them there and explained the gravity of the offense. "We could all die in our sleep, if our enemies fall upon us unawares. Like Mad Anthony Wayne at Paoli, but you're too young to remember. I met General Wayne once, when I was younger than you are now. When the Brits marched on Philiadelphia, he posted guards who fell asleep. British regulars surprised them in the night, bayoneted nearly everyone while they slept. Lord Gray, a peer of

England, ordered the slaughter. Banastre Tarleton carried it out. They were butchers, both of them. That's why there must be no sleeping while on watch. Sleeping, we are too vulnerable, easy prey."

The scars of the whipping still itched. Collins and Hall glared impassively back.

For the next three nights, Willard bore his pain courageously, but Collins and Hall disappeared each evening at the whipping hour. During the day, Collins performed all his assigned duties, cooked and hunted and axed and dug, but no amount of persuasion could make him remain within sight or earshot of the snake-like whip and the relentless count. He sat on a rock and counted the seconds out loud. His muscles twitched with each digit. His teeth clamped tightly as they had when the rod had struck the skin of his own naked back. It did not take long. He listened to the buzzing of the insects, the song of a bird, the soft ripple of the water. He counted twice the required number of strokes and waited still longer. Darkness descended like a shroud. Finally, long after he knew the whipping must have stopped, he rose, splashed a hatful of river water over his head, and walked back to camp. He stoked the cook fires, sliced and packed the meat for tomorrow's ration, and poured off a portion of grease for Alex Willard. By morning, it would cool and congeal and, used as a salve, would help heal Willard's wounds and stop the infernal itch.

Chapter Fifteen

Juan Sandoval was expecting reinforcements, the Spanish regulars that Governor Delassus had ordered from Santa Fé. They were overdue. Sandoval was losing men on his way upriver. Amos Leakins was the first, but Sandoval didn't count him as a loss. Sandoval had assigned Leakins to the ailing Botero whose strength had been diminishing steadily. Now Leakins was dead, and Botero stood before him like a prisoner in chains. Botero had stopped working. His emaciated form trembled slightly. Hat in hand, he anchored his eyes to the ground and said nothing. His very presence was an accusation. Sandoval lashed out at the frail one. "You think me heartless, eh, Botero? You await friends with favors from Santa Fé?"

"God approves or disapproves, *jefe*. I wait on his mercy. I have been idle these last years. The heavy work overwhelms my age. I'm sorry." The old man's face elongated, his eyes bulged, and wrinkles carved themselves more deeply into the folds of his sallow skin.

"Earn your keep, *viejo*, or we leave you to wait with the prairie wolves. See if they care. See if your God cares."

The old man dared to lift his eyes and whispered: "He is with me always, *jefe*. He is here. He does not desert me as your men would desert you."

Sandoval struck out. The blow caught Botero across the ear. He staggered and fell. "Say your prayers and go rot in hell!" Sandoval hated priests and the prayers that called down God's justice on his beastliness.

From that day, Juan Sandoval never spoke or set eyes on the old man again. Botero weakened daily. His skin turned yellow, then gray, and the toady eyes of scurvy stared out over hollow cheeks. His teeth had worn and loosened. He stopped eating. One day, he made the sign of the cross, lay down on the soft turf, and closed his eyes. After he fell asleep, they took his knives and his gun but not his ragged blanket. He was still breathing when they left him. It was the Indian way, the way of the savage land, when the old and infirm could no longer keep up with the herd. But for Sandoval, it was the easiest way to discard what he could not use. And it was a stark reminder that he had lost yet one more man and the troops from Santa Fé had not yet come.

He continued with his party upriver and warned the Oto chiefs against the new American invaders. The Otoes accepted gifts, listened perfunctorily, and lured away two of Sandoval's men who preferred life among the Indians to life under the tyrannical Spaniard.

With the Pawnees, Sandoval was more successful. These Indians were quitting the quiet riverbed for their annual buffalo hunt on the plains. They agreed to all his demands so as to receive the most lavish gifts. They would be gone from the river before the Americans arrived. Another of Sandoval's men disappeared the night the Pawnees departed for the hunt. Sandoval sent two more men to bring him back, dead or alive. All three never returned.

The Omahas and the Cheyennes had already departed for the hunt when Sandoval's party passed, but the Yanktons still remained and exacted exorbitant tribute which drastically depleted Sandoval's supplies. They were a clever, energetic tribe and collected their favors from Spanish, American, and English alike. They, too, promptly disappeared into the vastness of the plains. But they returned in time to meet the

Americans. The Yankton women were long-legged and beautiful, and three more of Sandoval's men deserted. With each loss, Sandoval restricted his men more, threatening physical pain and death. And every man less made the workload greater for the few who remained.

Sandoval hired Indians to replace the deserters, but Spaniard and Indian did not mesh well, and Sandoval's draconian rule exacerbated the differences. The Spaniards looked down on the strange customs and superstitions of the red men, expecting them to serve and obey. The Indians laughed at silly Spanish conventions and officious superiority. They obeyed grudgingly but never willingly, and only after dire threats. Resentments grew. The Spaniards cursed the lazy red men who rewarded their insults with still greater lassitude and defiance.

An open feud erupted the night the Englishman, Lassiter, entered the camp. It was cold and rainy when he arrived, but he brushed off the pelting drops like pesky gnats. The rain reminded him of England, of green lawns and shade trees. Lassiter was not used to the river country, although he had lived for years at Fort St. Peter, a North West Company post. Of late, he had taken a wife, a sultry Arikara maiden, but he lived with the Teton Sioux, the ruthless rulers of the upper Missouri River. Lassiter came alone. He had left his main party at the Teton village, far away from the influence of Juan Sandoval, and he had more men and horses camped a few miles upriver.

Lassiter was a tall, straight man, thin almost to the point of emaciation, with stringy, blond hair and beard, and watery blue eyes. He had come south from Canada to secure the northern reaches of the Missouri River for England and, in doing so, supplied the residents of the river with guns, knives, and whiskey in return for their allegiance and exclusive access to their trade. For the Sioux, it was important trade. England supplied the weapons with which the Sioux overpowered neighboring tribes. In trade and war, Lassiter had been eminently successful and assumed a position of considerable prominence within the tribe. It allowed him a latitude of word and action which few men could claim. Lassiter could state what he thought directly and succinctly without considering its effect on ill-tempered Sandoval. He could eat his fill and drink the Spaniard's best whiskey until his blue eyes sparkled and his cheeks flushed. Whiskey sharpend his wits. He spoke a clipped British English, peppered with the accents of the moor, in a high-pitched voice that Sandoval likened to the shriek of a she-wolf.

Now he walked with casual impunity straight up to Juan Sandoval. Sandoval repressed his distaste. No one, not even Juan Sandoval, dared contest a favored friend of the Sioux. Sandoval tilted his massive black head and twirled a pinky in his ear as if wax blurred the harsh alien sounds of Lassiter's speech. He disliked the Englishman and all his countrymen. They were haughty and cold. They needed strong drink to melt their reserve. Now he sat cross-legged opposite Lassiter, on a blanket spread over the damp ground. They were drinking, and the Englishman was speaking: "I have a man with the Tetons, a young chief we call The Partisan. For muskets and whiskey, he'll take the Americans over his knee, spank them soundly like the children they are, and send them promptly home, if he doesn't murder them first. Or he may throw their bodies in the river and let their bones float home."

Sandoval was as wary as the Britisher was confident. "The Partisan is not head chief, but an upstart, a seeker. He can only lead if his own people judge that he is worthy to lead, if he can gather enough warriors." Sandoval stopped, leveled a hard black stare at Lassiter, and announced: "I deal with Black Buffalo. He is the head chief of the Brulé, not your fawning, unproven Partisan."

Lassiter had not expected opposition. He stiffened. "The Partisan will be chief after I supply him with trade guns and whiskey. He will be the richest man in the tribe and will shower the warriors with riches, and he will do as I tell him."

"If it suits his purpose, if he does not already have enough guns, or if he must trade for corn with the Arikaras and for horses with the Cheyennes. How well have you paid him? How many muskets, how many rounds of ammunition, how much firewater did it cost your rich English company?"

Lassiter curled his lip in disdain and looked down his long nose at the Spaniard. "More than you can offer. More than the Americans have. I've told you, Captains Lewis and Clark are ill-prepared. The Partisan will stop them easily. The forces of nature and the lateness of the season can only help." His voice cut the thin air between them.

"Your Partisan will enrich himself first. I'll lay money on it." Sandoval snickered cynically.

Lassiter masked his impatience. He straightened. He didn't trust the burly Spaniard, and weighed every word carefully. New orders from Montreal conflicted with Sandoval's demands. He answered: "We will both profit from the bargain." The Englishman did not reveal his true intent: that the North West Company did not want to alienate the Americans, not while Napoléon was spreading his tentacles around Europe's soft belly. Better to have Louisiana in the unpracticed hands of seventeen disunited and disorganized states than bristling with bayonets under the command of Emperor Napoléon. But England and the North West Company wanted to push the borders of Louisiana as far south as possible, to reserve the rich fur-bearing rivers of the Missouri basin for Canada. Still, Mother England had suffered once when the Americans revolted, and she had incurred huge debts. She did not want to provoke another war on the far side of the Atlantic with the fledgling United States. Her hegemony must be more subtle. The blame for the failure of Captains Lewis and Clark must not incriminate England. It must lie with the Spanish and the tribes, or the river, the wild beasts, and the Shining Mountains.

Sandoval suspected Lassiter's duplicity, and his own inability to deal with it galled him. He avoided Lassiter's superior stare, picked up a stick, broke off a splinter to chew, and started to scrape thin shavings with his knife.

The Englishman's gaze circled derisively over the depleted camp. "You want an attack, you must provide more than sharpened sticks. You are far from your base, far upriver. Your supplies are low, but I tell you what you already know."

Sandoval stabbed his knife into the earth and grit his teeth against an upwelling of rage. Damn Delassus! Damn this English devil and his snobbish assurance! The man was too perceptive. He lifted a cup to his lips and downed its contents in one gulp. The whiskey burned, and he coughed.

Lassiter grabbed the jug and poured them both more whiskey. "The Americans will shrink like the frozen river as soon as the ice forms."

Sandoval downed another cupful and smacked his lips. "With powder and ball and a few Indian marksmen, I can lay them to rot. It is the only certain way." The big man should have been drunk, but the whiskey seemed only to sharpen the violence within.

Lassiter smiled and nodded. He lied with impunity. "I would gladly give you muskets, but I have only enough to bribe the greedy Partisan so that he will do the bloody work and we will be innocent of the deed and the intent. Trust me."

Sandoval's wide nostrils smelled betrayal. His black eyes smoldered. "Trust is expensive, my English *amigo*. You cannot pay the cost of my trust. Work your magic, but allow me to work mine." He drained a third cup and threw it to the ground. It lay there gleaming on the bed of shavings as he replaced his knife in his belt. When he stood up, his wide form cast a wide shadow over the Englishman. The whiskey bottle was empty.

Sandoval retired to his tent and pondered his predicament. Where were his promised reinforcements? Had they left Santa Fé, or, through some foul machination of colonial politics been assigned elsewhere or retained? Were they lost, delayed, dead? There had been no word since he had left St. Louis, and the season had passed when Delassus could send word. No Indian scout had reported a sighting. Sandoval cursed his superiors who had sent him on this ill-fated mission. They had forgotten him, thrown him like the slops into the sewer for rats to devour. He cursed himself for not having demanded payment in advance. He cursed Lassiter for the cheerful assurance that was a thin veil for scorn. He cursed his whiskey supply—he had only one barrel left.

Sandoval had chosen a wooded bottomland under a high hill for his camp. His Indians had erected only one lodge when thunder roared and lightning sizzled in the treetops. The Spaniards rushed to erect more lodges while the roaring wind blew water in sheets under the tent flaps and down smoke holes. The fires hissed and smoked. The Indians cowered in awe. They complained of spirits who wandered in the cold night. The slap of raindrops on lodgeskins echoed the patter of devil's feet. In his haste, Sandoval had not minded the spirits and had ordered the lodges placed with openings facing north toward the ice god, not east toward the rising sun. Evil ones traveled on the north wind and penetrated the warmth of the lodge. The Indians refused to sleep until a holy man had chanted an exorcism.

Sandoval sat through the night with his rifle across his knees, brooding, watching. After midnight, he threw a dry burl on the weakening fire. It crumbled swiftly to a glowing pile of coals. The Indians hovered morosely, claiming they saw ghosts in the fire.

Finally, a man they called holy took up a grass torch and waved it in a circle about his head. The smoke of the sweet grass, he claimed, would purify the lodge, but a gust of damp wind rushed in and blew it out. The holy man gathered his blanket and backed toward the entry. Others began to gather belongings to follow. They moved like shadows in the steamy dimness, dark silhouettes meshing hazily against the background of the smoking fire and the black of night.

Mutiny —Sandoval could smell its stink. "Stop, go to your beds!" His voice shook the earth like the demons the Indians invoked. He grabbed his knife and musket and blocked the way with his huge form. "Stop or the river will smell of your rotting flesh!" He felt eyes on his back. Lassiter stood rocklike in the shadows, calculating, watching. Sandoval turned.

In the instant's lapse, the holy man crouched, not with submission, but with cunning. He rose up and flung himself behind the fat Spaniard, out into the stormy night. Sandoval turned and fired. He missed. Unbelieving, he blinked his weary eyes. They could not penetrate the color of night outside. His voice echoed menacingly as he pointed his fat finger at the dark place where the Indian had disappeared. "He was the demon, and he is gone!"

Raindrops pounded on the canvas of the tents like drumbeats at a funeral. There were moanings outside, the soft noises of animals dying, cold and wet and without shelter. Wolves howled, calling in their comrades to the kill. Sandoval had stuffed his ears to block the awful sounds. Late in the night, after the Indians had finally settled, he fell asleep. He awakened suddenly in the early dawn and pulled the plugs from his ears. It was eerily quiet. A ray of sunlight swept across the earthen floor. It pierced a fresh cut in the lodge cover. Juan Sandoval leaped up and charged out into the light of day. The air was fresh, the river flowed in its quiet bed, but his Indians had faded like ghosts on the wind. Gear lay scattered around: a cauldron here, a saddle and blanket there, but no muskets and no horses! There had been no noise, not the slow roll of a gravel on stone, not the soft rustle of a sleeping animal, not a puff of breath. Juan Sandoval counted on his fingers the men he had left, seven, besides the accursed Lassiter.

Blind with fury, Juan Sandoval ran to the top of the embankment. Tracks, a broken branch, something must reveal which way they had gone. He would go after them. They were deserters. They deserved no mercy. There were no tracks, only rain-soaked streaks of mud as if God had combed all traces from the ground. He charged back to camp, ripped back the blankets from his sleeping men, shoved a musket in their bellies to prod them to hurry and take to the chase. But he knew instinctively pursuit was impossible.

Lassiter came up behind him. "You have no horses, friend. All the prints have washed away."

Sandoval turned on Lassiter with murder in his black eyes. "You! But for you they would still be here!"

The pale Englishman countered calmly: "You should have known when you set up the lodges." He had calculated his reply and shrugged. "With luck, we will replace them in the Teton camp."

"We? I will replace them! I hired them! I command them!" The Spaniard pounded his massive chest with a fist. He could not broach criticism or a challenge to his authority. He gripped the hilt of his knife, glaring at the grinning Englishman, but the knife remained in its scabbard.

Lassiter ignored the threat. "You'll feel better when you've had something to eat and drink. My camp is only a few miles upriver. I have a good supply of whiskey." He turned his back to the irate Spaniard and walked away.

Sandoval compressed the rage that welled up within him and retreated to a glade by the river to think. Had the Englishman plotted to usurp his position? The Partisan was in the pay of England. Lassiter had seen to that. Had Lassiter also fomented the desertion of his Indians? Juan Sandoval did not doubt Lassiter's complicity. But he didn't remember hiring that one they called holy, the one who waved the torch. There had been no difficulty before Lassiter arrived in the camp. The devils were the Englishman's convenient contrivance. Lassiter had spread the rumors and incited the fears. Spain and England had never been the best of friends. Hatreds dated back hundreds of years. They surged now within Sandoval's own breast, but he choked them down, balled his fists, swallowed his pride, and rose to follow Lassiter. He willed the Spanish expeditionary force to arrive. Survival first, then he would dispense with Lassiter decisively, once and for all. Still he did not comprehend the complexities of politics which ruled the tribes or the wily schemes of the North West Company. He did not comprehend the cohesive loyalties and the dogged endurance of the Americans. The pleasure of drink and the power of knife and gun, these he understood, and these he had always lived by.

England had never been a powerful force in Louisiana that belonged first to France, then to Spain, and briefly to the Emperor Napoléon. England depended on trade and affiliated companies, the Hudson's Bay and Lassiter's North West, for her influence. She chose to enforce her wishes by the use of economic power. She cajoled and flattered and bluffed and bribed, like a talented gambler. She was especially adept at persuading the tribes to act on her behalf.

Spain, too, had an elaborate bureaucracy and army in her colonies. In religion and government, the Spanish chain of command began at the top and filtered down through layers of officialdom. Decisions were final, discipline exact, and punishment swift, callous, and cruel, like the slaughter of the Pueblo Indians after their revolt. In the southwest, the memory was still raw. Thousands of Indians had died. Spain used the Indians, too, as slaves, and the Spanish army was fully capable of annihilating the American expedition and Lassiter, without leaving a trace.

But without that army, without reinforcements, Juan Sandoval was powerless. He faced not only the reprimand of Don Carlos Dehault Delassus if he returned to St. Louis a failure, but also loss of pay, or worse, imprisonment and death. The burly Spaniard had never failed. He would not stand by and let Lassiter assume the destruction assigned to him. He would not wait and watch until the tribes or the land or ignorance or ineptitude defeated the Americans. He was a man of action whose options were diminishing fast, and who did not fully consider more distant consequences. He must insure Spanish conquest, retain his good name and position, preserve his wealth, and avoid the brutal recrimination of superiors. He laid out his plans carefully. He would eliminate the Americans, lure them away from their posts one by one, finish the bloody job himself the only way he knew how, and collect Don Carlos's bounty for himself alone. He would return to St. Louis the victor, and Clamorgan and Delassus would reward him with riches, and his fatherland, Spain, would remain the absolute ruler of Louisiana. For now, he accompanied Lassiter and noted the Englishman's weaknesses.

Lassiter was a casual administrator. Indians, who often departed to visit relatives and wives, composed the majority of Lassiter's men. They came and went when they pleased. Others went to hunt if the buffalo were near because they preferred fresh meat to pemmican. No one asked permission. They kept what they hunted and shared willingly what they did not need. Lassiter exercised a relaxed authority and often sat with his men for hours while decisions were reached by mutual consent. To the iron-handed Spaniard, the system was tedious and ineffectual. And he resented the Englishman for always telling him what to do.

"Coming Juan?" Lassiter was kicking ashes over the dying fire. He'd interrupted the big Spaniard's brooding. "Have your men take down the lodge and douse the fire. I left a horse for you, but your men will have to walk."

Sandoval marched out and mounted the horse, a scruffy, arthritic nag with a stiff, jarring gait. He did not satisfy the Englishman with a complaint.

They cut across the open prairie to Lassiter's camp, a day's ride north. The sea of grass looked smooth, but, in fact, was riddled with ruts, stones, and clumps of stiff vegetation. Lassiter urged his mount to a swift, mileage-eating walk. Sandoval's nag had to trot to keep up. The Spaniard's fat legs did not reach the stirrups. They chaffed and rubbed. His buttocks slapped the hard wooden tree of the saddle. It softened, blistered, and bled. He gripped the pommel to steady himself. His six remaining men could not maintain the pace on foot. Two fell far behind, out of sight.

When they neared the first night's camp, the Englishman

smiled cheerily. "We've made good time. Two more days and you can buy fine mounts, buffalo chasers, if you need, from the Tetons."

Sandoval needed sturdy horses, weight carriers, not light buffalo chasers. He had nothing to trade for horses. If The Partisan failed to stop the Americans, Juan Sandoval could not waste his scant resources on horses. He glanced over his shoulder. The two stragglers had not caught up. He bounced along after Lassiter like a pumpkin on a cart, growing more angry by the minute. His thoughts clarified as his discomfort increased. The red-haired scalps of the two American captains, hanging from his belt, would make a good prize. So would the stringy blond hair of the Englishman. Indians respected scalps. Scalps would attest to his courage and the effectiveness of his command. Then he must find a boatman to float him downstream to St. Louis to collect his reward. His muscles cramped. His head ached. Finally, in agony, he dismounted while Lassiter rode on. The fat man envied Lassiter's long legs and good fortune, and he was certain that Lassiter had manipulated events so that he would have to walk.

Three days later, Sandoval arrived at the Teton camp. It was a humiliating, foot-sore entry, a fat man leading a scrawny horse. Lassiter had already spoken with the chiefs and portrayed Sandoval as maimed and defeated, the castrated, limping, former ruler of the pack. Lassiter had distributed his trade guns, powder, ball, and whiskey to each chief equally. What the Indians and Sandoval did not know was that Lassiter had met The Partisan and had given him twice the guns and powder as his rival chief, Black Buffalo.

Chapter Sixteen

Memory of the whippings faded as days passed. Increasingly, the captains worried that they had not met any natives. There were animals in abundance, but no humans. Drouillard suggested that they send a man in search of the tribes, and volunteered to go.

The captains refused to part with him. "You cannot speak Osage or Oto, and we depend on you to hunt."

"Some Indians speak French, and I know the signs. Others here can hunt."

"Others do not track as straight or aim as sure."

In the end, they chose a Frenchman, Joe Le Bartée, because he was the only one of the group who spoke the Indian language. He was an unfriendly, independent little man. The Americans could not pronounce his name correctly and contracted it phonetically to *Liberty*.

Days passed, then weeks. Drouillard and Collins back-trailed along the river to look for La Bartée and see if any natives had come in. All the camps were empty. The expedition had been gone over two months, traveled six hundred miles, and there was no sign of the native peoples. There were wild plums, grapes, currants, and berries on the hillsides, fat fish in the rivers, elk and antelope on the plain, provisions enough to make life sweet, but no sign of human inhabitants.

On August 2nd, Drouillard and Colter returned from the hunt with two horses loaded with elk. A cheer rose up in the camp. Collins and Whitehouse immediately began digging more fire pits to cook the quantity of meat, when another cry sounded the alert. To a man, they ran for guns! A delegation of Indians stood just outside musket range. An awkward gnome of a man stood at their head. He extended his arm in a sign of peace and addressed the company in French.

Drouillard recognized the scout, a hideous dwarf who stooped like Methuselah over a crooked staff. Collins could only think of the witches in the fairy tales his grandmother had told him, but the vision was human, and Drouillard marched forward with arms open in welcome. *"Eh Farfon! Qu'est-ce qui se passe?"* To Collins, the alien syllables sounded threatening as witchcraft.

The gnome shouted back, something which made the *engagés,* who understood, laugh. Farfon ran, short legs spinning like the spokes of a wheel, straight into the arms of Georges Drouillard. Drouillard's face turned red as they embraced like lost lovers.

The Indians stood by stolidly. There were six tall men of the Oto and Missouri nations, and they contrasted starkly with stubby Farfon. The Otoes were a stately race with long angular bones; the Missouris were slightly shorter with deep chests and stout limbs. They walked regally forward and took their places, cross-legged on a blanket that the captains spread over the ground. John Collins and Billy Warner roasted meat and served the entire group communally from a large wooden bowl.

The enlisted men had never seen a Western Indian before. The natives were dressed in their finest jewelry and buckskins, beaded and quilled in bright colors. The Americans stared with bullfrog eyes until Sergeant Ordway rebuked them for discourtesy. Captain Lewis fired his air gun, and all settled down for speeches and gift-giving. The captains announced the munificence and strength of the new father in

174

Washington. The Indians responded with speeches that Farfon translated into French, and Drouillard into English. Gradually, the Americans realized that these were lesser head men of smaller bands. It was a disappointment. The more powerful chiefs had refused to come. They had been warned to stay away.

When the Indians left for the night, Captain Clark shouted an order to strike camp, hoist the sail, and move upriver. He awakened Collins, Hall, and Goodrich from a deep sleep. They dragged themselves upright and manned the tow. Five miles later, the corps built a new camp and posted double sentries.

Conversation around the campfire that night resounded with complaints. George Gibson shouted for all to hear: "The captains drive us like slaves! Collins, Hall, and Willard, have stripes on their backs to prove it!"

Labiche, an experienced riverman, placated him. He speared a chunk of meat on the point of his knife and waved it to cool as he spoke. "This, my friends, could be your scalp. Look at Johnny Collins. They'd love his golden hair. And you, Joey Whitehouse and *mon petit,* Georgie Shannon, you would not grumble so loudly if you knew what a Teton war club could do."

The men fell silent. They were more hungry than worried, and they heaped meat into their bowls, sat, and ate. Labiche spoke again with his mouth full. "You will not have meat to fill your belly, if they steal our guns or our horses. You will have a knife here in the soft part of your belly beneath your ribs, and they will drive it up. You dream of feasting and soft breasts and long legs to warm and cushion you in the native lodges. Dream first of living to awaken the next morning. Come, we roll the dice. Winner take the beaver tail that Collins roasts on his spit."

175

Collins was not convinced. "We had a good site for camp. Two camps in one day is too many, and the beaver tail is mine, not yours to wager."

Labiche held out the dice. "Then cast the dice or cut the meat six ways, and let's eat." He tore off a piece with his fingers and stuffed it in his mouth.

Drouillard walked up. He had overheard. His face was grim, and he addressed his listeners solemnly like priest or confessor. "We're twenty-five days by horseback from Santa Fé." He stopped, waiting for each man's attention. They looked blankly up at him, like a class of recalcitrant schoolboys. "The Otoes tell us the Spanish have sent soldiers to pursue us." The men munched their meal distractedly. Collins measured out a gill for each and downed his own.

Drouillard frowned. His liquid brown eyes teared from fatigue. "Johnny, you remember the blood we discovered by the river, the day you shot your deer and saw your first buffalo?" Collins remembered. "Georgie Shannon, do you remember how we walked the hills and found the campfire only hours old?"

"Aye, I do!" George Shannon gulped the admission with a chunk of greasy tail, and choked.

Drouillard forced out the frightening words. "Spanish soldiers pursue us from behind. Le Bartée, the man whom we all know, who went to find White Horse, the Oto chief, has told us White Horse is in the pay of Spain and that there are others who want to stop us, Spanish sympathizers in the south and British traders in the north. We know how the British use the Indian nations. They maneuver until the Indians do the bloody work, then claim English right at the signing of the peace. We cannot sit like pigeons waiting for the eagle, waiting for Spanish dragoons, or Indian mercenaries to descend upon us. That is why the captain has moved the camp, so they cannot bayonet us as we sleep, like Tarleton at Waxhaws or Gray at Paoli. Or do you not remember? Your fathers and grandfathers remember. That is why your captains have posted a double guard." He turned and nodded to Labiche. "Labiche, here, he cheats at cards, but he does not lie." The grumbling had stopped.

Drouillard's voice trembled slightly as he continued. "I bring a message from the captains. They think we have outpaced the Spanish but not the English who now block our way. And if the Spanish have joined with the English, we must be doubly vigilant. Watch for strangers, report them immediately. Listen. Feel. Smell the scents on the wind. You heard the chiefs. Dangers are all around us, although we cannot see them. They are like the rain clouds or the gale winds or the bends in the river. We cannot avoid them. This is why the captains will demand great efforts of you. They do not mean to drive you beyond endurance. They have no love for Napoléon and his Spanish puppets or for the English whom your fathers and brothers fought bitterly not so very long ago. England let her colonies go reluctantly, and she is eager now to take them back. You all enlisted, knowing there would be risk and danger, deprivation and hardship. Your complaints can only increase our troubles and inspire our enemies. Enemies surround us. Have no doubt. Believe in them, although you cannot see them." He rubbed his weary eyes and fell silent. No one spoke. He leveled his dark eyes that pierced like arrows at the heart of every man. "You are strong men. Eat, fortify yourselves, load your guns, sharpen your knives." His voice faded, and he backed away to repeat the message to the next mess.

The men comprehended the intent if not the content of Drouillard's speech and quieted like chastened children. Sergeant Pryor himself was the first to break the stillness. "The

English will bait one tribe against the other. They have always used the red men for their own purposes. Drouillard's warning is real." There were no more complaints or grumblings that night.

The next morning, Collins awakened early and squirmed in his blankets. All the men in his tent were stirring. They itched and scratched. Some jumped into the river for cold relief. Labiche slapped himself and smeared bear grease under his armpits. The smell was nauseating, but he was the only one of Sergeant Pryor's mess who could stand still for muster. Lice had spread throughout the camp. Meriwether Lewis knew the signs. Over the next week, open sores and blisters covered the folds of hands, necks, and groins. The men begged for a post on the towline, where they could stay wet. They prayed for soothing rain. One by one, they began to use the bear grease. Labiche explained its effectiveness: "The bugs, they like only human blood. If you smell like a bear, they think you are a bear."

"They think you are a bear because you look like one!" Potts could say it because he was ugly like Labiche who was the ugliest man in the corps.

At the noon rest one rainy day, when he could stand the itch no longer, Collins took off his shirt. He turned his face to the storm, let the water pour over him, and opened his mouth to catch the drops.

Cruzatte stepped up beside him. "God gives us rain to cool the fiery itch. Then he creates the accursed creatures that feed on us." He shook his head, picked a louse from Collins's neck, and crunched it between his fingernails. "Come, I spread the grease on your back. Then we collect fresh raindrops for the coffee." Cruzatte insisted that rain water made the best coffee. They set out pots to collect the rain water and went to find more.

As they approached Ordway's tent, a man was fumbling with the cooking gear in the bright midday light. Only the superintendents of the messes, Thompson, Warner, and Collins, were permitted access to the pots and knives used to prepare the food that sustained the voracious corps. This man was not one of them. He was in violation of camp regulations.

The man was Moses Reed, and he spoke up to defend himself. "Me best knife is missing. Thompson said to look." He continued brazenly to rattle through the pots.

Collins countered: "Your knife's not there. Thompson knows his knives like I know mine and Warner knows his, and we count the equipment every night. What is it you really want, Reed?"

Reed snapped back: "I want me blade, and I intend to get it." He eyed Cruzatte narrowly. "Good sharp knife, mebbe you Frenchies stole it to add to La Bitch's collection." He mispronounced the name with stinging deliberation.

Cruzatte bristled. "You say that to Labiche . . . to his face, *cochon!*"

Reed seized the old man by the collar and jerked. "Call me *pig!* Think I don't hear what you Frenchies say behind my back. If I had my knife, I'd lay it across you skinny throat."

Sergeant Ordway heard the commotion and stepped up instantly. "He did say it to your face, Reed. Unhand the man."

Moses Reed let go Cruzatte and straightened. "Beggin' yer pardon, sir, must've left me knife back at the council fire. The Frenchie doesn't see so good, mebbe mixed it up with his own. Or mebbe the savages took it." He turned on his heel and backed away.

Later in the day, Captain Clark issued Moses Reed permission to go back for his knife to the place where they had met with the Oto chiefs. Reed promised to catch up. When

John Thompson counted his knives after the day's journey, two were missing and Reed was gone. Reports of Reed's insults swirled among the Frenchmen like chaff on a stiff wind.

Captain Clark was more concerned with finding the inhabitants of the vast land, and securing a peaceful passage upriver than with the disappearance of Moses Reed, which he supposed temporary. Worry carved itself into the smooth lines of his brow. The brief meeting with the Oto chiefs had been inconclusive. The younger Indians seemed brash, like brawling boys who enjoyed a good fist fight and did not hesitate to brag and steal if it meant inflated reputation or position. The older, wiser chiefs hammered at a persistent theme: they wanted the greatest quantity of goods for the lowest possible price. Indian friendship must be bought. The Indians would exact stiff punishment from anyone who tried to deny them their due. For Meriwether Lewis and William Clark this was a hard, unwelcome reality.

Each day, the corps waited for the return of Moses Reed. The word desertion began to circulate in the camp. Suspicion intensified when the captains sent out a party to bring Reed back. Sergeant Ordway led the search with Labiche as guide. Labiche gloated over the chance to apprehend the man who had insulted him. Collins watched the party depart in the early dawn, while thoughts of his own near desertion beseiged his brain. He wondered if Labiche would bring the man back dead or alive, if he would use his knife on Reed as Reed had threatened to slit the throat of old Cruzatte. Collins half hoped that Labiche would mark Reed so as to leave an ugly scar.

Labiche and the search party returned to camp the next day. They had found Reed with the Otoes, brazenly wooing the daughter of a chief. Reed had expected the Indians to shield him, but they turned him over willingly because Reed had taken the girl without payment. Captain Clark set up another court-martial, which convicted Reed and sentenced him to run a gauntlet of his peers.

" 'Tis an easy penance, easier than a whipping. His hands won't be tied." This was Cruzatte's contention, because Reed could run and dodge the switches that each man wielded.

Collins was doubtful. "Do you think forty men can lay on one hundred strokes?"

Drouillard knew better. "Reed insulted the Frenchmen. They'll lay on one hundred apiece!"

Reed ran the length four times. Only one man did not strike him: Charles Floyd because he was sick. The captains dismissed Reed summarily from the expedition, and Robert Frazier, a Frenchman from Deschamps's contingent, replaced him. It was the ultimate irony, replacement by one of the Frenchmen whom he despised.

A group of Indians watched the punishment of Moses Reed. The procedure shocked many of them. They protested the cruelty of their new masters in Washington who could so brutally chastise one of their own. What horrors would the new masters invoke, if one who was not of their own displeased them? The question circulated among the tribes. It was not a message Meriwether Lewis and William Clark wanted to disseminate.

The expedition pushed on to a round hill at the edge of the river, a place of death that made men cringe. Some said it was a burial mound, that its evil humors had invaded the mind of Moses Reed. Some said the devils who inhabited the stretch of water had invaded Sergeant Floyd's ravaged body. The Frenchmen pointed to the grave of an insatiable Omaha ruler who was buried high on a bluff above the river and whose restless soul coveted the boatloads of presents that ascended and descended the river. Floyd's illness grew worse still, and the superstitions multiplied. On August 20th, Sergeant Charles Floyd died, the towrope broke, and there was no cord left with which to replace it. Black clouds swept across the sky. Lightening bolts split the sizzling air. They hurried to moor the boats, climb out of the water, and carry Charles Floyd's lifeless body to shore. Cruzatte began to pray. Others joined in. At first Collins stiffened at the alien sounds, but, by nightfall, he was no longer embarrassed to utter the soothing prayer. He and all his companions, the sergeants and the captains, were afraid. Every man recited with Cruzatte: *"Notre père qui êtes aux cieux. . . ."* In French, the Lord's Prayer sounded softer, more convincing.

That night, Joseph Whitehouse wrote in his diary as he did every night. Whitehouse confessed sadly: **I record poor Floyd's death. He suffered.** Collins watched silently, sitting cross-legged beside his bunkmate and holding the bottle of precious ink. Whitehouse stopped what he was doing. "If you like, I'll show you the letters and their sounds."

"You must save your ink."

"We can draw the letters in the earth with a stick for a quill."

Collins nodded. Both men masked their true thoughts—that what had happened to Floyd could happen to them, a thousand miles from family and help, with only Dr. Rush's pills, Captain Lewis's kind hands, and their own mutual companionship for support. In the morning, they buried Charles Floyd.

They passed another mound a few days later. Cruzatte cried out when he saw it. "There, *mes amis,* it is the sacred place of the angels who remove the curse! Good spirits, this time, who will bless our passage!" They smiled at his innocence, but they covered sixteen miles in fair weather that day, and many knelt at sunset with Cruzatte, to thank God for their good fortune.

They built a bonfire which could be seen for miles to disperse the spirits and invite the tribes to gather. Drouillard spied an answer—smoke rising faintly from a distant hill. A cheer went up because smoke was a human sign, and luck and the good Lord were with them once more.

The Yankton Sioux had spotted the signal from their camp on the James River and rode in shortly after. They were friendly, jovial Indians. They laughed and sang and gambled and danced. The corps fired its guns, marched in formation, and prepared a feast. The Indians listened politely to the news of their new ruler, nodded agreeably to the words of peace, and awaited their gifts. They had already traded with the British and knew what to expect—powder, ball, and *milk*.

Hugh Hall snorted at that. "Milk? Would they feed whiskey to their infants? Do they think we can turn river water into wine?"

They laughed, but Drouillard's sobering voice broke in: "He's right. The captains give whiskey too freely. They did not bring enough to satisfy all the tribes."

Talk of peace continued, but the Indians' persistent request was for whiskey, muskets, and materials of war. When the captains acceded to the demands, food was plentiful, entertainment delightful, and the women beautiful and alluring. No one dared think about what would happen when supplies ran out and the captains refused.

Collins had not anticipated the friendliness of the women. Many were young, full-bodied, and eager, with copper skin, silken hair, and laughing eyes that tempted and excited. Their fathers and husbands offered them graciously in exchange for gifts. For Collins, Shannon, and some of the less experienced members of the corps, sexual freedom came as a shock, and they had no idea how to react. After Louise Bourgeron, Collins reacted with hesitation.

At first, the captains frowned at a soft hand under a shirt, a tender nip on the ear, or a soft brush thigh to thigh. Clark had fought Indians with his brother, George Rogers, in the Northwest Territories. He knew how the British used the Indians as spies for political purposes, especially Indian women, but he was powerless to stop the encounters, especially with the French *engagés* and the more experienced men.

He sent Deschamps to rouse the men from their embraces, out from under warm robes, and ordered the expedition to move on. Lewis tried to distract the men with the wonders of nature. There were prairie dog towns and herds of antelope, the skeleton of a fish forty-five feet long! Its mouth gaped like a death mask at the passing men. Cruzatte's superstitions resurfaced: "A harbinger of evil, teeth like a shark and a face like Labiche."

"But when I smile, I bring good luck." Labiche refused to worry. The Frenchmen laughed, and the memories of tender embraces and happier times endured.

But evil came to pass. According to Cruzatte, the fallen angel, Lucifer, awakened them in the night and shook the ground where they slept until it crumbled beneath them. Waters swirled in over the camp like the angry strikes of an offended God, punishment for the sins of the flesh. They ran for their lives into the waiting boats and cast off just as a mudbank came crashing down on the very spot where they had slept not minutes before. The boats careened in the boiling waves that heaved and sucked. Collins lost his boots, Potts, his hunting shirt, young Shannon a musket, but Labiche, one of the worst sinners among them, did not lose one single item. He winked presumptuously at Cruzatte. "I never wager against my God." Then John Colter arrived from the hunt, minus one horse. "Stolen," he asserted. No one had any doubt who the culprits were. Not devils this time. They were nearing the land of the Teton Sioux, the greatest horse thieves and most feared tribe on the river.

Chapter Seventeen

For the Englishman, Lassiter, it was good to be back in the Teton village with his Arikara wife nuzzled beside him. He threw off his buffalo robe. His wife was still asleep, and he was rested and well-fed. The hide lodge was warmer than the thin canvas tents of the whites, and he was sweating. He stretched, pulled on his pants and shirt, walked outside to relieve himself, and shivered.

The late September dawn was brisk, the sun was rising like a round red lamp over the eastern horizon, but the wind gushed out of the north. The village was stirring. Women were shaking out the sleep robes and kindling fires, sweeping out lodges, filling their water skins in the river. Some had begun to slice and lay fresh buffalo meat on racks to dry. Some were busy grinding corn and boiling squash for breakfast. The men were setting out to hunt. Young boys were driving the pony herd to the river to drink. Young girls were gathering to dig roots and pick the last of summer's berries. The sound of their voices carried on the cool morning air like the melodies of songbirds in spring. Dogs barked; babies cried.

A clatter of hoofs echoed through the village. A hunting party was riding in. Elk's Horn, a young brave of Black Buffalo's band, galloped ahead of the rest, tugging a fine horse behind him. The village matrons were instantly alert. Elk's Horn was a proud young man, unmarried, newly proven in battle, and the stolen horse would help him pay for a wife.

Abruptly, he jerked to a halt amid a broad circle of admirers to boast of his deed. His real hope was that Water That Whistles would hear. She was the young maiden of his choice.

He led the horse to her family's lodge and dropped its lead. His circle of listeners expanded as he described his exploits. Foreign men, white men, newcomers to the river, had abandoned the horse. He laughed gleefully as he spoke. "They let the horse wander off to join our ponies grazing where the grass is still green, in the valley of the river. The whites are walking up the river, pulling a huge boat behind them. They are wet and covered with mud." It seemed a thankless, frustrating effort to an Indian. To lose a good horse, to walk when one could ride and gallop like the wind across the open prairie and feel the thrust and speed of a powerful animal between his legs, Elk's Horn could not understand. There was more, and his voice rang with disbelief. "It was a heavy boat with a cannon on the bow and two on the stern and with a white winged sheet, like a bird."

"You've been drinking the white man's whiskey!" No one believed him.

Suddenly a loud, derisive voice shouted: "You could have taken a scalp, if they move so slowly." It was The Partisan, a lesser chief, one who was jealous of any young brave whose daring might eclipse his own.

Elk's Horn brushed off the insult. "I could have. Many have hair, red like the sunrise or yellow like the blooms of the sweet clover, handsome ornaments to hang from my shield, but they come in peace, forty of them, and I am one and I am wise. . . ."

"Wise or fearful?" The Partisan swelled his chest.

Elk's Horn bristled. "I will adorn my shield with the hair of opponents worthy of the name, not the pale heads of innocents. The river eats their strength. They are weak. They can bear us no harm."

"They trespass on our hunting grounds, interrupt our commerce on the river, carry weapons to our enemies, undermine the friendships we have fostered." The Partisan did not mention that he received British pay.

But Elk's Horn protested loudly: "Tell that to your British friends! The Americans walk like tortoises. You are not my chief. Our hunting grounds are on the plains. These Americans walk in the river. They are no threat. Black Buffalo commands me. He is greater than you, and he will acknowledge the value of my deed."

"When and if Black Buffalo returns from the hunt." The Partisan turned on his heel and stalked off to his lodge for breakfast.

Lassiter was waiting in the dimness of his lodge. He had heard the rumor that spread like oil on water around the village. "So they are coming, forty of them with a winged boat and baggage, walking." He laughed.

The chief laughed, too. "It is a wonder they have not drowned."

"Or died from the damp and cold. How many warriors do you have ready?"

"One hundred, if I choose." He held up the ten fingers of his hand and struck his wrist ten times and continued: "I have more warriors than you have given me guns. Those who must use bows will be jealous."

Lassiter acknowledged the complaint. "I have promised them more and better guns when the traders arrive in the spring. Besides, the river will snap up the Americans like a bear who swipes up his fish for dinner."

The Partisan's eyes widened. His lip curled. He had made his point, but his curiosity was not satisfied. "Have the Americans riches aboard?"

Lassiter downplayed the thought of American wealth, or any wealth that could compete with the North West Company's. He shrugged casually and responded: "I have promised you all the weapons you need, more reliable and more deadly instruments of war than the Americans will provide. Their powder is wet . . . their whiskey is weak, and the guns they carry jam and explode." He did not mention the cannon.

The Partisan was not deceived. "Forty foreigners against my warriors. No wealth, no horses, what will my warriors gain?"

"Power that only England can confer, and for you personally, the chieftanship of your tribe. Old Black Buffalo will return to find his position usurped."

The Partisan gloated. He was aptly named. Partisan was an ancient word. Long ago it denoted a double-edged sword that could strike two ways and cut an opponent apart. Mounted on a long shaft, it could strike farther than any other lance. The Partisan would strike out for power, for prestige, for wealth, for Lassiter and England, but the blade could easily swing back and slice the man who wielded it. Lassiter snickered to himself. He must be careful, but, for now, the ambitious chief was greedy, jealous of his rival, Black Buffalo, and ambitious enough to be manipulated to serve the cause of the North West Company and do Lassiter's bidding. Lassiter needed only to convince the chief that England's interests coincided with his own. He urged gently: "Stop the Americans and you will be doubly rich, with scalps and trade goods and whatever else they carry." But he had not witnessed the incident with Elk's Horn, and he had not been present when the last tribal council met.

Black Buffalo, head chief of the Brulé, returned early. He rode in triumphantly, with a dozen Pawnee horses loaded with fresh meat and four scalps hanging from his coup stick. By morning he had gathered his warriors around him and summoned The Partisan to parley. Other chiefs sat to his right and to his left and feasted on a rich stew of tender dog.

The Partisan entered Black Buffalo's lodge with oily confidence. But Black Buffalo left him standing and proceeded with his meal. The Partisan waited in silent fury. Finally Black Buffalo finished eating and spoke. "We have considered. If the Americans offer better prices than the British, we will exact a toll and allow them safe passage. And we will trade with both English and Americans until we determine who will profit us most."

The Partisan reacted aggressively. "They are rich, and they are weak. Lassiter knows. He knows a man who tracked them from the southern settlements. My scouts say they have guns and powder enough to ignite the hearts of our enemies. We cannot let them pass."

By interrupting, The Partisan had breached strict protocol. Black Buffalo barely raised his eyes. "We will wait to appraise their wealth with our own eyes and to hear their intentions with our own ears. After we see and hear, then we will act. We will not permit them to carry materials of war to our neighbors. I have heard they come in peace. In peace we shall receive them." It was a forceful but quiet rebuke. Black Buffalo spoke in the plural, in the first person, reminding all that he represented the entire tribe. The Partisan rose to his full height, nodded cursorily, and stalked out. Black Buffalo did not lift his gaze to watch him go.

Chapter Eighteen

The Americans anchored off the mouth of the Bad River. The water was brown, like dried blood and the sky, gray like gun metal. Old Cruzatte, the only man who could speak a smattering of the Sioux language, predicted disaster. His continual grumbling seemed to quiet his own fears, but it eroded the good spirits of others. Some chose to ignore him. John Collins used soft grass to plug his ears as he cooked the evening meal.

Labiche sat nearby, sharpening his knives and complaining: "You're *poltron*, old man, coward! We already know the Tetons fight like demons and have become rich as toll-keepers of the river. Sharpen your knife, not your tongue."

Cruzatte pointed to his one good eye. "I've seen Teton treachery. Yes, I cower." His fear hovered like a mist in a swamp, fouling all with its smell of decay. Finally, Sergeant Pryor sent Cruzatte to his tent to eat his meal alone. But the test for the corps would come shortly against this most powerful tribe. Captain Lewis ordered all guns loaded and primed, and doubled the guard.

The Americans made camp, raised their flag staff, and invited the Teton chiefs to talk. Three chiefs came with thirty braves, but communication was difficult. Pierre Dorion, the expedition's interpreter with the Yanktons, had stayed behind, and Cruzatte was a poor substitute. Every statement endured restatement, revision, and an infusion of the old man's fears. The Indians spoke to Omaha captives who spoke

191

to Cruzatte who translated the Omaha into French, which Labiche translated into English. The captives laced their words with complaints of brutality and privation, while Cruzatte added his own prejudices and superstitions. The captains' replies filtered back like fruit through a sieve—the pulp remained while only the sweetened juice seeped through. They presented medals, beads, and whiskey. They appointed Black Buffalo as head chief, and showered him with gifts—a red military coat and a cocked hat, a medal, and more whiskey. To the haughty lesser chief, whom the English called The Partisan, they gave less. His warriors grew impatient, rose from the parley, and sauntered brazenly about the American camp. Their eyes and hands were everywhere, darting from the shiny brass swivel gun, to muskets, whiskey barrels, knives, and pots. Their glances pierced tarps, unwrapped packs, and assessed the hidden wealth of the white man and his willlingness to defend it. Indignant and proud, The Partisan demanded more. He spoke in broken English. Captain Lewis gave him whiskey to appease him and invited him with Black Buffalo aboard the keelboat. The Partisan gulped down his drink, and paraded boldly about the deck. He inspected the rudder, the oars, the rigging of the sail. He pushed men aside and fingered the weapons that they held in hand. He broke open a crate and seized one of the new Harpers Ferry rifles. It wasn't loaded.

Captain Clark's patience finally broke. He cocked his gun at the unruly Indian, and instantly every American did the same. Collins stood only ten feet from The Partisan and trained his weapon on the Indian's belly. He sensed Drouillard come up beside him, then Colter and Whitehouse. The angry chief did not change expression. He backed away, downed the contents of an entire whiskey bottle, staggered, and smashed the bottle against the mast.

Collins, who had lost his boots when the camp flooded, stepped on a shard of glass that cut through his moccasin into his heel. He cursed as pain shot up through the muscles of his leg, but he held his gun steady and his eyes glued to the Indian until Drouillard drove a gun barrel into the chief's ribs and prodded him bodily off the keelboat into the white *pirogue*.

Captain Lewis rushed up with more whiskey and poured it over Collins's foot. "Sit, press the skin together until the bleeding stops." Then Lewis was gone to ferry more Indians to shore.

On land at the campsite on the opposite shore, Labiche replaced the injured Collins at the cook fire. Captain Lewis came to inspect the wound. "You must keep the foot elevated. If you lower it or walk on it, it will reopen and bleed."

The incident was a hard lesson for the impetuous, young frontiersman—he had never before not been able to walk. He felt inferior and emasculated. And Lewis warned of further troubles. "They will touch your weapons, rifles, and knives, and they will touch you. Do nothing. It would be a provocation, a breech of their courtesy. You must endure abuse, even pain for the sake of peace. But not theft. Lock away your valuables." Lewis's words flew ominously over the heads of the men. They took precautions. Labiche hid his knives in the bottom of the hold. Collins stationed himself with leg propped across the locker that held the pots and knives for butchering and cooking. He strung the key on a thong around his neck and sat, immovable, while the Tetons jostled him until his injured foot bled. Hugh Hall sat beside him, complaining: "Tickly fingers crawl over my skin like fleas on a dog, worse than the god-damn lice."

They took an inventory, when the Indians finally left. A

knife was gone that John Thompson had not concealed, a pot here, a ramrod there, a mirror—but the guns, whiskey, and powder were locked away and accounted for. They spent a watchful night afloat in the middle of the stream, near the mouth of the Bad River whose name seemed to curse the very air they breathed.

Next morning, Captain Clark called for volunteers to go ashore. Labiche, Colter, Hall, and Reuben Fields, all good marksmen, stepped forward. Collins, Drouillard, and Joe Fields covered them from the keelboat. They took interpreter Cruzatte, and rowed off in the white *pirogue*. The Partisan, the double-edged sword, was waiting at the landing with angry warriors. The warriors cocked rifles and drew arrows from their quivers. Old Cruzatte screamed a warning, but his shrill words blew away like pollen on the prairie wind as the Americans sighted their guns.

John Collins gazed grimly down the barrel of a new Harpers Ferry rifle. On shore, Colter and Fields had dropped to one knee to steady their aim. Cruzatte was trumpeting his litanies. Collins could see his frantic lips at work. Captain Clark's lips were moving, too, but whether he was addressing the Indians or his own men, Collins could not hear. He was angry. His outstretched leg throbbed. His trigger finger quivered. He rested his gun barrel over his knee and trained it on the recalcitrant chief. A surge of raw power coursed through his veins. He wanted to fight this high-handed Indian like he had fought Jacques Bourgeron, but he could not walk.

"Hold, Johnny, no fire now." Drouillard sensed his mounting frustration.

Captain Lewis called the men to battle stations and trained the swivel on the threatening warriors. They rowed the keelboat into the shallows to better aim their guns. The stand-off was complete. They stood like pillars, white man and Indian, in stark battle lines, both brave, both disciplined, both waiting, not twenty feet apart, ready to pounce for the kill. Suddenly, yelling a string of curses, The Partisan lunged for the anchor cable. His warriors jumped for the keelboat.

William Clark was a patient man. He lifted a staying hand to Lewis, and spoke loud enough for all the Americans to hear. "Be still, no shooting, no insults, no violence, and we will pass from here." To The Partisan, he proclaimed: "We bring you news of a powerful new father in Washington who wishes you prosperity and peace!" Cruzatte squawked the awkward translation.

The Partisan had also heard the exhortations of Lassiter, the Briton. He bore the scars of many battles against the Pawnees and Omahas, battles fought to defend trade with good Mother England. The word "father" challenged his loyalties and undermined his ambitions. He stood defiant in the shallow water, as if carved in stone. Seconds stretched like the river into long-flowing minutes. They stood, they stared, the fiery young chief and Captain William Clark, until Collins felt his every muscle twitch. He was hardly aware that his heel had opened and his blood dripped steadily into the planks of the keelboat.

Suddenly, a regal figure in a long buffalo robe appeared. Black Buffalo walked like a messiah between the rows of warriors and weapons, lifted his arms to shoulder height, and held the flat side of his palms toward the lines of Indians. Slowly, they parted and lowered their bows. The Americans shouldered their guns while Captain Clark stepped bravely forward with outstretched hand in friendship. Black Buffalo shook Clark's hand with flourish. He shouted rudely at The Partisan, whose eyes flashed pure hatred. The Partisan stepped back. They hauled the keelboat nearer still. Captain

Lewis walked bravely ashore, and the parley began. John Collins felt his own breath drain as the men on shore eased gradually back to the boats and the safety of the opposite shore. They kept their guns primed.

At day's end, safely afloat on the keelboat, Meriwether Lewis called a muster to commend his men for their restraint. "You have performed well this day, with great responsibility and discretion, but our trial is not over. The British have taught the natives that we Americans are scoundrels, greedy for land and pelts. The Spanish priests call us infidels. The great chief of the Tetons, Black Buffalo, has many suitors. He holds flags of France, England, Spain, as well as our own. We are not the first. We are the fourth, but we are the ones who will endure!"

The mood among the men was bleak. "Bloody thievin', deceivin' liars!" Hugh Hall could not resist. He voiced loudly what John Collins and others were thinking. "Keep sittin' there, Johnny, on your perch, and they'll pick you off like a pigeon on a fence."

Pryor interjected a vein of sanity. "They think the same of us, that we are the liars."

The following day, Black Buffalo returned, spread his long arms in a gesture of friendship. He was a tall man, a true native prince, taller even than William Clark. When he signaled, the warriors dispersed. The Tetons motioned the Americans to come ashore a second time, brought roasted meat and furs, and set up a shelter for a conference. Captain Lewis landed first and raised the pipe of peace to the four directions and heaven and earth. They smoked. The Indians sang and danced, and Lewis invited the chiefs to board the boats once again. They came, but their change of heart was contrived. Hall growled another protest. "One minute they want our scalps, the next minute he invites them for an afternoon sail.

We don't impress them. They'll tempt us with sugar, then shoot us down like geese on the fly soon as we show 'em our tails." John Collins agreed.

But Potts found cause to tease. "I have no tail, Hughie Hall. Now Collins there, with his bum foot, he sits all day on his." They laughed nervously. It was small relief.

Collins laughed with them. It eased the throb in his foot and the pounding in his head, but body and brain were too tired to find a clever response for Hughie Hall.

Days passed, and he tried walking again, but only on the ball, and he stumbled frequently. Whitehouse had fashioned him a crude crutch from the crook of a cottonwood. At dinnertime, clamping his jaw tightly against the pain, he pushed himself erect and went to prepare the meal. He served the meal, but the effort strained, and he fell asleep over his plate. They let him sleep because it would restore his ailing foot.

When Drouillard awakened him, it was night, and he jumped up with a start. "The captain wants you to take the second watch. You're rested, and you don't need to walk in order to watch."

Collins rubbed his eyes. Drouillard handed him a cup of coffee. "Captain says we can't post a reliable watch if everybody's falling asleep. He's ordered us to rotate chores and sleep time, so we always have some who are alert."

"What about the captains?"

Drouillard shrugged. "They can never shut an eye."

Collins sat through his watch, morose, vulnerable, ready to roll aside and grab gun, knife, club, spike, or the nearest weapon to hand. He lowered his foot and let it throb and bleed because it kept him awake.

When they pushed off next morning, hundreds of curious Indian faces watched from the shore. The gauntlet of staring eyes wore on all their spirits. The sheer numbers humbled and intimidated, because by comparison the Americans were so few. There was more grumbling, more resistance to the captains who subjected them to the evil eyes and the torrents of abuse.

They hove to in the lee of an island to avoid the ever-present eyes. A little of the old camaraderie returned, and complaints settled into the dust. But no hunters had gone out for days, and there was no fresh meat. Dry stores did not fill a stomach, and the grumbling revived. Labiche was loudest, shouting that the *cuisine* was fit only for prisoners and Irish pigs, that the cornmeal grated his gums like dry sand. Clark heard the commotion and placed Labiche in charge of meals so Collins could rest. The result was a black crust on the bottom of the cook pots that soured their food for a week. The men cursed Labiche, but they ate or went hungry.

Collins was munching on a blackened rib, when the boat heaved to starboard and he tumbled to the deck. He heard Howard scream: "Bloody redskin must've half-cut the anchor cable! I seen 'im!" They used the anchor during the tow to offset the backward pull of the current, when the men needed rest.

Potts had just hoisted the sail, when the boat swirled and a wave struck across the beam. Captain Clark swore: "Release the god-damn' sail!" Potts let go. Cruzatte crossed himself. It was the last movement Collins witnessed. The halyard zinged loose, and yards of heavy canvas crashed down over the deck. It knocked Collins through the hatch and into the hold, onto the bales of stores, and pinned him helplessly in the boat's belly. "Now straighten 'er!" He heard the cry from above, and prayed that Labiche, at the helm, steered with the current. He was trapped. Howard was still shouting: "Knife was dull or that damn' Injun would've sliced clean through, and we'd be floatin' down the rapids on our way to hell!" Fear choked John Collins. The boat was loose in the current—if it capsized, he would drown. A blistering stream of French invective blasted from the stern. That was Labiche at the tiller that was flapping free.

Labiche cursed as the boat heeled dangerously, and Collins rolled sideways. "Steady now! Don't rip the sail!" Clark's voice howled, then was silent. Collins heard Cruzatte confessing his sins, and his heart froze. He shouted for help, but his cry was lost in the clatter on deck. He heard himself mumbling and realized it was a prayer. But the boat steadied.

"I need a second man to hold her steady!" Labiche again, he had caught the tiller.

"Collins, you there?" Drouillard's voice resounded from the deck like an angel from heaven above. Pushing back the heavy canvas, Drouillard peered down and held out a hand. Collins climbed out, unhurt. Drouillard pushed him forward. "Saw you go down. Anchor cable snapped again. Grab an oar if you can. Row like the devil was chasing you and damn your sore foot." The boat ran aground gratefully, on soft sand, in the lee of an embankment. Labiche's face was white, his shirt soaked with sweat. The rowers breathed with relief.

The Tetons had followed all the way, laughing at the predicament and hurling prickly taunts. But as night fell, convinced that the foolish Americans could go no farther and that they were now the proud possessors of all that the expedition carried, the Indians drifted away.

The Americans pushed on. They rigged a substitute anchor, refitted the sail, and unloaded the boat to lighten the load and pull it off the bar. By torchlight, the desperate work progressed. Only two men were left on board: Howard with a pole in the bow and Labiche at the tiller in the stern. Even Captain Lewis put his shoulder to the tow, and the keelboat backed away slowly from the soft silt until she floated free.

Next morning at dawn, the Sioux returned, hundreds strong, but the Americans had sailed on. The Indians caught up and ambled to the slow progress of the tow, cackling and yelling. Because their prize had escaped, their mockery intensified. Women threw stones and sticks and ran along the dry ground, mimicking the tired, wet men wading through deep river mud. Sexual innuendo laced gesture and word. When the Americans ignored the jibes, the innuendo turned physical. Cruzatte didn't need to translate. Tempers flared and began to erupt. Potts, Goodrich, Labiche, and Hall charged the bank, but the sergeants ordered them back. Even the stiff reserve of Meriwether Lewis broke. "Heathens, demons!" For an instant, he shook his head madly and aimed his rifle at a wildly gesticulating Indian, but Clark deflected the gun before the shot was fired. Through it all, John Collins writhed in his corner of the keelboat. He, too, grabbed his gun, lifted it, and sighted down the long barrel. But his foot gave way, he nearly fell overboard, and the gun clattered across the deck.

Cruzatte screeched continuously over the din. "They place bets on us, who will slip, who will drown, whose hair will make the finest ornament! They pick those of us they will enslave and those they will crucify!"

Collins's head was pounding with little hammers behind his eyes, and his foot cramped in spasms of pain. He screamed at Cruzatte: "Shut up, old man!" Even prayers were better than a constant barrage of doom. Finally, Potts had had enough. He smacked Cruzatte hard across the mouth and sent him sprawling on the deck.

Clark helped the old Frenchman up. "Let him speak. We need to know what the scoundrels are thinking. Words are less dangerous than sticks and stones or arrows and lances."

Collins plugged his ears. He felt the bile in the pit of his stomach rise and make him want to retch. He sat perched now on a locker near the bow, cleaning rifles. Hall was nearest on the towrope; Hall, whose stripes had healed into reddened welts like his own; Hall, whom a good whipping could not intimidate and who always spoke his mind. Hall was shirtless, and he could see the ugly red scars. Veins pulsed blue over Hall's red-scarred shoulders. Collins wondered which was worse, the whipping or this terrible, endless struggle against the river and the degrading mockery of the Teton tribe.

The captains suffered along with the men. Most exhausted of all was Captain Clark, who blinked and staggered from lack of sleep. The sergeants and Captain Lewis urged him to rest and eat, in vain. It was Captain Lewis who drove the corps forward now with one obsessive thought—escape from this hellhole of river to kinder ground where a people lived who would honor their new father in Washington and treat his envoys respectfully, and let them sleep and heal. Lewis came to care for Collins's foot.

"One more step, one more pull, one more bend in the river . . . ," Lewis's words echoed poetically and lent a rhythm to the tug and slack of the tow. Still they entertained three chiefs on board, chiefs who did nothing to end the insolence of their people.

Collins held a gun and watched mutely, but Hugh Hall, as always, raised his voice. "They treat the savages like gods in heaven while we honest men grunt like mules in harness. I'd like to cut out their wagging tongues."

Labiche concurred: "I will sharpen the knife for you."

But the presence of the chiefs was a necessary precaution. Captain Lewis explained it as best he could. "The Sioux will not injure us while one of theirs is with us. We entertain the chiefs as insurance against attack." John Collins was thinking of what would happen when the last chief departed and both captains and men collapsed from exhaustion. No welcome guests then. Only combat, enslavement, massacre, death— they were chilling thoughts. But he was too tired to think. His chin fell to his chest. His eyes closed.

Slowly, the Indians grew bored with the snail-like pace and the prodigious, repetitive labors of the white men. They melted away, and the captains finally put the last chief ashore. The Corps of Discovery pushed inexorably onward for one more day. The muscles of their legs cramped from the strain. Their backs ached. William Clark's eyes had sunk into deep, ghost-like hollows in his skull. His skin was gray, his muscles soft as wet sponges. Captain Lewis feared for his life. That night, they had to carry Clark to his berth, and he fell asleep in their arms. He did not awaken even when the boat jerked and scraped the river's bottom.

They made their camp there, where the boat stopped. They hoped the river would rise and wash the boat free by morning. John Collins's hands shook as he tried two or three times to kindle the fire. The kindling was dry, the flint new, and his head nodding from exhaustion. He stumbled, lost his crutch, stepped inadvertently down on his wound as pain shot like a flare from heel to hip. Potts struck the spark and sent George Shannon to the river to fill the pots. No one spoke. Whitehouse and Pryor, the sergeant, fell asleep on their feet. Men dropped their heads into the food on their plates or spilled rations into the dirt for the dog to lick. Drouillard collapsed on the shore. The next day was little better. They had to haul the boat off the bar. They plodded on, pulling each foot mechanically through the sticky mud, leaning on each other, scanning the banks with half-open eyes, expecting attack around every bend in the river and wishing only for an end to the pain.

A shout went up suddenly. Collins hardly lifted his head. A shadowy form stood on the bank, a man. They groped for the guns, fumbling, shaking themselves into wakefulness. But Deschamps stood up in the red *pirogue*, took off his hat, and waved. "Here, Vallé, how are your *bâtards?*" It was a Frenchman named Vallé, and he was a friend of Deschamps.

Vallé paddled out in a tubby round boat and brought welcome news. There would be no more encounters with the Teton Sioux. "They have gone to the plains for one last hunt before the snow falls and the tree trunks crack from the exploding ice." Friendly words! No symphony could have been more beautiful to the exhausted men's ears.

They stopped right there, trudged up the bank, and stretched out on the sand. They slept soundly for the first time in a week. They were too tired to question Vallé about his bastard children or the cracking tree trunks. The Arikaras were near. What would be their reception with this tribe? It was October. Would they stop to prepare a berth for winter or would the captains push relentlessly on? The cold was increasing. Even in their blankets, they shivered at night. The water's temperature was falling, too. Soon they would trade mud for ice.

Captain Clark's health improved. There was frost one morning, heavy frost the next, and howling wind which swept gunmetal clouds across the sky. It was the diminishing time of the year, when trees and grasses yellow and die, and animals migrate and cache their food. Great flocks of geese blackened the sky. Bears sought their dens, and the plague of insects vanished. A thin veneer of ice frosted the backpools where the water lay still. They passed an abandoned Indian camp with canoes and baskets ready for use, but no human resident in sight. They spied two emaciated natives, fed them, and sent them on, wondering how they would feed themselves during the winter. The laughter and enthusiasm of the summer were gone, blown away with the mockery of the Sioux. Apprehensiveness and worry replaced them. Now men crowded around Collins, Thompson, and Warner at the cook fires and stuffed their moccasins with grass for warmth. The days grew shorter. But the hunting was good, they regained their strength, and Collins's foot was healing well.

"Ice has formed in the high country." Captain Lewis announced it one frosty morning at muster. The men could not see mountains, only the empty plate of prairie, but they felt the chill of cold water, and their wet clothing froze against their skin when the north wind howled through the bottomland. Now they could sleep in peace, but coughing, congestion, chaffed and chapped hands and legs tortured them. They could only dream of warmth and good health.

An abandoned village hovered on the shore. They looked with longing at the snug earth lodges and the strong palisade, but it was disease-ridden Captain Lewis said, and they dragged the boats past. Around a bend in the river, Drouillard discovered another village on an island. This one was peopled, and its residents emerged like ants from a hill, to wonder and stare. Captain Lewis ordered the corps to battle stations, summoned volunteers, and prepared to go ashore.

Chapter Nineteen

The Arikara village lay at the mouth of the Grand River, in a series of humps that dotted the landscape like dunes on a barrier beach. The earth lodges were large, round dwellings, with tunneled entries and smoke curling from holes in the roofs. Cultivated fields stretched on either side in the rich bottomland, but they were yellowed now. The harvest was in. A horse herd grazed peacefully on the prairie beyond.

A huge assemblage of Indians crowded the shore. Some came out to greet the expedition in tub-like boats that bounced and swirled jauntily in the eddies. Some stood on the curved roofs of their lodges for a better view. Some waved a greeting. They were a noisy, colorful, laughing lot, dressed in leggings and robes, adorned with beads and the brightly dyed quills of porcupine and gull.

The anchor hit the muddy bottom, dragged, then caught and held below a high bluff. William Clark's voice droned the orders. "Guard the keelboat. Watch the *pirogues*. Ordway, Shields, Drouillard, Collins, come with me." Streaks of blood blotted Clark's eyes because he had lost sleep. A black fly, the last of the season, landed on an eyelid. He did not lift a hand to brush it away. They climbed into a *pirogue* and rowed out into the river. Instantly they were engulfed by a host of the strange tubs, full of jabbering, gesticulating Indians.

A burly Frenchman met them at water's edge. He was smiling. He wore a wide waxed mustache that lifted the edges of his eyes and spread his pink bulbous nose across a mass of black whiskers. It wiggled like a rodent's when he spoke. "So the Sioux have made you wary, *messieurs,* but not wary enough to turn back!" He laughed heartily and arched a shaggy, black brow. "They let you pass, the greedy Sioux? How much did you pay?" He didn't wait for an answer but held out his hand. "Joseph Gravelines, North West Company, welcome to Sawahaini village! And this is Lassiter, our English friend, who arrived yesterday and brought us news of your coming." A tall, thin, buckskin-clad, white man stood behind him. "And Pierre is over there!"

Indians crowded in. The white men shouldered their rifles as a path opened through the press of bodies and Pierre appeared. He spat out a viscous glob of chewed tobacco. His raucous voice rose among the chatter of onlookers. "Hello, American! *Me voici,* Pierre Tabeau!" His speech was strongly accented but clear. A thick beard and thatch of black hair hid any facial expression except for his eyes which were bright, twinkling blue. He held out a friendly hand.

Clark's relief was obvious. "Bill Clark, Captain, Army of the seventeen United States." He took Pierre's hand, then Gravelines's.

Lassiter was the last to come forward and nodded suspiciously. His handshake was firm, but his eyes were distant and his words unsettling. "Your men can put up their arms." William Clark frowned.

Meriwether Lewis came ashore next with a friendly greeting. His eyes locked on Gravelines, then wandered to the curious Indians. "Can you speak to these natives, gentlemen? Our interpreter has stayed behind." He motioned toward the curious Indians and smiled broadly. Lassiter retreated into the crowd.

Pierre answered: "I will gladly speak for you. Joseph cannot. He speaks like the river in flood, too much, too fast, and without thought. But come, bring tobacco, chew, smoke. These are good people who will trade fairly with you." His eyes brightened. "They think you blessed by the spirits and very brave for having come this far."

Captain Lewis corrected him. "We are not traders. We are explorers. We seek passage to the western ocean."

"But of course." The response was mechanical. Gravelines did not believe him.

Lewis took three men, Labiche because he spoke French and two others, and followed Joseph and Pierre.

John Collins waited apprehensively with Clark at the river's edge, while Lewis proceeded to the village. Clark paced nervously and refused food. His tension wore on the waiting men. They raised tents, lit fires, and started pots to stew. They cleaned and sharpened weapons and listened to old Cruzatte mumble his litanies. Collins served a tasteless meal of cornmeal and salt pork steeped in day-old venison broth that boiled away and left their mouths sour as stale brine.

They were still washing the mouthfuls down with river water, when Labiche returned. He was exuberant. He had feasted on fat buffalo and rested in a warm earth lodge under a thick robe, in the arms of the long-legged, buxom, young daughter of a medicine man. The ugly Frenchman did not hesitate to embellish the details of his languorous afternoon. "It was dark in the lodge. She was supple as a lynx and soft as beaver fur with skin that smelled like sweetest grass." It sounded like a fairy tale.

Old Cruzatte shook his head with disgust. "He won her in a game of chance. She could not see his *visage de gargoyle* in the twilight of the lodge, but God could see his sin."

Labiche ignored the old man and addressed the younger. "Come tomorrow, Georgie Shannon in the light of day." He laughed. "The handsomest maids in the tribe will line up ten deep to couple with a pretty yellow-hair like you. You, too, Johnny Collins." Labiche tossed a carrot of tobacco into their midst. "See what they give me for my efforts. There are no whipping posts in Indian villages. Let the old man pray for salvation. I take my heaven like my whiskey and tobacco, now." This last was intended for Collins.

Collins stared straight ahead into the sputtering flames. A hot fire, a warm blanket, dry clothes, three days' ration of fresh meat, six days' sleep, and a wholesome foot, he was satisfied with simple pleasures. It was getting cold. The fire was warm. He did not look up.

Labiche turned to Shannon. "Wash and comb your hair. Come with me tomorrow."

Shannon hesitated. "I've never bedded a woman."

"For a roll of the dice, it's easy."

Shannon looked for support to Collins who didn't lift his eyes. He was comfortable, well-fed, his foot had healed, but he felt vulnerable, especially in front of fickle women. He wasn't betting.

Arikara women were not deceitful like Louise Bourgeron, nor hostile like the Sioux. The Arikaras believed that the sexual act transmitted the magic of the white man, a powerful medicine that resisted disease, produced firearms and metal objects, mirrors, and colorful glass beads, which comprehended and spoke many tongues. Husbands sought out partners for their wives, and fathers offered their daughters in an effort to acquire the precious powers for themselves. The Americans reciprocated eagerly. Freed from the threat of Sioux violence and lured by warm lodges and fresh food, they were eager as stags in rut to oblige. Captain Clark was too exhausted to stop them. He gave all who requested leave. Only the two captains, the sergeants, Drouillard, Collins whose memories of betrayal still rankled, Bratton who was married, and saintly old Cruzatte stayed in the camp. Clark rolled up in his blankets and fell into a deep restorative sleep. The rest rotated a perfunctory guard. Collins hobbled drearily about on his painful foot, prepared food, stood his watch, and retired early to bed, while the bawdy sounds of revelry in the village echoed in the night air.

The temperature dropped, and a stiff wind picked up. It blew beneath tent flaps and billowed the canvas like a luffing sail. It invaded blankets and clothing, chilled the skin, and made teeth chatter. Collins awakened shivering. He thought of his comrades in the sturdy earth lodges, protected from the incessant wind. The fire had blown out. He rose and rekindled it and set out water to boil as the dawn ascended ominously like a great gray dome, with dark, enveloping clouds that blotted out the light and robbed the air of heat.

Slowly, the men drifted back to camp. Negotiations began in late morning after all had returned. Collins spread the canvas sail as a windbreak and roof over the meeting place. Shannon ran the American flag up the mast. It snapped briskly in the strong prairie wind. The Indians arrived with ceremony, and the captains cut open a bale for distribution. The native people had never seen such a wide variety of goods, not even when the English came to trade. There were vermilion, mirrors, needles, razors, wire scissors, and cloth of every hue. The gold-braided coats, tricorner hats, and medals were reserved for chiefs.

The men of the expedition had mustered in two rows and presented arms. Two chiefs, tall and powerfully built, with a retinue of warriors, arrived at midday. They wore leggings and thick buffalo robes and elaborate hunting shirts painted with scenes of past victories. Bracelets and rings adorned their ears and arms, and the black feathers of the crow anchored their hair. Crow at Rest, chief of Sawahaini, and Man Crow, chief of Rhtarahe, welcomed the expedition, but other chiefs were absent, warned away by Lassiter. They came belatedly, after Pierre implored them, and talks began in the early afternoon.

The ceremonies were dignified as in any court of Europe. The two captains, Gravelines, and Pierre saluted as the chiefs approached the camp. Howard fired the swivel. Bratton fired the air gun whose silent discharge awed the Indians. Disbelieving, they ran to see where the noiseless ball had struck. While the captains talked, the enlisted men enjoyed themselves. Drouillard played a Jew's harp. Labiche walked on his hands like an acrobat in a circus. They danced and sang. The music was sweet, like memories of summer and home.

Collins stood rigidly, hardly daring to blink, but Drouillard grunted, and Labiche coughed nervously and swung his head to the side. Collins followed with his eyes and instantly recognized the newcomers. Two Sioux warriors from the Teton village, delegates and spies, haughty as the lords of a fiefdom, appeared behind the second Arikara chief.

The captains spoke their prescribed words. "Children, your new father in Washington will keep the river open to all who want to trade in harmony and peace. You will have riches such as you see here in exchange for your good grain, pelts, and, above all, your friendship." Lewis raised his voice to emphasize the impact of his message, but the inflection was lost in translation. He denounced any who tried to curtail trade and stop the expedition's progress. The chiefs stared stoically at the earthen floor as he questioned the presence of the Sioux. "Are these your friends who tried to stop us?" His meaning was plain. He continued: "The Sioux exact payment for Arikara safety and well-being. The river gives you drink, waters your gardens, and enriches you with wealth and friends. The Sioux have cut off your access to the southern reaches of the river which has brought you life since your fathers and grandfathers were born."

The first chief listened solemnly and carefully considered his reply. The Arikaras were an agricultural nation, he explained. "The earth is nourished by the river and brings forth corn and squash in abundance. But we are few because of the attacks of those you call our friends." He referred to the Mandans and Hidatsas but glared at the Sioux delegates who avoided his eyes. Antipathy rose like a slow tide, first toward the delegates, then toward the entire Sioux nation and their British and Canadian allies.

The second chief, Pocasse, revealed the reality. "The Tetons came with the North West man, Lassiter, to persuade us that no American should be allowed to proceed upriver. We were not fooled. We were a great and wise nation once. We remember with respect those who came before us, the fathers and grandfathers whom the pox and war have struck down in their wake." He inhaled slowly and drew back broad, muscular shoulders. "We have come like the thin smoke of a waning fire from nine powerful villages, with feet that dragged like stones along the ground, and we have gathered here at the mouth of the Grand River, in these three villages. They are all that is left." He glared darkly at the Sioux braves, and his voice rang with accusation. "We were rich and numerous before the theft of our birthright. We give of our corn for a meager supply of white man's guns and always you demand more, more corn, more hides! And we become fewer each year. The effort strains. We pay because we cannot feed and defend ourselves from your greed without the precious guns and powder. Now the Americans come and I, Pocasse, welcome them! But these Americans must not betray our trust!"

The first chief, Kakawisassa, nodded, then raised his voice again to address Captain Lewis. "You say you bring goods to all tribes on the river. You exact fewer pelts than the Sioux, fewer than the English from Fort Saint Peter. Can you promise to bring health, not sickness?" He stopped. His question rattled like dry leaves on an old tree. He added: "Too many have died. I myself am scarred." His hand rose to brush the pockmarks on his face.

Both chiefs worried for the survival of their people. They worried that a change of allegiance would reshuffle the delicate trading partnerships of the upper Missouri. They could not afford more casualties, but neither could they afford to lose a lucrative trading partner. Captain Lewis had called them children. They were far more astute than innocent children.

Lewis sensed his mistake. "The smallpox scars our people, too. We come to all nations in peace. We come for your welfare and your increase."

Kakawisassa, chief of the Sawahaini village, raised his head. "But you come also to our enemies. You come to the Mandans and Hidatsas."

"Today they are your enemies. Your new father in Washington will make of them your friends."

Kakawisassa showed neither doubt nor belief. Another Sioux had entered the camp and scowled at this last exchange. An Arikara-Mandan alliance would undermine Sioux domination and threaten the British monopoly of trade on the northern reaches of the river. The council meeting had fallen silent. But Lewis, the negotiator, did not let discussion drop. "Travel with us to the Mandan nation. See for yourself how we will effect a peace for all nations."

More silence. Kakawisassa took his time. "Yours is a fair request. I will come with you so that the tears of my people may wash away in the river, and my people may smile in the sweet flood of spring." He lifted the pipe, took a puff, and passed it to Lewis. Lewis inhaled and replied. "It is a brave thing you do, setting foot in the land of your enemies. Let your safe return be proof of your new father's good will." The Sioux delegation rose and walked out.

The captains returned to their camp with gifts of fresh buffalo meat, squash, and corn. The aroma of roasting hump-rib wafted over the hungry men. They ate heartily as they had not eaten in days, and slept soundly by a blazing central fire. Late in the evening, several of the men departed for the Indian village. Collins, Drouillard, Pryor, and Cruzatte stayed behind, but young Shannon went with Labiche, eagerly this time.

The fire cast an eerie glow across Drouillard's dark features as he lay by the fire propped on an elbow and spoke to Collins. "You remember Louise, Johnny? Betrayal pains more than whipping. Has she so injured you that you no longer care for the caresses of a woman?"

Collins chewed off a strip of meat and swallowed before answering. "Why didn't you go with them?"

Drouillard averted his gaze, then murmured: "I have my own prickly memories." He turned back to Collins. "You can still join them, still sleep in a soft embrace. All women are not like the witch, Louise Bourgeron. Cruzatte and I will tend the fire."

John Collins could feel his organ harden. He pictured the pleasures of the night, but he still felt the sting of rejection. He shook his head and whispered: "I go if you go."

Drouillard yawned, lay back on his elbows, and laughed. "I am going to sleep."

Drouillard had the uncanny ability to fall asleep at will, but Collins lay awake for hours. He imagined the kiss of

Louise Bourgeron, the soft press of her breasts. Cruzatte would have condemned him to hellfire for the lustful ramblings of his imaginings. He fell asleep finally and awakened in a sweat in the early dawn. A buffalo robe lay over him, and a body, alive, warm, and naked, lay next to him. He felt the touch skin to skin. He rolled away out of the blankets and stood shivering in the cold air. He looked down on a mound where had slept, a sweep of silken, black hair and a round face staring at him in the dim light of the fire. It was a woman, and she lay waiting. He tried to speak, but he fumbled over words she did not understand, and she laughed. He looked for help. Cruzatte was snoring steadily. Drouillard lay with an arm outstretched, and an Indian maid draped across it. Except for the officers, the others were all absent in the Arikara village.

The girl in his blankets was speaking softly in strange, cacophonous, incomprehensible syllables. She motioned him to lie down, moved toward him. The blanket fell away from her shoulders, and he stared at the softness of her breasts, then at her eyes. She touched his arm. The brush of her hand was warm. He shivered, but not from the cold. His breath came in gasps; his chest swelled. An iciness ate into the marrow of his bones until his teeth began to chatter and his body shake. He tried to pull her up and away, but she resisted and would not go quietly. Finally, numb from the cold, not caring who she was or why she had come, he climbed back under the warm robe and, in a violent physical thrust, made passionate love, and fell off into deep, recuperative sleep.

He awakened warm and rested, when the sun was high. The Indian maiden was gone, and he wondered if he had been dreaming and she had existed at all, if she was the invention of an imagination tortured by days of excruciating pain and privation. He lay dozing pleasantly, savoring the sensations of the night. The smell of her was still in the blanket, a sweet, rancid aroma of the bear grease she used to dress her hair. He inhaled deeply, drawing the sweetness into himself, and felt himself aroused a second time. The rest of the camp was still asleep. He rose and set his weight on the injured foot. He walked without pain as he went to fetch water for breakfast.

Chapter Twenty

The Corps of Discovery left the Arikaras reluctantly. Horns and fiddles accompanied the festive departure, but many of the men were sorry to relinquish the soft buffalo robes and the sweet slumber of the village. The Arikara chief sailed with them as a delegate of peace to the Mandan nation, and the days of trudging and hauling resumed. Now winter was approaching fast. Insects had mercifully disappeared, the wind shrieked like the ghosts of tortured souls, and signs of dying were all around. Game became scarce. Some days the hunters killed one deer only, barely enough to feed eight men.

They met Indians slaughtering antelope in the river. Herders on both shores chased the struggling animals into the water where swimmers killed them easily with bare sticks. It was wet, cold, bloody work. It reminded Collins of his own fragility and that of the whole corps against the backdrop of the unknown. He was a stranger in these alien wilds, especially now with winter coming on, much like the sleek, swift antelope in water, unprepared, unadapted, and easily destroyed. He mentioned the thought to Drouillard, who agreed solemnly to consider the morale of his fellows and not to speak his fears. It irked Collins at times that Drouillard was so placid, so unresponsive, so self-possessed. Collins disliked having to depend on the stoic Frenchman for support, yet he loved and admired the man. The Indians came to the camp that night with the fresh-killed antelope, and they feasted and sang. Labiche danced on his hands and made clownish faces to see if he could make Drouillard laugh. Drouillard snickered—Collins had hardly ever heard the sound.

The weather grew colder still. Old Cruzatte led prayers each evening. He prayed for a wind from the south to fill the sail, for health and warmth and fair weather and blind luck. No one mocked the saintly Frenchman now.

Their muscles ached, and their noses ran. They coughed from the damp and cold. There was always at least one man on the keelboat, too sick to pole or pull, even to stand. Drouillard, Collins, and a few who maintained their health took turns ranging ahead each day to hunt, prepare camp, and light a welcoming fire. The men came off the tow nearly frozen. They stripped off their wet clothing and wrapped themselves in dry blankets and soft buffalo robes and huddled miserably around the fire. Sleep did not come easily in the open where the wind blew choking smoke over the men in their slumber, and the cold river threatened to undermine the camp. During the day, sandbars and sawyers barred the way. At night, coughing and wheezing interrupted kind sleep. The wind did shift in answer to Cruzatte's implacable prayers, but it was as frigid as the ice in the lowest tier of hell.

They passed cornfields and abandoned villages. Indians began to appear on the shore in small, tight groups. One man was missing two fingers. He had cut them off out of grief for his dead father. An Englishman named McCracken accompanied him, and there was a third man, who did not reveal himself, from the British Fort St. Peter, the North West Company's post. The Indian had three handsome women with him. Labiche and others took note.

Matootonha, the first village of the Mandans, came into view like a medieval castle out of a mist. It was an impressive sight, hovering on a high palisade fifty feet above the river. The sun's slim rays slanted obliquely over the round roofs and dusted the hump-like silhouettes with pink and gold. Collins and the corps looked up wondrously from the shadowy shore like sinners at the gates of heaven.

Captain Clark took a small contingent and climbed the embankment to meet with the chief. Lewis waited with the corps below. Collins kindled a weak fire and stewed some meat. It was a thankless task because there were neither trees nor ample driftwood to burn. Each man nursed his own grim apprehension. Would they be welcome with the Mandans as with the Arikaras? Or would the glimmer of friendship snuff out abruptly, and the Indians threaten like the Sioux and force them to retreat? Would the captains stop here for the winter or push ahead into the teeth of the oncoming cold?

They feared for Captain Clark. "Looks like a starvin' horse, all ribs and pointy haunches." Hall stated what they all knew. "He's wasting. Doesn't eat enough to maintain himself."

Collins volunteered: "Eats his ration like everyone else, but vomits it back up."

"He needs sleep, that's all." This from John Colter.

"He needs a warm quiet lodge and God's blessing." They no longer ignored Cruzatte.

Clark returned from the village pale and worried. "My stomach churns. They are offended. I could not eat." He downed a dose of Dr. Rush's pills that the men called thunderbolts because they produced explosive, immediate results. He sent Lewis back to explain his refusal and warned: "There are Englishmen here. They watch us." Lewis went into the village with tobacco and gifts and the message of peace and prosperity that he had recited to the Osages and Arikaras. He returned and ordered the expedition to move on.

Hall and others objected loudly: "We passin' them by . . . I don't believe it . . . with the smell of snow on the north wind

218

and ice formin' in the shallows."

Howard concurred. "Can't steer the boat when ice stops the rudder. Where we goin' to find shelter on this barren plain in the dead of winter?"

Each man had an opinion. Drouillard quietly stated the obvious. "The captain looks for wood to build and to burn. There is none here. We could stay, but we would freeze."

"We had good wood in the bottom camp four days ago and no more since."

"The captains are too stubborn to retrace our steps."

"So they push us until we drop, until Clark himself is thin as a thorn . . . with six men sick, and ten more weak and brittle as drought grass. We'll be winterin' on block ice in the middle of the river with stiff frozen sheets for cover, or buried and dead under ten feet of snow."

They came to a second village, Rooptahee, smaller than the first, then a third, Mahawha, and still there was no wood. At Mahawha, where they rested overnight, the prairie caught fire. Now the corps were glad for their boats and put off into the river to escape the flames. The Indians in their bobbing bullboats joined them.

" 'Tis devil's work! No hellfire ever spread so fast!" Cruzatte stood in the bow, squinting with his one eye at the conflagration that lit the sky. "It means animals will flee, that we'll have salt pork and rodent to eat. It means there will not be grass enough for buffalo and elk."

Captain Clark finally called a halt, and they made camp and set up negotiations. They hired an interpreter, René Jusseaume, who had lived with the Mandans for many years. In the next few days, while the captains parleyed, Drouillard scouted the territory ahead for a site with wood enough to build winter quarters. There was none. For the first time, the expedition retreated back downriver.

They chose a flat prairie on the opposite shore from the first village. Here, there was cottonwood enough for a simple fort and the fuel to warm it. Their efforts redoubled, felling trees, chopping and splitting wood. The Indians, too, were regrouping for the winter, into smaller, more snug lodges, in the lee of the riverbank.

The air grew steadily colder. Brilliant lights appeared like ship's beacons in the night sky, and ice thickened in the river like logs in a jam. Drouillard, Collins, and Colter ranged out thirty miles to hunt enough meat to supply the hungry men. Word went out to the hunters to hurry back before the freeze sealed the river's flow. The hunt was good—thirty-two deer, twelve elk, and a buffalo—but the river's flow was slowing to a trickle, the hard ice swelling.

On their way back to camp, the hunters met three chiefs. They were grave, haughty men and explained to Drouillard in signs that their people were in danger. The Sioux had attacked an Arikara peace delegation and stolen their horses. The enemy had moved north past the Cheyenne River and threatened the Mandans. The chiefs had come to alert the captains and beg military support with gifts of corn and fresh meat.

Drouillard escorted the chiefs to the captains' shelter. Black Cat, chief of Rooptahe, told an ominous tale. "There are men among us who say you come from the Sioux to destroy us, and seven traders from the River Assiniboin and the North West man, Lassiter, who denounce you. Even Laroque, the Frenchman, makes gifts to us of British flags and medals." Captain Lewis went back with the chief to his village to reassure him.

One morning, when the sun's rays cracked through the clouds, shimmering ice encased every branch of every tree.

Every rock, every blade of grass sparkled. The whole landscape glittered like a thousand mirrors. Ice weighed on the
tents. The canvas, moldy and worn from hard daily use,
ripped, and tent poles cracked. Dry kindling for fire was impossible to find. No longer could anyone sleep in the open.
Yet winter huts were not finished. They had felled trees,
dragged the heavy lengths through mud and over ice,
chopped and sawed until their backs ached. Now, they
moved into the shelters before they were complete and dug
deep into the frozen ground for mud to daub the openings
between the logs and seal out the biting wind. Their fingers
froze. Their knuckles turned blue from the cold. It snowed,
and they used the snow to seal the cracks. Shields sprained
his back. Pryor dislocated his shoulder. Georges Drouillard
cut his right hand, and McNeal sliced his leg with an axe. The
crowded huts were dark and smoky, but they were protected
from the brutal wind, and they were warm. During the next
week, two feet of snow fell.

Collins was standing guard near the gate, when he heard
the cry. A robed Indian stood on the opposite shore, a mes-
senger who was signing frantically, in the manner universal to
the tribes. Collins could not interpret the signs and ran for
Drouillard to translate. A nub of fear anchored in Collins's
throat as Drouillard sent him running for the captains. The
news was grim. The Sioux had attacked, and men of the
village had been killed. More frightening was the inescapable
conclusion: the Sioux would attack again. Where? When?

It was an opportunity William Clark could have prayed
for. He called for volunteers. John Collins and twenty-two
others stepped up promptly. They marched in ranks to the
village and offered to mount an attack. But the Mandan
chiefs refused to fight in winter and invited the captains to
talk while the corps retired to various lodges.

John Collins had never visited an earth lodge. He followed Labiche who ducked into the entry passage of a nearby lodge. They stepped around the windbreak into the dim interior. The winter lodge was smaller than those he had seen on the bluff above, but it was firmly built, and warm. A fire blazed in a pit beneath a central smoke hole. The air smelled deliciously of roasting meat and steaming vegetables. Two dogs growled. Collins rubbed his eyes as they adjusted to the dimness. Buffalo robes and dressed skins covered cots, and grass mats warmed the hard clay floor. Tools, weapons, and baskets of corn, squash, and beans hung from beams. A gourd in the shape of a child's doll lay on the floor. Children's laughter filled the air.

This was home to a family. Collins had been too long in the company of rough men. He had not heard a child laugh for a year. It was a pleasant sound and reminded him of brothers and sisters and the close bonds of blood, of his mother, and the humble touch of his sister's hand.

He blinked. A harsh voice sounded, and peals of laughter stopped abruptly. He stepped back as an old woman turned a hard black stare on him. Her eyes shot daggers like shards of ice. But a young woman straightened and smiled. A boy gave a whoop, leaped aside, grabbed a small bow, and pulled back the string in challenge. A little girl scrambled to snatch up her doll.

Labiche grinned, nodded to the forbidding old woman, and mumbled to Collins: "Their man is absent. Pay respects to the old woman. The lodge belongs to her." John Collins nodded dutifully to the haughty old hag, but shrank back from the steely stare.

The younger woman thrust her hand forward, palm up, at Collins. Impulsively, he took the hand in his and smiled back.

"Now you've done it." Labiche's harsh voice intruded.

Collins turned dumbly as Labiche explained: "You don't take their hand without giving them something in return . . . a knife, a mirror, beads, a button, especially one who's young and pretty. She wants a favor. Better tell her you've got a girl back home and you're marching off to war come spring." He pushed past the old woman to warm his hands at the fire.

"I can't tell her anything." But it didn't matter. John Collins held the hand gently. It was soft, like velvet to the touch, warm and slightly moist, and sent a tingling sensation the length of his spine. She had bright, liquid eyes and even features in a round, cheerful face. When she spoke, her voice was lilting. Collins grinned stupidly back, wishing he could communicate what he felt, wishing for all the world that he had listened when Drouillard tried to teach him the meaning of the Indian signs.

The old woman scowled harder as the girl came toward him. She wore a buckskin sheath belted narrowly at the waist and falling gracefully over the curve of her hips. A string of beads lay against two small mounds of breast. Her long, raven hair hung loosely over her shoulders. He repressed a sudden urge to touch it and held happily to her hand, enjoying the smooth feel of the dainty palm until she laughed and drew her hand away and spoke again in a flood of sounds, striking her breast with her index finger.

"That's her name," Labiche interrupted impatiently.

She reached up and touched one of the pewter buttons that held Collins's linsey shirt closed at the neck. It was black and grimy from the river mud because he had never polished it. On impulse he took his knife, cut the threads that held it, and gave it to her. Her eyes flashed, and he knew she was pleased when she laughed again lightly. He enjoyed the sound of her laughter, like the plucked strings of a harp. He laughed, too. It seemed the natural thing to do. Then he took his fist and hit his own breast and spoke his name. He felt foolish and decided that it didn't matter whether or not she understood. It mattered that he please the old woman. He took another knife from his belt and handed it to the her. The old woman barely cracked a toothless smile.

The girl repeated his name softly several times, then replied in another unintelligible onslaught, a splattering of syllables that he could neither remember nor pronounce, but he sensed instinctively that she had welcomed him. She turned away and stooped to ladle a bowl of broth and handed it to him. He thought how she moved gracefully as a doe, and she might be named for a deer. She sat on a grass mat by the stone perimeter of the fire pit and motioned for him to sit opposite on the puncheon bench in front of the fire screen. The stew was made of boiled meat and corn cooked in a fatty substance. He picked out the chunks on the point of his knife, swallowed them nearly whole, tipped up the bowl, and drank the liquid. It was hot and delicious. He was very hungry.

Collins didn't hear the call to arms. He was devouring his third bowlful. Labiche had to walk over and kick him. Collins fumbled for his rifle and scrambled to his feet. Without taking his eyes off the girl, he addressed the old woman: "May I come back tomorrow?"

The old woman grunted, but she did not frown. She could not have understood, but it didn't matter. He was coming anyway. The young woman had dropped her eyes submissively.

When they were in the open, Labiche snapped at him: "What did you say that for?"

Collins shrugged. "Say what? They didn't understand and neither did I."

"Yes, you did understand, and so did that girl, but not in words."

Collins didn't answer. His imagination was far away, in Maryland, in the home of his boyhood, with his mother and sisters and brothers gathered around and the smell of apples baking and meat roasting. He was thinking of the long, snowy winters of his youth when he lived with a family like the one in that Indian lodge, like the one he had known before his Army days, before his mother had died and his father had withered, a family with bonds of blood and brotherhood, and traditions of co-operation and caring, the young for the old and the old for the youngest. He mumbled to himself: "If we do not have to fight, if the captains give me leave. . . ." But he was dreaming.

Labiche slapped him with cold reality. "You don't even know her name."

John Collins looked back. There were twenty, maybe thirty lodges nestled in the river bottom, and each brown hump was exactly identical with its neighbor. The village was a maze. He had come only twenty paces from her door, and he could not find her again.

It grew colder still. The Sioux retreated. They did not have to fight. But the forthright offer to repel the Mandans' enemies earned for the corps the trust and respect of the village chiefs. It earned for each man the friendship and hospitality of the Mandan people.

John Collins did not sleep well that night. He tossed in thin blankets on the hard surface of his bunk while prickly questions tormented his brain. Had it been so long? Had he forgotten what a home was like? Had he come to regard all members of the female sex as spiteful and selfish? This girl did not disguise her feelings. There was a humble, refreshing innocence about the Indian lodge and the young woman who lived there. Her openness inspired confidence and trust. It inspired in him a desire to protect and shield. He could not

deny the warmth that filled him when he looked at her, and he
made up his mind to visit again in the morning. He went
about his chores with her image in front of his eyes. The
pressure in his breast grew until he could not eat, as if a tight
cord had coiled around his heart and someone, somewhere,
was drawing it in ever more tightly, like the inevitable,
rhythmic heave of the tow on the heavy boat against the current of the river. He was the weight on the end of the rope that
was pulling him like a stubborn colt, in a direction he did not
want to go. He could not resist the pull because it was powerful and persistent, and the girl in the lodge was beautiful
and warm. He would ask Labiche where to find her and hope
Labiche didn't broadcast news of his passion all over the
camp.

Chapter Twenty-One

Alexander Heney arrived at the Awatixa Hidatsa village on the Knife River days before Lassiter. Heney had come from Fort Assiniboin in the Canadian north, and he had traded with the Mandans and Hidatsas before. Because the Sioux blocked trade from the south, the two neighboring tribes depended on English traders from Canada for guns and whiskey, powder and ball. The Sioux discouraged contact with the southern tribes. The restriction of trade enhanced the profits for the Hudson's Bay and North West Companies at their bases in Canada.

Lassiter had come from the camps of the Sioux and Arikaras, enemies of the Mandans. He had hoped to intercept Alexander Heney on his way into the village and enter as one of the party from Fort Assiniboine, but Heney had arrived early. Now Lassiter tread warily into the village, alone. The sentries called to him to halt, took his rifle, knife, and tomahawk, and marched him forward under guard. Fortunately, Alexander Heney himself was in council with the chief, when they brought Lassiter in. Heney spoke up for his fellow North Wester. "He is one of ours, a friend. I will vouch for him."

"He wears Arikara moccasins and carries a Sioux tomahawk." Black Moccasin, the chief, was not fooled. The sentry sat him down on the cold perimeter of the lodge but did not return his weapons. When Heney got up to leave a few hours later, he picked up Lassiter's rifle and knife. The chief kept the tomahawk in payment for Lassiter's freedom. Shivering with cold and humiliation, Lassiter followed Heney out.

When they were beyond hearing of the chief's lodge, Heney confronted his comrade. "You're lucky to be left with your hair. What are you doing here?"

"There's important news. The Americans have purchased Louisiana. They're here on the Missouri."

"I know. They arrived before you. It's a miracle they've come this far. At least they've banished Emperor Napoléon from the continent of North America." Heney dismissed Lassiter's account with impatience and disgust.

Lassiter protested: "You trust too easily. The American presence here will establish a claim to this place. The Spaniards understand. They've sent soldiers to stop them."

Alexander Heney laughed. His voice rang with cynicism. "And what has an army got our Spanish friends, except expense and waste? We're a thousand miles from the farthest settlement. Armed Spanish soldiers are far worse a threat to us than these bumbling Americans. Look at them. They are sick and illiterate. They scratch and sneeze. Our former colonies are nothing but a bickering bunch of rascal states, untutored, undisciplined, unsettled in their government."

"They will compete with us for trade."

"They are forty men, with one boatload of supplies, a few guns and gadgets to impress the natives, some tobacco, some whiskey. They'll run out of powder and lead. They must survive in total wilderness without reinforcement, among unknown and unpredictable natives, in the dead of winter." Heney was laughing.

"Sandoval wants me to destroy them."

"Who's Sandoval?"

"A Spaniard in the pay of Clamorgan. He has spies with the Americans. You do know Clamorgan?"

"That old pirate! Ask him where is his army of soldiers.

Ask him who will pay for his spies. Not me." Heney snickered cynically. "And the Cheyennes tell me that the Pawnees wiped out a starving group of Spaniards months ago. They brought Spanish guns when they came to trade. I believe them."

"I didn't know."

"Your Spaniards were more likely in the service of Napoléon and his henchmen. I've no love for Frenchmen. The French are notorious enemies of England." The outburst silenced Lassiter, and he bit back his tongue. Heney was still speaking: "And this man Sandoval, where is he now with all his spies and soldiers?"

"He left me in the Arikara village."

"His spies have either deserted, stayed behind with the Sioux, or joined the American brigade because they wanted to survive." Snickering, Heney shook his head in disbelief and dismissed Lassiter with a casual wave of his hand. "These Americans say they're going to the western ocean. They must pass the war-like Blackfeet, the mountain ranges, the rapids of the Columbia River. They've neither adequate boats nor horses nor provisions nor accurate maps, and they'll get no help from us. I'll see to that. We should pity them not punish them."

Lassiter sucked in his lips. He had made the same argument to Sandoval in the Sioux villages. Now he said nothing.

Heney continued: "Go back to your Arikara squaw. Pretend you never heard of Sandoval. If Clamorgan complains, if you ever see him again, tell him we're devoted subjects of the British Crown and loyal employees of the North West Company, that we protect British interests and British trade, that we will not be indebted to the throne of Spain which is only a thin veil for the French Emperor Napoléon. As for Sandoval, if he turns up, avoid him, disable him." He did not add *kill him*.

Lassiter changed the subject. "How many pelts will you ship next spring?"

"Several hundred bales."

Lassiter bit his lip nervously and drew blood. "I will not have as large a supply."

"That's because you dabble in politics."

Lassiter writhed at Heney's insinuation that he had neglected business and the true interests of Mother England that he should turn a profit by every available means. Lassiter could trick with alcohol or bribe with guns. Drunk, the Indians would trade away their life's sustenance, mortgage the welfare of their families. Guns would encourage them to make war. But Lassiter's wife was Arikara. The Arikaras were a proud and industrious people, good trappers who could easily replenish his inventory if pressured. They rejected the whiskey that made them foolish and the guns that made them violent. Lassiter himself had encouraged them not to drink. Finally he spat an angry reply back at Heney: "I trade guns so they can hunt and protect themselves. I do not trade whiskey or the future of my children."

Heney nodded. "As you wish, but don't come to me when the company slashes your allotment."

It was a powerful warning. Lassiter fell silent. He had been out of touch, too attentive to Sandoval and his winning words. The real threat was here with the North West Company he served. He could be cut off too easily. They had arrived at Heney's lodge. Lassiter stepped aside and held the tent skin back for Heney to enter first. It was a gesture without humility, smacking of assumed superiority. Lassiter refused the brandy Heney offered, lay back on the hard clay floor of the lodge, and rested his head on his hands. He had much to contemplate.

Chapter Twenty-Two

John Collins was up early. A restlessness churned through his veins. He was going visiting. He fueled the cooking fires and chopped ice to melt over the fire. When it came to a boil, he added meal and let the brew thicken. He spitted chunks of fat venison. He collected the dripping fat in a pan, poured it into the soup with herbs and spring salt, and turned the meat until it was brown. Men drifted in from their chores. Each had his preference. Shannon ate his meat almost raw. Pryor liked it charred. There were always complaints. "Too hot!" "Boiled grass, if you ask me!" "Sand from the river!" "Let a bloody Irishman cook an' he boils it all to piss!" This last remark was aimed directly at Collins, and he retorted angrily: "I cook what you shoot, same as Thompson and Warner! You don't hit anything. You shoot grass. I cook grass." He held out the ladle to Labiche who voiced the loudest complaint. "You cook! I hunt!"

Sergeant Ordway heard the commotion and headed off an argument. "François Labiche, go eat with Warner's mess." Warner was the worst of the three cooks.

Labiche snapped to attention and saluted. "Request permission to eat with the *engagés,* sir." It was what he had wanted all along, to eat with the Frenchman who knew how to spice a dish. Ordway's cold glare leveled Labiche. "Permission denied."

The cry went up when breakfast was finished and Collins was warming his hands at the fire. He heard yells first, wild, furious alien shouts, like war cries, that sent fear threading down the length of his spine. Hoofs thundered outside the stockade, and Indians swooped back and forth in front of the gate, waving weapons like banners in a parade. Collins recognized Big White, chief of Matootonha village, and a great crowd of warriors. A vision flashed before him of his captains and comrades and Drouillard, his mentor, scalped and riddled with arrows, as the Indians charged the fort. He ran for his gun, checked his powder horn and pouch of lead balls. Drouillard came running with Captain Clark and Sergeants Ordway and Gass. Hooting, yelling, signing madly, the Indians drew up in a cloud of snorting, prancing horseflesh. All was confusion until Drouillard jumped up on a stump and shouted: "Buffalo on the plains!"

A cheer went up. Hats sailed in the air. Old Cruzatte whooped like an Indian and kicked up his heels. Howard dropped his dram of whiskey. Buffalo meant feasting and dancing, warm hides for bedding, hump-rib and steak instead of boiled cornmeal, salt pork, and dried soup. Everyone was running to collect arms for the hunt except Bratton and Shields who watched enviously. They had to tend the forge. Even old Cruzatte volunteered, but he was ordered back to guard the camp with Corporal Warfington's contingent, because he couldn't see far enough to shoot accurately.

The group gathered as the Indians on horseback galloped away. Drouillard, Hall, Colter, Whitehouse, Goodrich, and Howard crowded the captains like eager children competing for places on a team. William Clark shouted to enforce order: "Warner, Collins, collect the guns . . . the guns! McNeal, bring sledges for the meat. Labiche, get the butchering knives. Where's Jusseaume?" Clark needed an interpreter.

Jusseaume rushed up, panting. "Calmly, calmly, no rush. They'll share the meat. It is the custom. Go softly. *Doucement.* The approach is as important as the chase."

His counsel fell on deaf ears. A buffalo hunt was active, thrilling sport after the drudgery of chopping wood and hauling boats. The men raced ahead, shouting, tramping noisily over the frozen ground, vying with each other to over-take the Indians. They came to a sudden halt. A line of thirty mounted warriors, their faces painted black for war, guns raised, arrows strung in their bows, blocked the path.

Hall raised his musket. "No bloody savage gonna keep me from shootin' my share of meat for the winter." Others fol-lowed suit.

With a cruel swipe, Jusseaume knocked Hall's gun from his hands. "Fools! You'll scare the game. These are the Black Mouths, enforcers . . . you call them police." His eyes locked on Captain Clark. "Tell your men. They must follow the hunt leader, single-file, with humility and gratitude for the sacrifice of these brave animals. The buffalo are the gift of Old Woman Above who will reward us with plenty, if we show respect, but who will deny us and leave us to starve, if we are wasteful and careless. That is the rule. Obey, or these warriors will stop you."

William Clark took in the situation at a glance and shouted above the din: "Go quietly! Obey them as you would me! We'll stampede the whole herd, if we descend on them like a pack of wolves! Then no one will eat, and we'll shiver through the winter! Worse the Indians will blame us for their empty stomachs!" He paused, red with anger and ended with a threat: "Help where you can! If any man interferes with the proper conduct of the hunt, I will personally administer one hundred lashes on his naked back!" A naked back in the freezing cold was a terrifying thought. They quieted at that, drew up in a tight line, and marched off double time after the Indians.

The Mandans began the hunt like an army drill. The

mounted hunters went first. They approached the herd in a semicircle, from upwind, clinging to ravines and wallows, so as not to reveal themselves and startle the shaggy beasts. They carried long, sturdy lances, bows, and quivers filled with arrows. They rode small, agile horses that worked, instinctively, like hunting dogs, senses exquisitely tuned to the wild impulses of their prey. Their riders concentrated intently on every hint of movement and breath of air. As soon as the buffalo caught the scent and bolted, the horses leaped from halt to gallop, closing a circle around the herd. It was not a free-for-all chase. Each man rode two or three revolutions while the huge beasts milled, and he selected the animals he would kill. The sick or lame were chosen first, cut from the herd, and slaughtered. After ample meat was secured, faster, stronger animals were put down. That was when the sport began and the chase was on. The Indians vied with each other in acts of daring. They would torment an enraged bull before administering the final blow.

It was a display of horsemanship like Collins had never before witnessed. The Indians darted bareback, with only a thin blanket for a saddle and a strip of leather for a bit, in and out of the lumbering herd. Their mounts matched their pace and stride to the speeding buffalo, horse's nose at the buffalo's shoulder, exactly parallel, so as to assure the best shot. Legs wrapped tightly, the Indians dropped reins, rose on their knees, arched their backs, pulled back their bows almost to breaking. One false step and they would be trampled and gored. Some shot their arrows powerfully home. Others drove lances deeply into the hump. Sometimes wounded animals, two thousand pounds of muscle and nerve, turned on their pursuers. Riders anticipated their sudden challenge and let fly arrows again and again until the huge animals sank on their haunches from exhaustion or loss of blood or until a mighty thrust struck the soft heart. Collins gaped in awe as he watched an Indian jump on the hump of a raging bull to strike the fatal blow with the tomahawk at the back of the head. It was a feat of incredible agility and audacity. For the whites, it was madness. For the Indian, it meant prestige, recognition, pride and the adulation of his peers.

The whites could not match the co-ordination or athleticism of the Mandans. Their muskets were not powerful enough to kill a bison with one shot. They lacked the physical stamina and instinct to race after a ton of shaggy beast, and no white man would dare stand face to face with an angry buffalo. They lagged far behind.

Collins's hands were so cold it was nearly impossible to shoot. He dismounted to steady his aim and shoot his first animal. He fired. It did not fall. He reloaded and aimed another shot directly between the eyes. The ball struck, but the thick-skulled bull shook it off like a ticklish fly, rose up, and charged. Collins ran in panic. Drouillard was shouting: "Not the head, shoot the heart!" Drouillard's gun went off with a deafening crash. The ground trembled when the animal fell. Collins's whole body shook, and his heart was pounding like the blast from a cannon. He stood heaving and watching his own breath spill out like smoke from a billowing fire into the frigid air. Drouillard came up and struck the final blow and put a hand on Collins's shoulder to steady him. The next time, he aimed for the heart, and dispatched two bulls and a cow.

The hunt was nearly over, the buffalo herd had fled from the bloody business, and every man was killing the wounded animals that still lived and struggled. The Indians began the butchering with gusto. They cut out first the liver, then the tongue. The liver they ate raw; the tongue they reserved for the man who had made the specific kill. The rest of the animal was free for the taking to whomever assumed the hard labor of butchering. Collins met Jusseaume licking his lips and holding out a generous slice for him to taste. "Liver, the best part." Collins gagged at the dripping blood.

A horde of people—squaws, old men, older children—descended on the scene with knives and axes, sledges and pack horses and dogs to complete the work the hunters had begun. They worked quickly, before the precious meat froze. Their implements were in bad repair. Some were dull, others broken or sharpened so often that the blades were thin and would not slice the thick hide. Some used the sharp brown flint of the Knife River shores. They started at the top of the hump, sliced out the hump-rib, then cut open the length of the spine and peeled off the wet hide to the right and left. They worked swiftly lest the hide freeze and stiffen. It was brutal, bloody work.

More women arrived with dog sledges to collect the meat and carry it back to camp. They sang as they worked, laughed, and teased. There was no resentment, no shirking, no complaining of the intense cold. Young and old alike exerted the very best of their endurance and skill.

When darkness started to fall, the men lit fires to light the plain and repel nocturnal predators. They toiled on until cold or exhaustion slowed them. Some built crude shelters to store and guard what was left. Nothing remained for the scavengers.

When the captains came to collect the members of the corps, many could not be found. Their muscles ached and they were numb from the cold, hungry and tired, but they had ranged far and wide helping the Indians butcher and pack.

John Collins had started back on foot, tugging his heavily laden sled behind him. He was passing the carcass of a huge bull, where the Indians were still at work, when he recognized the Indian girl from the old woman's lodge. He was surprised he recognized her at all, bundled as she was from head to foot in skins and furs. It wasn't her face or form, but her movements and the sound of her laughter that attracted him. She was happily at work, her hands and forearms and the front of her tunic bloody and stained. A fur hat had anchored her black hair tightly behind her ears, but long wisps had escaped in the blustery wind and swept across her face. She looked up. The twilight threw a gentle glow across her brow. He remembered the eyes, dark, bright, and alive with life. She brushed away the hair from her face and waved. He swore he heard her shout: "John!" She had remembered his name.

Collins called back eagerly. He heard his voice crack stupidly in the brittle air.

She held a thin, dull blade and was slicing a flank into smaller chunks for a dog to carry. He took out his own knife and held it out to her. She took it and gave him back her own. He stammered: "Bratton will reinforce and sharpen the blade." He ran his finger over the blade to illustrate his words. She nodded and went back to work. He looked around. The old grandmother, black eyes hard as flint, was staring at him. She motioned for him to help.

Captain Clark saw her gesture and called out: "Collins! You have my leave! Help them!" Collins missed the curfew that night. So did Labiche and Shannon, and stolid Drouillard who had never missed a curfew.

The temperature dropped quickly. The cold, like a tide, rose in Collins's veins, but the Indians seemed impervious to the temperature. He worked frantically to keep warm until the meat was loaded and the Indians began breaking apart the bones. Later, they would carve the bones into hoes and scrapers, spoons, and drinking vessels. The skulls they placed over the portals of the lodges or added them to medicine bundles to bring good fortune. The night was dark when they started back to Matootonha. It was a cold, arduous struggle to bring in the kill by horse, by dog, by their own strong backs.

It started to snow, and a three-quarter moon reflected soft, silver light on the powdery snow. Collins trudged behind the young woman. He could see her form clearly in the moonlight. Wrapped in skins, she bent under the weight of her pack and leaned into the wind with supple grace and an amazing lightness of step. Gently, with a stick, she prodded two dogs.

Suddenly, she looked back, caught his eye, and laughed. The sound sang out like a church bell. She reached down and scooped a handful of snow and, with a jump and a yip like a playful pup, tossed it high in the air. The wind scattered the feathery flakes and blew them back into his face. Her laughter pealed merrily as he shook the snow from his eyes. She tossed more and ran ahead. Collins jumped to the chase and ran after. The cold flakes seemed soft on his skin, the pack lighter, the moon brighter, and the sparkling snow a dusting from the gods. He was laughing euphorically. His blood surged as much from the joy of contest as from a visceral, sexual attraction. He caught up to her, tossed his own snowy flakes. She ducked but not soon enough, and the snow blew glittering silver crystals on the frigid updraft across her laughing eyes. It frosted the wisps of her hair and settled like a halo over her hat. He caught sight of her face. Her smile was radiant. His hand rose to brush the tiny flakes from her brow. He would have kissed her, but the old woman was glaring. There were too many people. Still the long walk to the village passed like the blissful ending of a fairy tale.

When they arrived at her lodge, the old grandmother stood like a pillar of stone, guarding the door. The girl went in. Collins waited for a grudging nod to enter, but the flint-eyed old lady, tough and heartless as a general, voiced a sharp order and stopped him in his tracks. After a pause, she motioned him forward.

The girl was inside the entry, shaking the snow from her robe. It was warm inside, and the robe had begun to drip. She dropped it where she stood, and the old woman hung it over a post to dry. John Collins was staring. The girl wore a loose skin tunic that molded subtly to the contours of her body. Soft white fur at the neck reflected the fire's glow on the smooth skin of her face. Collins followed her avidly with his eyes. The old woman walked between them to the fire, ladled some hot broth into a clay bowl, and offered it to him. He hesitated, then drank. The liquid scalded his mouth. For the first time he realized how cold and hungry he was. Gradually he became aware of other people in the lodge: an older man, two middle-aged women probably his wives, and three or four children, and the girl. A baby was asleep in a cradleboard propped at the edge of the central fire pit. He wondered if the child was hers. She seemed so young.

The girl motioned for him to leave his coat on a post and sit at the perimeter of the fire. The girl sat opposite. She touched her breast with an index finger and spoke. It was a sweep of vowels and consonants that he could not understand, but he sensed innately that she was telling him her name and repeated the sounds. The children giggled and the old woman frowned, but the girl laughed and so did he.

The old woman reminded him of his own grandmother who policed the raucous Collins's household with a stout locust cane. The children ran from her in terror when they misbehaved, but, when they were good, she told wonderful stories, and they would gather around her by the hour, listening. She told them how, as a young girl, she had arrived on

the Maryland shore in a sailing ship and how lonely she had
been until she had met a Delaware girl her own age. He
thought how he had arrived in this vast sea of prairie and how
he would have been lost in the cold and dark except for this
girl. And he thought of his sister, Sarah, whose suitor came to
visit, and how his grandmother had stared with hostile suspicion. He knew this girl reciprocated his feelings. He could tell
by her gaze and the subtle motions of her form. He could feel
the force of his own desire pounding within his chest while
the eyes of the grandmother glared down.

The girl rose and spitted some of the fresh meat to roast
and placed a pot over the coals to boil. They sat in silence
until the meat was cooked and she served him from a great
horn bowl. He ate ravenously and drank his fill of steaming
broth and marveled how she, too, must be hungry but waited
patiently with the other women until he and the man had
finished.

He watched her eat, his mind filled with anticipation for
the long hours of the night. Where would he sleep? Would she
invite him to her bed? In the end, the grandmother showed
him a bare spot of hard clay floor and placed her own pallet
between him and the girl.

He did not immediately fall sleep. His thoughts ranged to
the night at Sawahaini village when the Arikara woman had
crawled under his blankets. He listened to the breathing of
the dogs, the snoring of the grandmother, the grunts and
gasps of the man and his wife. He studied the interior of the
lodge, the beams, the pallets, the stones encircling the pit,
and the strange bundle that hung in the place of honor above
the firebreak. He counted the stars that shone through the
smoke hole. His eyes burned when the smoke blew back on a
downdraft. He coughed, but no one awakened. He craved
sleep. He could just perceive the outline of the girl against the

background of the fire, and he studied the rise and fall of her breathing. He counted each swelling intake of air, and sleep crept up on him finally like the soothing fingers of a healer, near dawn.

He slept late and awakened to the hum of human activity. The man was busy passing sticks through a hole in a piece of bone, straightening arrow shafts. The women were cutting meat into strips and hanging them over racks to dry. The old woman was skimming the fat from a boiling pot. The girl pounded cooked meat into fine powder for pemmican. The dogs were everywhere, begging for scraps, and the children chased them away. The girl stopped when she saw him and handed him a cup of broth. She looked furtively at the grandmother, who nodded and handed her a packet wrapped in doeskin. She held it out to him. He took it and unwrapped it carefully. It contained his old knife and his button. Disappointment seized him, a weight on his heart that pulled him deep down as the ecstasy of yesterday had raised him up. He said nothing, ate, drank, paid his respects, and left.

The rejection stung. He walked ponderously the four miles back to Fort Mandan. Drouillard would know what it all meant. But the first person he met was Labiche who was hard at work, slicing meat and bragging about a new conquest. Drouillard had not yet returned. Collins took out his knife and joined the butchering. Gradually his story spilled out.

Labiche sympathized. "A knife and a button, it was not payment enough. Ask Jusseaume."

He asked Jusseaume. "Her father is Stands in the River. He owns the Snowy Owl bundle, powerful medicine. The grandmother is the daughter of Furred Hat, a chief, and this girl you speak of was married to Raven's Wing, one of the warriors the Sioux killed. The child is hers."

"What is her name?"

"Laughing Water." Jusseaume explained: "She is free to choose another, but he must meet the price. She has not rejected you, Private Collins. You were part of the group that wanted to avenge her brother whom the Sioux killed, but the gifts you offered are not enough. If you want her to be your wife, you will need horses and fine robes. She cannot be had cheaply. This is their way. It is for the good of the family and the clan."

John Collins stared open-mouthed. A wife! Here? Now? When he must leave with the expedition come spring? It was too much like buying a slave.

The Frenchman continued blithely: "She comes of a good family. That is why they demand valuable gifts."

Collins stammered: "I have no horses, and the only robe I possess is stiff with age and full of holes." He walked away with a sinking heart.

Jusseaume called after him: "It is not so impossible, if you do not despair."

For a week, Collins did not go back to the village. He dragged somberly about the fort and stood by as other men went out regularly. Hall, Shannon, Potts, even Drouillard and righteous Ordway visited women of the village. Sergeant Ordway was even the cause of a domestic quarrel when the jealous husband came to camp with murder in his eyes.

Whitehouse and Warner returned one morning mildly drunk and leading a horse. They had won the animal in a game of chance. They laughed and congratulated each other until Captain Lewis confronted them. "How, gentlemen, do you expect to feed the beast? We have no forage for a horse." When the two men could not answer, Lewis muttered: "I suggest you give it back or turn it loose." But they did not give it back. They traded the horse for two exquisitely tanned buffalo robes.

An idea jelled slowly in Collins's mind. Was it possible for him to win enough horses and robes to impress the old grandmother? Whitehouse and Warner gambled and won, but he, John Collins, had always been an unlucky gambler. He avoided the village now like a chastised child. Still the girl consumed his imaginings like a ripening fruit, held just beyond reach, made more desirable each day by the thought of its sweetness. John Collins could not erase his desire for the woman, Laughing Water.

Chapter Twenty-Three

John Collins's restlessness did not go unnoticed. His cooking deteriorated. Sergeant Pryor assigned him to saw wood for sledges. His axe nearly sliced his foot. They sent him out to hunt. He aimed and missed. He couldn't sleep at night, and he would walk outside to count stars and wander in the snow, talking and laughing to himself, and come in numb from the cold. Drouillard found him once by the light of the moon, pawing the snow like a playful colt, and thought he was drunk and led him back to his bunk and tucked him in like a naughty child. Sergeant Pryor shook his head. "He's in love." Even dour Drouillard chuckled at that. Another time, Sergeant Ordway found him loitering outside the gates without a hat. Ordway upbraided him. "Your ears are white. Cover them. They're freezing." Collins shrugged him off. Ordway had to order him to wear a hat.

Captain Clark summoned the sergeants to discuss the problem. "Keep him busy." "Wear down his horniness." "Confine him to camp." "Send him to hunt." It was Nathaniel Pryor who suggested the most creative solution. "We could buy Collins a bride."

Cruzatte heard of it and objected: "Purchasing favors? . . . that's whoring."

Nathaniel Pryor disagreed: "No different than giving my sister a dowry."

Tom Howard commented cynically: "Buy her with what, a dram, two drops o' your whiskey? Coin money's no good."

Howard was right. They had nothing of value.

François Labiche, who owned a set of dice and a deck of cards, had overheard. "He could win a wife in a foot race. Haven't had a good race in a month."

"You want him to race in snowshoes? Worse than sloggin' through mud in the river." Pryor's frown was a flat dismissal, but he went off to confront Collins, while Labiche skewed his ugly face in a broad grin.

Young Shannon was sitting nearby. "You're matchmaking, Labiche. You did it to me. I laughed, but Collins won't like it."

Labiche shrugged. "I throw brush on a fire that's already burning. I make a little harmless entertainment in a dull winter camp."

Shannon's blue eyes ignited. He jumped up and took off for Sergeant Gass's mess. In minutes, news of Collins's plight and its possible remedies had spread like a grass fire to every mess in the camp. Wagers proliferated, and sexual speculation spiced every conversation.

Labiche sat alone away from the campfire, hunched, with a wide, stupid smirk spread like butter over his ugly face. He had placed his bets carefully, distributed them around the camp, and he could not lose.

Collins marched up, ablaze with anger. "François Labiche, you've made me look the fool in front of the whole expedition."

Labiche rose. He spread his hands, palms outward in front of his chest, and dropped his voice. "Because I win you pleasure and pride? It's harmless gossip. It relieves boredom, Johnny. In the end, you will love me for it, and others will love you."

"You play with me like your deck of cards. You rob me of self-respect. They're placing wagers on the workings of my heart."

"Because you wear your heart like a badge? Because you let it cloud your reason? Because you frustrate yourself with bad memories? Trust me. In the end, I will bring you luck."

An angry blush crept up Collins's neck. Like I trusted Louise Bourgeron? Labiche was right. Frustration boiled in his veins. Finally he muttered: "Tell me, Labiche, how do I regain the respect of this corps?"

Labiche smiled and reached for his dice. "With these and your lady luck."

Collins laughed. It was hard to stay angry with Labiche.

Shannon came back. He said nothing, but a suggestive smirk plastered itself like a poster over his baby face. Collins snapped at him like a weasel. "Where've you been?"

Billy Warner interrupted softly: "Have some soup, Georgie. It's hot."

Shannon took the cup and sipped, but Collins pushed Warner aside.

Warner reacted. "You blaming me now, Johnny? You drag around the camp like a sick puppy. Have I met this beauty? Has Shannon? Has Labiche?"

Collins blasted back. "Labiche saw her the day we went to fight the Sioux. We waited in the lodge. She couldn't stand the sight of an ogre like him. Gimme some soup."

Labiche let the insult dissipate. A grin still pulled at the crooked angles of his face. "I remember. The two of you tittered like nesting doves while I sat with the bear of a grandmother." He puffed out his cheeks and pounded his chest. "For a cup of soup and a siren's glance he throws away his heart. Says he met her again the day of the buffalo hunt. Was her soup better than Warner's?" Everyone laughed except Collins. Labiche winked and continued: "Just stop waking me in the night to go bring you in like a calf half-frozen in a blizzard."

Another steely silence. Collins bottled his anger, but there was an edge to his voice and he had balled his fists. "You run at the mouth, Labiche, like the mud in the river."

Labiche's good humor persisted. "But the mud smoothes over the rocks and fills the holes. It makes the way easier."

Pryor stepped up to prevent a confrontation. "Johnny, we all know how you brood. If the camp is talking, you have yourself to blame. Your attitude wears on the spirit of every man in this mess, in the whole camp. Sit." He pressed Collins to a nearby log. "Labiche, come here. I have an idea . . . but Labiche has to help, so don't provoke him. Johnny, you need horses and robes that you do not have and that you have very little hope of ever obtaining." Pryor took a breath. Collins stared morosely at his toes. Labiche's crooked grin covered the lower half of his face.

Pryor went on: "You've seen Labiche with the dice. He never loses."

Collins spat back. "And I never win."

"Because I play better than you." Labiche smacked his lips.

"Because you cheat!" Collins was yelling.

"You lie!" Labiche jumped up and reached for his knife.

Shouting, Pryor separated the two. "Quiet, both of you. That's an order!" Nathaniel Pryor let moments lapse and hot tempers cool. "I will blame your insolence on lack of sleep, Private Collins. As for you Labiche, draw a weapon on a duly appointed member of this corps and I will see you brought before the court and whipped." He turned to Collins. "Labiche has never cheated you out of more than your whiskey. Sit and listen, both of you. Control your tempers. See if you can help each other. There is a man I know, a rich man, rich enough to barter horses in a game of chance."

Collins growled insolently: "The captains have forbade us to cheat the natives."

Nathaniel Pryor's keen eyes narrowed as he explained. "Not an Indian. An Englishman. One of the lordly ones who bled our colonies dry. Englishmen love a good match, and they wager high."

It was tempting. Labiche licked his lips. "They bask in their wealth like lapdogs, but they'll risk all they own, robes, horses, guns, as freely as ice runs in the river, if it inflates their bloated pride."

Pryor continued eagerly: "There is an Englishman at the Awatixa village, with the Hidatsas on the Knife River, not far from here. I've heard the Frenchman, Charbonneau, talk of him. Heney is his name. You and Labiche will pay him a visit. Labiche will challenge him to a game, lure him with drink. He will play for horses. When Heney loses, Labiche will give you his winnings to present to the girl's family. After you have wed your bride, Heney can buy the horses back from the family, for the North West trade guns that the British at Fort Saint Peter supply him so freely, and everyone comes out richer." Pryor and Labiche were both grinning broadly now. "And you, Johnny Collins, will have satisfied your lust and become a responsible member of this company again." Pryor slapped Collins hard on the back. Collins winced.

It took a moment for Collins to digest the plan. *Wed*, it was a short word for a very scary proposition. It sounded terribly permanent.

Labiche spoke up with a flip of the hand: "In the Indian fashion, you marry her. You bring the family gifts. If they accept, they invite you to live with her in the lodge or you can bring her here to the fort. There are others who have already done as much and the squaws are very helpful to us."

"And what happens in the spring when she is fat with my child and we leave for the Shining Mountains?"

"*If* she fattens. . . . We'll probably pass back this way again in a few months on our return. Then you can decide whether you want to stay or go. Think on it until sunset."

Collins left them and retired to his hut. It was warm inside, and he was grateful for the few moments alone to lay back on his bunk. Whitehouse was scribbling silently. Collins ignored him. The image of the Indian girl loomed up before him like a tantalizing dream, but an alliance here, now, seemed impractical, a denial of harsh reality. He pondered Labiche's motives. The Frenchman and his strange countrymen took their pleasure with enthusiasm, unfettered by any sense of remorse. His heart ached for the girl, not with a visceral lust as it had for Louise Bourgeron, but with a finer compulsion, almost a reverence, and he doubted if he were worthy. The more he doubted, the more he desired. He lay sweating on the cold bunk, watching Whitehouse who lay on his side with his quill, an open bottle of ink, and a crumpled notebook, writing by the light of a single candle. Collins wondered how Whitehouse did not spill the ink or set fire to his blankets. He listened to the steady clawing of the quill. Writing, it was a talent Collins always aspired to learn. It was an eminent act of civilization. Here in the wilderness, it was reinforced in its importance. So with marriage. The cruel loneliness of geography reconstituted the institution. He thought of the girl. He saw her face in the candle flame, her liquid eyes, the curve of hip, the long silky fall of hair, and let his heart dictate. Marriage to an Indian beauty was a very desirable way of surviving the winter. Besides, success would probably elude them all. But he had convinced himself that this girl loved him and that he could love her deeply in return. And there was a pernicious possibility that he could drive the scheming Labiche to jealous frustration. It would be a just revenge for the Frenchman's mockery.

At sunset, he found Pryor and Labiche preparing the

mess. He trembled when he accepted: "I will do it. What do you want from me?"

Pryor grinned back sheepishly. "There is a condition." He hesitated. "Labiche wants payment for his efforts."

Collins backed away, but Labiche did not hesitate. "Your dram of whiskey every day from now on."

Collins snapped back instantly. "Every other day."

Pryor prompted the young man insidiously: "Which do you love better, the girl or a few drops of your precious drink?"

Labiche parried: "You will have the soft body of a beauty, robes, and a family to wrap you in warmth and comfort while ugly me must rest here on a hard cold plank. I'll give you your whiskey every third day."

Collins's eyes flashed, but he was grinning greedily, his heart thumping. He reacted swiftly, on impulse. "Done. But you'd better win. Don't lose. Now where is this man, Heney?"

Pryor elaborated: "Only a few miles beyond the mouth of the Knife River but he comes here often."

"To spy on us and laugh at our weakness." Like Pryor, Labiche had no love for Englishmen.

Collins questioned: "What will the captains say?"

Pryor shrugged. "They want to end your distractions. They've told us to befriend the natives. They owe nothing to the bloody English, and this man Heney can only accuse us, if he catches us. I doubt anyone would whip us over a woman, when nearly every man in this camp has taken his pleasure with the native women on the way upriver. But not a word to the captains or the other sergeants or your friend, Drouillard, or that saintly fool, Cruzatte, whose mouth runs like a spigot. Go quietly and we risk very little."

"I'll desert before I'll submit to whipping!" It was a

sudden, defiant outburst for Labiche.

Collins answered with a sneer: "How would you know?"

Labiche leveled a withering glance at Collins. "I know." He stood up and let fall the thick robe that covered his back, loosened the thong that held his shirt at the neck, lifted the it over his head, and turned his back to Collins and Pryor. The skin was rutted and red with deep, furrowed scars that could only have come from the barbs of the cat-o-nine-tails.

Collins backed away, astonished. "My God! I'm sorry!"

"It happened on a French brigantine off Martinique. I was a seaman." Labiche's voice cracked. "An English brigantine demasted us. The captain needed crewmen. I had a choice . . . the British naval service or a prison cell in the tropics. I would not have survived. The brig's captain was a brute. I had to bargain for food, and, when I refused to man a gun against my own countrymen, they hauled me before the mast, tied my hands and my feet, ripped the shirt from my back and the skin from my spine, and threw me in the hold limp as a dead fish. I should have died for all the pain but for a kind ship's surgeon. Ever since, I have avoided the sea, and so I follow the river inland." Labiche sucked in his lips to a thin red line. His eyes narrowed, a vein at his temples pulsed, and every muscle of his face seemed to contract hideously. Collins recoiled. He waited for Labiche to compress the hatred within him. The Frenchman's face finally cleared, and he continued. "Tomorrow or the day after, we will go hunting . . . the captains will agree . . . they usually do. We will visit the Englishman, and I will win horses for you. It will be like a settling of old scores." Labiche drew his knife across a stone so that it made a shrieking sound that pained a man's ears. The wind lifted the scrapings that sparkled in the bright sunlight on the clear, brittle air.

Collins winced and waited for his eardrums to clear. He wasn't finished. "If I live in her lodge, who will cook for the mess?"

Sergeant Pryor's lips curled slightly. He had already conceived the answer. "Labiche, here, who complains so loudly about his growling stomach. Labiche should make a fine cook, and he will have extra whiskey to spice the pot." Pryor turned to Collins with a self-satisfied leer. "Or you, Collins, can entice your fair spouse to spend her nights here with us. You can build a suitable shelter. Others already have. She can help cook."

"I won't share her services with him, if that's what he's thinking." Collins pointed a bony finger at the ugly Frenchman.

"No one will interfere with your domestic bliss. I shall personally see to it."

Grinning, Collins went back to the cooking fires. His hand shook nervously as he ladled fat from off the top of a boiling cauldron. Buffalo hump was in the pot, and he took a taste and licked his lips. Suddenly he felt his appetite sharpen, spooned out a bowlful, and ate like he had not eaten in days, like a happy, hungry man. When his stomach was full, lethargy consumed him. He lay back against a log, closed his eyes, and let his thoughts ramble. What kind of foolishness had he spawned? *Wed*, such a tiny word, so packed with commitment and force! He had handed over one of life's most important decisions to a pirate and a gambler. Who was this François Labiche? He had a quick eye and had hoodwinked many of the party. He was physically strong—he entertained them all by walking upside down. But where was he from? No one really knew. When had he learned to deal cards, cast dice, and speak English? Collins could see the man now through the open doorway. The wiry Frenchman was sitting outside the storeroom, humming mildly to himself, polishing his knife with an oily rag. And what about the Indian girl? Why not Louise Bourgeron or another easier choice who sought his attentions openly? Why not one without a forbidding grandmother? What if the Englishman refused to play, and what if the captains discovered that he and Labiche and Pryor had created the colossal hoax? What if the captains refused her presence in the camp? What if her family refused his gifts? One irate husband had already threatened to kill Sergeant Ordway. The prim and proper sergeant, the one man in camp bound so rigidly by laws and conventions had seduced another man's wife! Captain Clark did not think the husband who came to camp with murder in his eyes and a tomahawk in his raised fist was a laughing matter. The scandal humbled and humanized righteous Sergeant Ordway. And what of Labiche? Collins sensed with instinctive certainty that Labiche responded to an old ingrained hostility: the Frenchman enjoyed snubbing his Gallic nose at any haughty son of prim and proper England.

Tomorrow arrived, but hours passed and Labiche did not come. Collins went with Shannon and the sledges to bring in the meat of eight buffalo that the hunters had killed the day before. It began to snow lightly. They hurried back, and Collins resumed his cooking assignment. He moved with nervous impatience that he could not hide.

Drouillard returned from the hunt and came to the cooking fire to warm himself. "You getting married? The news is all over the camp." When Collins nodded sheepishly, Drouillard laughed loudly and exclaimed: "I helped you escape from Louise Bourgeron. This time I wash my hands of your affairs of the heart." But he softened and asked: "Who's the young lady?"

"Laughing Water, widow of Raven's Wing who died."

Drouillard lifted an eyebrow, turned his back, and walked away.

Labiche finally arrived shortly before noon, and the two left immediately for the Hidatsa Village. They crossed the Missouri on the ice and pushed steadily through the river bottom, clinging to the shelter of the trees in the face of a growing storm. Labiche halted once to cut willow stems for snowshoes and again to shoot a white hare that he skinned and used the fur to shield his face from the biting wind. He gave half to Collins whose own nose was reddening. The storm intensified; the wind howled at gale force. Except for the definition of the trees and the scale-like crust of the river, all was a frigid, milky haze. The sun, the sky, the contours of the land, the very light of day blurred into indistinguishable grayness.

They climbed up from the bottom into the force of wind. Labiche stopped and pointed. "There is the pony herd. We are near." A hundred horses stood, barely distinguishable, blurred silhouettes in the dim light, shaggy with winter coats, tails tucked into the wind, like ice statues. The heat of their breathing rose like smoke and blew off in a stream of thickening haze. Collins could no longer feel his toes or the tip of his nose. The skin on his face tightened. His breath froze in icicles on his beard. He was very cold.

They retraced their steps back down into the bottom out of the wind, and plodded on. The winter village of the Hidatsas lay at the foot of a high bluff, protected from the bitter, relentless gale. But snow was fast filling the spaces between the lodges, and no one was outside. Dogs barked a warning. Two men muffled in thick buffalo robes emerged from the first lodge, armed with muskets. Labiche made the peace sign and held his gun in one hand over his head. The Indians nodded, called off the dogs, and invited them inside. Women came, offered them hot broth, and beckoned them to the fire. They drank, and Collins felt rosy warmth invade his tissues and the cold stiffness within him soften and ease. Labiche inquired for Heney. The Englishman was only two lodges away.

Chapter Twenty-Four

Alexander Heney was surprised to see them. He was a short man, built squarely, with a round red face and blue, dancing eyes. He rose when they entered and greeted them first in Hidatsa, then in English. There was a lilt to the clipped syllables of his light tenor voice. "You did not come for high tea, gentlemen. Shake off the snow and warm yourselves." There was a table and four chairs—Collins had not sat upon a chair in months—but Heney did not invite them to sit down. A four-poster mahogany bed, covered with thick buffalo robes, stood incongruously back from the fire. Crates and casks of supplies were stacked neatly about. Heney explained with characteristic understatement: "I permit myself small luxuries, even here." He waited, grinning broadly, while they stripped their outer garments. He was a jovial man with a round paunch swathed in a bright belt like Deschamps, and light blond beard that reminded Collins of a Saxon Saint Nicholas, but he was a snob.

Labiche nodded obsequiously. "Privates François Labiche and John Collins, sir. We are members of the American expedition."

"I have heard. It is a pleasure and a relief, gentlemen, to speak the English tongue. Do you bring news from the colonies?"

"I have no news that is not already six months old, sir. We come for a horse."

"I have many horses. I trade them for guns or whiskey, whichever you offer as tender."

"The horse is not for me, sir. A man in your employ, a *Monsieur* Charbonneau, has in his possession a horse that Bold Medicine of Matootonha village lost the day of the buffalo hunt." Labiche could lie like a smuggler when it suited him and pretend friendship like a politician.

Heney chuckled when he answered: "Charbonneau, that rascal! He told me he found the horse, a big black, running loose. You passed the pony herd coming in. Did you see the animal you seek?"

Labiche's eyes narrowed. He answered with calculated courtesy. "It was cold, sir. The wind was blowing. We were hungry. We did not stop to look. We beg your hospitality for the night." He bowed submissively.

Heney nodded. "Of course." Heney's manners were impeccable. No man could deny a request for food and shelter in the winter in a storm, still Heney's lack of British reserve surprised the Americans. He motioned them toward the chairs and table. An Indian woman came forward and stirred the ever-present pot. They sat, and Heney poured out three cups of rum. "Drink. You will warm faster. I have casks enough to last the winter."

Labiche emptied his cup, stretched out comfortably on the soft mat, and fell instantly asleep. Collins had another drink to loosen his tongue. Heney enjoyed hearing himself talk. He motioned to the sleeping Labiche. "An ugly bloke that one." Collins shrugged, and questioned Heney about living under a king for a ruler.

"The whole world obeys a king except for your rebellious colonies. It is only you Americans and now the French who reject the tradition and right of a proper monarch."

Collins felt the criticism and made no reply. Heney sensed Collins's unease and gradually dominated the conversation. He pried open a crate lifting out a bottle of French brandy.

"My best brew. Imported all the way from Liverpool. I'm told it was captured off a French privateer. The French are superior distillers. Too bad they're such a fractious race and make such frequent war."

The liquor tasted sweet and burned the insides as Collins swallowed. He had never tasted brandy and drank eagerly.

Heney paused and raised his glass to the light of the fire. The golden liquid sparkled like a jewel. He smacked his lips and resumed: "So you Americans have purchased Louisiana. You must not replace good brandy with your distilled corn or let the Frenchmen loose like a pack of dogs."

Collins's head was fogging. He nodded stupidly as Heney clapped twice. An Indian woman brought bowls of a rich soup. Heney grinned. "Taste it. Almost as good as a French *pot au feu*."

It was. Collins complimented the cook and commented blandly on the rich furnishings.

"We live well here, better than in the East after the damn' refugees from your thirteen rebellious colonies crowded loyal Canadians out of the lands and positions that should have been ours. As hungry a bunch of damn' thieves as I ever met! Tell me, how does one govern a pack of thieves?" Heney slapped the woman lightly across the rump, and they both laughed, but Collins laughter was forced.

Labiche awakened suddenly to the laughter. "I smell brandy."

"It's gone, Frenchie, drunk to the dregs by two more handsome gentlemen than you." Heney handed Labiche the empty bottle without looking at him. It was a deliberate snub.

Labiche did not intimidate easily. "You have another bottle? I play you for another."

"Aren't you already poor enough, eh, Frenchman?" Heney took another bottle from the crate. "Let me see what an ugly Frenchman will wager."

"A musket or a good knife." Labiche filled his cup, sipped gingerly, and reached inside his shirt for his deck. He flicked the cards with his thumb. They made a crisp, snapping sound. "Or if you prefer dice. . . ." He rummaged in the fold of his shirt.

Heney grinned through his yellow beard. "Dice mix better with drink, no staring faces to make you blink, only dots that dance before your eyes." He smoothed the floor in front of him and spread an elkskin for a playing surface. Labiche passed him the dice, and he rolled. "Six, a neat, single digit." Heney's blue eyes beamed with satisfaction. He rolled again.

"Two, snake eyes." Labiche said it for him, and Heney passed him the bottle.

But Heney was undaunted. "Now you, Collins."

John Collins groped for an excuse. He had drunk rum, then brandy. His vision was blurred. Labiche was nodding eagerly. "Pet them gently, make them love you like you love the woman."

Collins's fingers fumbled with the cubes. He held the dice between his palms, stopped, rubbed his red eyes, then blurted drunkenly: "I have nothing to wager."

"You have lead in your pouch. It's worth a cast."

Collins rolled the dice. The little black dots tumbled hazily in front of his eyes, swimming, floating like leaves on an updraft. He lost. Labiche popped the cork from another bottle, filled his cup, and downed the contents. "*A la bonne chance, et aux belles femmes!*"

The toast jangled irrationally like tinkling sleigh bells in Collins's ears. The foreign syllables echoed meaninglessly. His eyelids drooped, he felt his chin slam against his chest, and he was caught in a powerful current, twirling in the river, spinning, drowning, sucking for precious breath. His muscles went slack, and he passed out face first over the game.

Labiche pushed his limp body aside and covered him with a soft buffalo robe. He picked up the dice, rolled them between his palms, and blew. He threw a two and a six. He threw again and went to open another bottle.

Heney stared with bloodshot eyes, his weight of head swaying like a ball on a string. He drawled: "No more for me, Frenchman. You finish it. Your friend will sleep until morning, but I must stay awake to win back my losses."

It was morning when Collins awakened. Little hammers pounded his temples, and sourness filled his stomach. He sat up, and a cannonball rolled back and forth in his skull. He pulled himself dizzily erect and stumbled outside to relieve himself. A ray of sun, a reflection from off the pristine snow, assaulted his eyes, and he fell to his knees and crawled the rest of the way and scooped handfuls of cold snow and held it against his aching head. The pain eased.

He came back in to warm his freezing hands. Heney was snoring loudly, one arm draped over the body of his squaw. She was awake. When she saw Collins, she edged out from under her mate and took up her station at the cook fire. Collins watched silently while his head steadily cleared. It was pleasant to watch a female form bend and straighten as she sliced chunks of meat into the pot, stirred and skimmed the grease from the top. The mixture looked like boiled yellow glue, but it smelled and tasted delicious. He ate and refilled his bowl twice and thought of Laughing Water.

Labiche walked in a few minutes later. Collins hadn't realized he was gone. He was dressed in thick furs, and, at first, Collins thought he was an Indian until he spoke. "It's late, my friend. Are you so rich, that you can bask in sweet slumber all day?"

The Indian woman held out a bowl. "She's a good cook . . . better than me." Collins was still hungry.

Labiche gulped the contents and pushed the bowl away. "Put your coat on. I have something to show you."

Collins snapped instantly alert. "You won?"

"Six horses and eight robes, more than you need. The Englishman was so drunk he lost count. Get your gear and come quickly. I don't want to be here when he awakens. We want no rematch until after you have presented the gifts to your bride." He turned and left.

Collins dressed, grabbed his pack and musket, and ran after Labiche. Gradually his eyes adjusted, but not before Labiche had disappeared around the neighboring lodge.

The wind had died, and the snow lay even as frosting on a cake. Labiche's trail was clear as thumbprints in a pie. Collins caught up as they came in view of the pony herd from the top of a rise. The sun was strong and reflected in broad prismatic shafts off the frosted coats of the animals. The horses stood out starkly, pawing the snow, to feed on the rich grass beneath. It was a peaceful, wintery scene, worthy of the finest landscape painter. Three human figures stood by the herd, with three animals packed for travel. One was a man. The other two were women, and one was very pregnant.

Labiche pointed. "That's Charbonneau. He's coming with us. . . . Over there, that black one and the two sorrels and the spotted mare, those are my choices. The black horse is a buffalo runner. I'll keep him. I leave the last two selections to you. Choose a gentle one for your bride. The fat one can ride it to Matootonha village."

"The women are coming with us?" It seemed preposterous to Collins.

"The Virgin rode a donkey the day before she gave birth to the Christ. The woman can ride better than she can walk."

Collins chose a stocky, white-faced bay that walked up to him and did not shy away when he approached. Many of the horses had not been used since the buffalo hunt, and now did not want to submit to halter and shank. He caught another larger gray, for himself, and watched as Labiche passed a leather thong over the black's lower jaw and leaped aboard.

"Catch!" Labiche threw another thong bridle to Collins, whose horse bolted at the flying object. Collins pursued, tripped on a hidden mound, and sprawled face first in the snow.

Labiche, Charbonneau, and his three wives roared with laughter. Humiliated, Collins cursed. He lay a hand on another animal that threw its head high and swiped sideways with a rear hoof. He jumped away.

Labiche was growing impatient. "Choose a gelded one, and let's hope your woman is more willing." But Collins fumbled again until Labiche entered the herd, caught a little bay, bridled, and held it steady while Collins mounted. Labiche couldn't resist another jibe. "If you value your pride, don't fall off when you enter the village. How will you handle a woman, if you cannot hold a horse between your legs?"

John Collins bristled at the mockery. He wrenched the rein around, twisting the animal so hard that it nearly lost its balance. But Labiche and the others were riding away, pushing their animals swiftly ahead, their ridicule ringing raucously in the cold air. John Collins dug his heels into the animal's flanks. At least in the Indian village, he would not be a laughingstock.

Labiche stopped at the outskirts of Matootonha village. "Do you remember which lodge, Johnny?"

Collins remembered only vaguely, but nodded because he knew Labiche would embarrass him again. His hands were shaking, his temples throbbing, the doubt in his heart pounding like the hammer on Bratton's anvil. Villagers, alerted by the shouting and the thumping of hoofs, had come out of the lodges to stare.

Labiche turned to him with uncharacteristic concern and urged him forward. "They love gossip, Johnny, like a bunch of Irish biddies. Go on. Go find her. Go to your lady love." Collins sensed a hint of envy and sadness in Labiche's voice as he rode forward.

The Indians crowded around. They seemed to know why he had come and, in their enthusiasm, pressed him on to Raven's Wing's lodge. He led the horses to the door, dismounted, and dropped the leads. When the old grandmother stepped out, he drew back, but her iron glare settled on the animals, not on him. She came over to inspect them, swept her hand over the soft winter coats and down the muscular shoulders and over the rumps. Finally, she smiled and a hint of lost youth and beauty softened her face.

John Collins did not know the customs or language of this alien people. He could not speak his desires. He could not question their motives. A circle of Indians drew up around him and fear choked off the air in his lungs. The blood drained from his face, and he stood immobile as the ice in December's river. It was the old lady who reassured him. She took his horse by the rein and him by the hand and led both into the lodge. He went woodenly.

The girl was standing by the fire, adorned in a white doeskin dress beaded with flowers the blue color of the summer prairie sky. Word had traveled. She had known he was coming. Her dark hair was braided and shone like fine silk in the firelight. She held out her hands in welcome as he walked forward. She brought him first drink and then food, and he ate and drank. He held her hand and minutes melted into hours, and he felt the gaze of the old woman like the scourge upon his back, but she was smiling now, a faint lift at one corner of the mouth and a swift, deep glance of eye.

The girl led him to a soft bed of buffalo skins. They undressed slowly and lay upon the soft fur, and he caressed her gently, afraid at first, inhibited in his movements by the presence of humanity in the lodge. Their love-making would not be private. But her touch and the soft sounds of her voice reassured him until, finally, the noises diminished in the night and he took her to him. They loved passionately, their pleasure heightened by months of loneliness. For Collins, the dismal memory of his betrayal, the exhausting trip upriver, his disobedience and punishment grew dim and lost itself in the present delight. He was glad that he had come. He thanked God for giving him this wondrous woman who lay at his side. He desired no other.

The next day, the grandmother ushered out the other residents from the lodge to give the newlyweds time alone. They spent the day in the warmth of their passion, gently, patiently learning the secrets of each other.

On the third day, Drouillard came by with orders. "The captains are summoning all hands to help free the boats from the ice. Bring your lady with you, and she can tend the fires and cook. She can join Charbonneau's wives. They will welcome her."

Over the next weeks, they slaved to free the boats from their encasement of ice. They chipped, they melted, they slipped on the hard, slick, sharp shards until their limbs bruised and froze. It was wet, cold, thankless work that no man could endure for long. The indomitable river came flooding inevitably back in as soon as they chopped it out, and refroze as solidly as before. But, for Collins, the vain struggles of each day were made bearable by the ecstasies of the night.

They built canoes for their trip upriver where it would grow shallow and narrow and the keelboat would no longer serve. With axes and staves and hot brands, they hollowed heavy cottonwood trunks to fashion boats sturdy enough to withstand the power of swirling rapids.

Collins and Laughing Water built their own shelter just outside the fort's stockade. Hall, Shannon, Ordway, even quiet Whitehouse, and many others had Indian consorts, but not Labiche. His grotesque visage and sharp tongue discouraged close personal relationships. He visited Collins often and took some visible pride in having engendered the match, but even Laughing Water was afraid of him, as if he possessed some mysterious medicine that was better invoked from a distance, and he was left to satisfy his desires with village cast-offs and old women.

In all, it was a pleasant, busy, friendly winter. The Mandans were a handsome, noble, hospitable race. They taught the captains and men how to hunt the strange new animals, how to harvest the herbs of the prairies, where to find precious water and salt and edible fruits and roots. They told of waterfalls and rapids on the river that led to the high, glistening mountains in the west where other tribes who came to trade lived.

The hardships of the winter knitted the men into a tight, self-reliant unit. The cold tempered the rectitude of Sergeant Ordway and allowed the captains to sanction frivolity and companionship. It convinced delinquents like Collins and Hall that obedience, co-operation, and temperance were necessary for the livelihood and survival of all. Most of all, it gave the men precious time to fraternize and to understand themselves, to meld English and Irish, French, Indian and slave, and treat all as equal companions and fellow travelers, and the native peoples as friends. The trip upriver had weeded out the malcontents. Now the long months of isolation cemented respect and friendship.

Lewis and Clark hired Toussaint Charbonneau as interpreter, because he spoke Hidatsa and Crow and could translate into French. The English traders tried to buy back his talents and deprive the expedition of his considerable skills. In the end, it was Labiche who convinced him not betray his Gallic blood, that to work with the Americans was to strive for the glory of his French forebears and against their traditional enemy, England. But, at first, Charbonneau could not communicate well and relied on Deschamps and François Labiche to translate for him.

Charbonneau's pregnant wife bore a child. Captain Lewis himself and Laughing Water aided in her delivery of a strapping baby boy. She cried out when the contractions seized her, in a language no one had yet heard. Laughing Water declared it was Shoshone and explained that Charbonneau's wife was a captive, taken as a very young girl from the Shining Mountains that were the corps' destination. Captains Lewis and Clark immediately invited mother and child to accompany them on their way.

The weather changed suddenly. Warmer winds penetrated the cold air, the ice broke in the river, and the boats swung free. The rush of spring melt left the detritus of winter washed up upon the banks. There were whole trees and rocks and dead and frozen bodies of animals that had fallen through the ice. One was human. The corpse was bloated and black but otherwise preserved. It was the body of fat man. By his beard, they knew he was not Indian. Heney came to view the body and declared: "Not French, not English. He's Spanish, I'll wager, a freebooter of no consequence. The

Spaniards could never stand the cold. They have no business here."

With the warmer weather, the men were eager to be on their way. The keelboat was the first to leave with Deschamps and his *engagés*, Richard Warfington and his army contingent. They packed Captain Lewis's specimens and notes and set sail southward, downstream from where they had come, to St. Louis.

The day came for the expedition, thirty-one men, one slave, one dog, and one woman to leave. Laughing Water, her grandmother, and Cone Flower, Charbonneau's second wife, stood at the gates. John Collins kissed his bride for all to see while his fellows cheered him on. Labiche was loudest. "Lips sweeter than whiskey!"

Collins wasn't listening. He stared longingly into the deep dark pools of her eyes. "I'll be back before the ice runs again in the river." He felt a pang. He would miss Laughing Water, but he had given his word. He turned, and the excitement of the departure affected him. He was a vital member of corps, necessary to the effective function of the whole. Laughing Water smiled wanly. The old grandmother glared stoically. Indian wives endured the departures of their men, for the hunt or for war. It was their way.

John Collins picked up his musket, shouldered his pack, and took his place in the column, in front of John Colter and behind William Bratton. Captain Clark gave the order, and they marched in formation to the waiting boats.

Jane Candia Coleman

THE O'KEEFE EMPIRE

Alex O'Keefe has a dream. Fired up with visions of an empire and millions of acres for the taking in New Mexico Territory, he sets out from Texas to make his dream a reality. His wife, Joanna, becomes caught up in her husband's enthusiasm, sells the family holdings, then boards a train to meet him. She has no idea what lies before her. When Joanna arrives, her own dreams are nearly shattered. Alex is dead, murdered by an unknown killer. And the empire they had planned is threatened by exorbitant cattle fees charged by the railroad. But dreams die hard. Joanna will do whatever she has to, even if that means taking the cattle on a brutal overland trail drive to San Diego, across the Mojave Desert.

___4859-0 $4.50 US/$5.50 CAN

Broken Ranks

Hiram King

The Civil War just ended. For one group of black men, hope for a new life comes in the form of a piece of paper, a government handbill urging volunteers to join the new Negro Cavalry, which will soon become the famous Tenth Cavalry Regiment. But trouble begins for the recruits long before they can even reach their training camp. First they have to get from St. Louis to Fort Leavenworth, Kansas, a hard journey through hostile, ex-Confederate territory, surrounded by vengeful white men who don't like the idea of these recruits having guns. The army hires Ples Butler, a grim, black gunfighter, to get the recruits to Fort Leavenworth safely, and he will do his job . . . even if it means riding through Hell.

___4872-8 $5.99 US/$6.99 CAN

TREASURES
OF THE
SUN
T.V. OLSEN

The lost city of Huacha has been a legend for centuries. It is believed that the Incas concealed a fantastic treasure there before their empire fell to Francisco Pizarro's conquistadores in the 16th century. So when Wilbur Tennington comes upon a memoir written by one of Pizarro's men, revealing the exact location of Huacha, visions of gold fill his eyes. He wastes no time getting an expedition together, then sets out on his quest. He should have known, though, that nothing so valuable ever comes easily. He will have to survive freezing mountain elevations, volcanic deserts, tribes of headhunters, and murderous bandits if he hopes to ever find the . . . treasures of the sun.

___4904-X $4.50 US/$5.50 CAN